CONTENTS

BEYOND THE GATE

DANIEL KENNEDY

PROLOGUE

THE END

I don't remember much about the house... at least not after my Nan died.

Back when she was alive I do remember it being too hot all the time; probably because she never turned the central heating off. I suppose the older a person gets the colder they must become; I don't know why, and it doesn't make much sense, because my Nan was quite fat when she was old, and you'd think that layers of fat would keep a person warm, as if they were wrapped in two or three duvets all at once. When she was younger my Nan wasn't fat at all; she was thin, and very beautiful, at least that's what my mother says. I expect she was never cold back then either, even without all those extra layers. Like I said, it doesn't make much sense, but then there are lots of things that don't make much sense; that's why I never stop asking questions.

And it smelled funny – the house I mean – not in a bad way, just sort of *different* to our house. I didn't know what that smell was for years and years until finally I discovered something called *Imperial Leather*. It's a type of soap if you're wondering, and the entire house smelled of it. I've never much bothered with soap myself; water seems to do the job well enough on its own (of washing things I mean). Soap just seems like a lot of extra effort to me... but I suppose my Nan must have liked it an awful lot.

That explains why the place was so spotlessly clean; she was good at cleaning, my Nan. And she liked wearing pink rubber gloves while doing it. I've no idea why... it's not as if hands aren't water proof, is it? Maybe she was allergic to soap or something. It wasn't just the rubber gloves though; there were funny things everywhere which I never really understood; like elastic bands on door handles, and not just one or two, but hundreds, all clumped together, as if that's where they were meant to be; and extra bits of carpet shoved under doorways to 'keep the draft out' – that's what she always used to say. But there was no draft, and even if there had have been, it would have been the *hot* sort, which isn't exactly a draft at all when you think about it. Then there was the pantry... we didn't have a pantry in our house, we just had cupboards like most people. It was the only room that was ever cold; not that I was allowed in there much. The pantry door was always locked. I can even remember a big iron key which my Nan kept hidden somewhere. And it's no wonder why; there were sweets in that pantry – *real* sweets, the old-fashioned type that old-fashioned shops used to sell in big transparent jars. I remember my Nan used to give me one or two every time we left, but always in a sneaky sort of way, so that my mother couldn't see. She did once trick me though, by giving me something called *aniseed balls*. They were probably the most disgusting thing that I've ever tasted... apart from marzipan that is, and for some reason everything that my Nan made *had* to have marzipan in it.

And there were lots of other strange things about that house; I suppose my Nan just spent a very long time making it perfect – perfect for *her* I mean. It was always just the right temperature, the drafts were always kept out (even the made-up ones), and everything was just where she expected it to be; the elastic bands on door handles; the old coats that hadn't been worn for forty years on the hat stand; the hats that probably hadn't ever been worn on the dresser. As for the smell... well, maybe she liked it; I can't say that I did, but then at least if ever I want to remember her, all I have to do is go sniff a bar of soap.

Like I said, I don't remember much about the house after my Nan died; only the garden, because that's where my Granddad seemed to live, come rain or shine or snow or hail. And I suppose the most interesting thing about a place is the people who live there, because they sort of make that place come alive. My Granddad didn't used to spend all his time in the garden, not when my Nan was alive. I suppose when she was in the house he had a reason to be there, even if he did pretend to be miserable all the time when 'caged up inside', as he put it. I think he just liked complaining – I've noticed that most old people seem to like complaining. And he was very good at it, especially to my Nan. I don't think she really paid much attention though; she usually just smiled and nodded, or laughed – she had the heartiest laugh I've ever heard in my life. I can still sort of hear it now. I'm glad I remember that. And I'm sure they were both very happy living there; after all, it had been their home for a very long time – since before even my mother was born. Of course, my Granddad pretended not to be happy, but really he was. I don't know how I know that, but I do.

When my Nan died things changed. My Granddad changed. He stopped talking, even to complain, and spent all his time sitting alone in the garden. I wasn't the only one to notice, my mother did too, which is why we started visiting much more often – every month in fact. That might not seem like very often to you, but that house was an awfully long way away from ours – hundreds of miles. And up until that point we'd only visited three or four times a year, mostly on special occasions, like Christmas or Easter; come to think of it, maybe that's why there was always so much marzipan on things. Anyway, I've no idea where the house was exactly, I never really paid any attention to the route; in fact at the time it didn't even occur to me that there was a route between our house and theirs. It was far too far for that. I don't think I got through a single car journey without falling asleep, but not proper sleep, more like the kind where you're slumped awkwardly against the window half awake and half dreaming about something. I hated those car journeys, and I always felt just a little bit sick, but not sick enough to actually *be* sick... that would have been much better, because then my mother would have been forced to at least *pretend* to care. It might have been all right if I could have sat up front, because the front seat bent backwards, so I could have actually slept like it was a proper bed. But my sister never let me; she was five years older, and told me that it was illegal for me to sit in the front seat because I was too small, and if we crashed into a lamp-post I'd go flying through the windscreen and die; and even if we didn't crash into a lamp-post, and I didn't go flying through the windscreen and die, those cameras on the motorway would still see me, and then a policeman (or lady) would come to our house and arrest me for breaking the law. I didn't believe her of course, but still... would you have taken the chance?

My Granddad was blind – at least he was almost blind. If he sat by the window, or outside, and squinted really hard at something held five centimetres from his nose, then maybe he could just about make out its shape. He had something called Glaucoma; it's a disease that people don't seem to get any more. I know that because every year my mother has an eye test to check for symptoms. I suppose it's quite sad to think that my Granddad probably lived half his life without being able to see just because nobody bothered to give him eye tests. Still, I never heard him complain about it, which is quite strange really, considering how much he complained about everything else. After my Nan died my mother didn't think that he could look after himself in that house. After all, it wasn't one of those houses designed for old people – a bungalow, with no stairs, or steps, or loose floorboards; it had plenty of all of those things, and a lot more besides. She wanted him to go into something called 'a retirement home' where she said he'd be looked after, but my Granddad insisted that he already lived in a retirement home, having retired twenty years earlier, and that the kind of place my mother was talking about was somewhere people were sent to die, and if he was going to die, he'd much rather do it in his own bloody house, without a lot of fools to watch him. That's what he said. I remember asking my mother later why she hadn't shouted at him after he'd said that – she'd certainly have shouted at me, and probably stopped my pocket money for about a year too. She told me that when a person gets very old, so old that they can't really walk, or see, or hear, or do much besides sit and feel sorry for themselves, they've somehow earned the right to say whatever they want. My Granddad was eighty-seven at the time. He couldn't even do a jigsaw. I always imagine old people doing jigsaws when they're alone... but he couldn't.

My mother finally decided they'd have 'a trial period' to see how he coped by himself, which I think was just her way of feeling a bit more in control, even though it really just meant that my Granddad had got his way.

My Nan died in the spring, which I always thought was stupid, because that's when things are supposed to be born, not die. Anyway, it was then that we started visiting every month; so my mother could check on my Granddad, and she and my sister could help out with anything he couldn't manage or be bothered to do (which turned out to be quite a lot). I don't think she used the same soap as my Nan, but that smell never did go away. I was only nine at the time, so I managed to avoid doing much of the work, thank goodness, but I do remember every one of those visits as if it was only yesterday. I expect Neil Armstrong and Buzz Aldrin remember the time they spent on the moon in much the same way.

Important stuff sticks in your brain. And discovering a new world, well... what could be more important than that?

APRIL

1

BEYOND THE GATE

Everything had started growing.

I remember standing in the kitchen, watching my Granddad out of the window. He was sat in the garden on an old deck chair – so old that it was even going a bit mouldy. I don't think he'd noticed though; it's not like you can really *feel* mould, is it? My mother and sister were upstairs somewhere; I could hear a vacuum cleaner. Every now and again it would stop and my mother would say something like 'if it's this bad after a month, just imagine what it'll be like after a year'.

I was bored.

My Granddad was sat slumped in the deck chair, with his back to the window not doing a whole lot, but then I suppose he couldn't have even if he'd wanted to, being blind... and eighty-seven. It was a big garden – much bigger than ours, not that ours was small exactly. And it was one of those gardens in which everything was sort of overgrown, but you could tell had once been very orderly. Things were sort of *arranged*, or had been years earlier, like the rose bushes. And if you looked hard enough, through all the bits that had grown where they probably weren't supposed to grow, you could see things like plant pots, and bamboo polls, and bits of string used to tie branches together, that were now so old and crusty they looked more like straw than string. But I didn't really think about those things; it's only now that I remember them. What I did think about though, quite a lot in fact, was the gate at the end of the garden – except, to my eyes, it wasn't the *end* of the garden at all.

You see, it didn't end with a hedge, or a fence, or a wall, like most people's gardens (even ours), beyond which is somebody else's garden, or a house, or a road, or something terribly dull like that. Beyond the gate, it just sort of... *went on*, getting wilder and wilder as it went. First there was an orchard, with a whole lot of apple trees and pear trees; and then, at some point somewhere, the orchard became a forest. Not like the sort of boring forest we used to visit near our own house, with stupid footpaths made of gravel, and sign posts everywhere telling you where to go and where not to go. That's not a *real* forest at all. But this was. The kind of forest where there were no footpaths, at least not made by people like you and me, and the trees were all different types: some small, some big, some really big, and some so gigantically huge that it seemed like they might have been there for a thousand years. I suppose it was the kind of forest that I'd always imagined when reading stories, except a lot more real, and not just because it *was* real. I don't suppose that makes a whole lot of sense though. I couldn't see it in much detail of course, not from the house, it being quite a long way away, but you don't always have to be close to a thing to know what it is. I could just tell... even before everything my Granddad told me.

The house was built on the side of a great rolling hill; that's how it was possible to see everything beyond the gate. It sloped down into a deep valley, with a lot of little glades and meadows at the bottom. I remember them being mostly white that April, as if covered in snow. They must have been filled with some sort of wild flower in bloom – daisies I expect, they're white. Beyond the valley another great hill rose, and there the forest continued on, until right at the top, which was stoney and bare. It looked very windy up there, but then there wasn't a whole lot to be blown about, so I suppose that's just a guess. You couldn't see beyond that, even with extra powerful binoculars (not that I had any extra powerful binoculars), because the hill blocked everything out, apart from the odd cloud. It was just one huge valley, sort of hidden from the world. And in a funny way, I think it was right and proper that you couldn't see what was *not* in it, and what *was* in it, at the same time. I don't expect that makes a whole lot of sense either, not yet anyway.

"Go and talk to him."

"What?"

"Your Granddad... go and talk to him. Sat out there by himself, he'll be glad of the company. And it's not like you're of any use standing there gawping out the window."

It was my mother. She could be very direct at times. People are always telling me that I'm the same way, and

4

that I must have somehow *got it* from her. But I'm pretty sure I wouldn't have said a thing like that; after all, there's nothing wrong with looking out of windows... how else are you supposed to see what's on the other side? And besides, people wouldn't bother making windows out of glass if they weren't meant to be looked out of.

"I don't want to."

"Why not?"

"I don't know what to say."

"Don't be ridiculous; he's your Granddad. It doesn't matter what you say."

"Yes, but he seems... *different*."

"What do you mean?"

"You know... since Nan died."

I looked at my mother then. I wanted to see what she was thinking, and sometimes if you look at a person's face you can tell what they're thinking, even though they might say something totally different. She looked as if she wanted to cry; except my mother never cried. I suppose she must have spent a lot of years practicing not to.

"Then go out and play."

"Where?"

"In the garden of course. Go out and play while the sun is out. I don't want you getting in my way while I clean this floor. Go on."

I looked down at the floor, and wondered why it needed cleaning. There might have been one or two muddy footprints, but then floors are there to be walked on; that's the whole point of them, the reason they exist, which makes footprints a natural thing, which should be there too. Not to mention the fact that my Granddad was blind. But there was no point telling my mother that; she wouldn't have understood. She never did.

So anyway, I went outside.

I probably shouldn't have told you all that – I expect it's all a bit boring – but then that's just how I remember things. And like I said, the important stuff sticks in your brain, so I guess I might as well tell you everything.

The garden wasn't especially wide, at least it didn't seem like it was, being so long; and there were a whole lot of bushes on either side. Not like a hedge though; more like the sort of thorny bushes you get in wild places, like the tops of cliffs by the sea. I think it's called *gorse* or *heather* or something like that. It was all tangly and overgrown, and seemed like it might have been eating the garden, even though a lot of it was brown and dead-looking. There were lots of nettles there too, particularly at the front. I don't know why; it's not as if those bushes needed guarding or anything, but that's what it looked like to me.

"Who's that?"

"Me."

"What?"

"Dylan."

"Dylan?"

"Yes."

"What do you want?"

"Nothing."

"Good."

There wasn't anything to play with in the garden: like footballs, or tennis balls, or rugby balls (the worst kind of balls because they don't bounce straight). But even if there had have been, I'm not sure I'd have bothered anyway, especially not if it'd been a rugby ball, because I'd probably have ended up kicking it into those wild bushes, and then someone would have shouted at me no doubt. Or worse still, I might have kicked it into my Granddad's head, and knocked him clean out. It's not that I'd have been trying to of course; I just knew that my mother wouldn't have seen it that way. She always preferred to make up her own reasons why things happen. So anyway, I remember spending quite a while wandering about, just sort of *looking* at things, but I have to admit, it was better looking at them up close than through a window. I didn't know what anything was called – the plants and the trees I mean. It's annoying that, when you see something and don't know what it's called. There were quite a lot of birds about, whistling and singing. In fact, the whole place seemed extremely noisy, as if it was one big living thing, when really it was lots of little things all sort of working together. I couldn't see any of them though – the birds I mean. I suppose they were just hidden beneath leaves and branches and flowers and what not.

I think I sort of *drifted* down the garden, without really meaning to; probably because I was more comfortable the farther I got from my Granddad, who seemed to be watching me (even though he was blind); and because, like I've said, the garden was very long, and didn't really have an end. Except, to get to the orchard, you had to go through the gate; not that it was locked or anything, and I could have even climbed over it if I'd wanted to. It's just that I didn't. Some things are fun to climb: like trees, and bunk-beds, and gates that *are* locked, but if a gate isn't locked you might as well just walk through it. So that's what I did. Or at least, I was about to.

I think it must have creaked. I don't remember that part.

"DON'T YOU DARE GO THROUGH THAT GATE."

For all that my Granddad liked to complain about things – usually things that didn't seem to matter – I think that was the first time that I'd ever heard him shout. And I really mean *ever*. He normally talked so quietly that you couldn't hear half of what he was saying; so to hear him shout like that... I was scared. But I don't think it was really because he was shouting; anyone can shout without it being scary. It was more the way he did it. I suppose he was angry. But there was more to it even than that... I think *he* was scared too. I didn't notice any of that at the time – well, I mean I must have, because otherwise I wouldn't know it now, would I? But it's not like I thought about it or anything; I just froze, and felt a bit like crying. I didn't though. I'd been practicing not to you see... so I could be more like my mother.

2

A PROMISE

I never used to like the word *magic*. It seemed liked one
of those annoying words which people always call things
that they can't really explain properly, either because
they're too lazy, or because they just don't know. Not
that there's anything wrong with not knowing things, but
I think it's better to just come out and say that, rather
than making up stupid words that don't mean anything.
Of course, that was before I understood what magic
really is. You see, it's not really a word at all; it's a
feeling. And I think it's probably the best feeling in the
world (at least, I can't think of any better ones). It's not
the sort of feeling you get when some old man pulls a
rabbit out of a hat, or guesses a card right, or makes a
coin appear up your nostril – that's just annoying,
because it doesn't make any sense. But that's not what
magic is, things that don't make any sense. Like I said,
magic is a feeling, and it has nothing to do with whether
a thing makes sense or not. Besides, everything makes

sense if you ask enough questions.

"Dylan?"

"Yes?"

"You didn't go through the gate?"

"No."

"Good. I mean, thank you. And... I'm sorry if I shouted at you. I didn't mean to. Well, I mean, I did mean to; there's no point denying it. I just didn't mean... well, you know what I mean, don't you lad?"

I'm not sure if I knew what he meant or not, but I knew that he was back to normal, and that I didn't feel scared any more. And I even knew that if something really scary had happened to me, like a big wild hound had jumped over that gate and started trying to eat me, then he'd have somehow got in the way and fought that hound off, even though it might have killed him, because he was blind and eighty-seven. I knew that, because I knew that he was my Granddad and that he loved me. Not because he told me that he did (because he didn't) or because other people told me that he did, like my mother. No. I knew it, because I felt it. And it was a good feeling; there might even have been some magic in it. Yes, at least one quarter I should think.

That's when I became unfrozen (there's no point being frozen if you're not scared) and went to sit with my Granddad. I remember wanting to talk to him, and for some reason, talking seemed very easy all of a sudden.

"Granddad?"

"What? I mean, yes? I didn't upset you did I Dylan?"

"A bit."

Well he had. And I don't see the point in lying; it just makes things more complicated than they really are. And most things are already too complicated as it is.

"Oh. I, I really am very sorry about that. I didn't—"

"I know."

"You do?"

"Granddad?"

"Yes Dylan?"

"Why can't I go through the gate?"

He didn't answer for a long time, but when finally he did speak, I suppose it was sort of like that first small step, which is really a giant leap... you know, the one Neil Armstrong took on the moon.

"Because you might never come back."

He wasn't lying. I could tell.

"Why not?"

"What?"

"Why might I never come back?"

"Because things that go through that gate don't always come back. That's all."

It wasn't much of an answer; sort of like calling something *magic* without explaining it. But one thing I've noticed about very old people – the ones I've met at least – is that they seem to like talking a lot, probably because they can't get distracted with doing stuff. Now, that's not necessarily a good thing; the trick, I've learned, is to keep on asking them questions. That way, you can get them talking about the things you're interested in, instead of the usual rubbish they drone on about. This doesn't work with people that aren't very old, like mothers for example, because they're so busy *doing* things that when they talk, it's only ever to *tell* you something – usually something you knew anyway. Of course, even old people can only answer questions about the things which they know about. Luckily my Granddad was eighty-seven at the time, and knew about an awful lot.

"Do you mean like a ball?"

"What?"

"Or a stick? It doesn't have to be a ball."

"What are you talking about Dylan?"

"If I threw a stick over that gate, it might get lost in a big bit of grass, or stuck up one of those apple trees, and then it wouldn't come back, would it? Not unless someone went and got it. And why should they do that for a boring old stick? Unless it's a special stick with a lion's head carved into it or something."

I seem to remember my Granddad thinking about this for quite some time. Come to mention it, I suppose he did that rather a lot when I asked him questions. It's probably because old people's brains work slower. You just have to put up with it I suppose.

"No, not like that at all."

"Why?"

"Because that's true of throwing something anywhere. A stick can't walk, or even think, which means that it can't even try to get back. But you can try; you've got legs haven't you, and something to control them with?"

"So you mean to say, even if I *tried* to get back, I wouldn't be able to?"

"I didn't say that; not exactly."

"Yes you did."

But he hadn't. I knew as soon as I said it that he

hadn't.

"You should pay better attention lad."

He was smiling now. I've no idea why. I was tempted to ask him, but the whole question of the gate was far too interesting for distractions.

"What I actually said, was that you *might* not come back. And that's very different, because it means if you tried, you *might* also succeed, but as this is my garden, I get to make up the rules as to who does what. And as I'm an old man, I don't much like taking risks any more. So I should prefer it if you didn't go through that gate, all right?"

"All right."

It was my turn to think. He'd answered my question well enough, and it wasn't as if his answer didn't make sense; and yet, I still didn't know exactly why I couldn't go through that gate. There was only one thing to do.

"That's all well and good..."

I remember feeling very clever when I said that, because my mother said it all the time when trying to make it seem that what she was about to say was far more important than what I'd just said.

"... but I still don't understand why I *might* not be able to come back through the gate; I mean, if I really were trying. Of course, some big catastrophe might happen, like an earthquake might swallow me up, but that's just as likely this side of the gate as it is that side of the gate. What I want to know Granddad, is what exactly it is about going through that gate that means that I might not come back? And if at all possible, I'd rather you tell me straight up, instead of beating around the bush and what not. I suppose it's because I like being direct – at least that's what people keep telling me."

He laughed.

"Shall I tell you where you get that from?"

"No thanks."

He laughed again.

"Well, Dylan. It's a complicated business, but now that you've caught the scent, I suppose there's no keeping you from the hunt. So I might as well just tell you the whole of it. But only on one condition..."

"What?"

"That if I tell you... *everything* that is, you have to promise me that you won't sneak off sometime and go through that gate when I'm not looking."

"Granddad?"

"Yes?"

"Can you really see things when you're blind?"

This time he grinned.

"You bet I can. Well... what's it to be?"

I promised.

3

MAGIC

I never make a promise unless I mean it. That's the whole point of a promise... that you really mean it. If you say it, and you don't really mean it, then I don't see how it's any different to lying. And like I've said, lying just makes things too complicated. But he looked at me, my Granddad, to make extra sure I suppose; just like I look at my mother to see what she's really thinking. Don't ask me how he looked at me, being blind... but he did.

"Very well."

I suppose he must have been satisfied that what I was thinking and what I said sort of matched up.

"That gate is a doorway, you see..."

Of course it was a doorway; it was a gate. Gates *are* doorways, except with gates instead of doors.

"A gateway, you mean?"

He looked confused, but not for very long.

"The point is lad, beyond that gate is a place that

ordinary folks don't know about. It's dangerous, and it's scary, and most of all, it's very *very* real. As real as you or I, sitting here now."

I looked at the gate. I looked at the orchard beyond it: the trees, and the grass, and the nettles and weeds. I looked even farther, to the dark forest, and down into the valley with green and white fields. I even looked up at the really big hill on the other side of the valley, which seemed more like a mountain than just a hill. I looked, and I thought... really quite hard.

"Granddad?"

"Yes?"

"You're beating around the bush again."

He made a strange noise, like a sort of cross between a sigh and cough; or a bark, if it had been made by a very old dog.

"It's different Dylan, beyond that gate. Because, well... it's a *magical* place."

There was that word again, except back then I still didn't know what it really meant.

"Is that because you don't understand it, or because you're too lazy to tell me about it?"

I suppose that was a bit rude of me, thinking about it now. I remember he looked a bit shocked, but that was okay, because he never got cross – not my Granddad – well, except for that one time I already mentioned, but I don't think that really counts.

"You really don't know anything, do you lad? But then I suppose you are only... what, eight?"

"Nine."

"Same difference."

"No, it's not. I know much more than when I was

eight."

"You don't know about magical places though do you?"

"I know that that word doesn't really mean anything."

"What word?"

"Magic."

He spat out some air, as if it had no right to be in his mouth.

"Only when some ignorant fool says it. Do I look like one of those to you?"

He didn't, not that I really knew what an ignorant fool did look like, I suppose more or less like an ordinary person.

"No."

"No. Because I'm not. And I'll tell you something else; there are some words, very special words, which most people use far too often. *Love's* one of them. And *Magic's* another. And that's because they mean powerful things, so people that really are lazy use them to make what they're saying *seem* more powerful too. But when you use a powerful word to mean something else, well... soon enough it loses its meaning altogether, or people forget what it ever was, and then it has no power at all."

"Is that why you never tell me you love me?"

I don't think he was expecting that, but it just sort of came out.

"No, Dylan. It's why when I *do* tell you, it means so much."

"But that's never—"

"Yes, well never mind that; I'm trying to explain something important here. You see, Magic does mean something, you just don't know what it is, because you've only ever heard ignorant fools say it; so when someone like me says it, who knows just what he's talking about, you don't take it seriously, because you think it means something else, or nothing at all. Do you understand?"

"Yes. It's sort of like painting."

I think it was my Granddad who didn't understand.

"What has painting got to do with it?"

"My mother says that to paint something properly you've got to have lots of layers, because real things have lots of layers. Like a leaf; it's not just green. It's a hundred types of green, and some white too, and even black."

"Go on..."

"So whenever I paint something now, I add a hundred different colours, and white, and black, just like my mother said. Except then it doesn't look like the thing it was supposed to at all; it just looks like a big whitish-black blob."

"Aha."

He smiled.

"And where's the meaning in a big whitish-black blob, eh lad? I'd much sooner have a green leaf."

"Exactly."

"Exactly."

And that's when it appeared – the bird I mean – except it wasn't really a bird at all. That is to say, it *was* a bird, but it was also more than a bird. Not that there's anything wrong with birds that are just birds. But this wasn't just a bird, and even if it had have been, it certainly wouldn't have been an ordinary one. I expect

There was this bird you see, and it flew really fast up the garden, landing on an upturned plant pot a few feet away from my Granddad's deck chair. Then it cocked its head, and looked straight at him, but only for a second or two. Then it did the same to me, but for even less time, as if it really didn't consider me worth looking at. And it didn't chirp, or tweet, or sing a little tune, or anything like that. But it did pluck a bluebottle from a spider's web which hung on the stalk of a nearby dandelion. The strange thing about that, was that the bluebottle was almost as big as the bird; not because it was a very big bluebottle – it was the normal size I should think – but because the bird, which was quite unlike any bird that I've ever seen, before or since, was as tiny as a twenty pence piece, and not much fatter than a hazelnut. And if you've ever seen a twenty pence piece, or a hazelnut, then you'll probably find that just as astonishing as I did.

"Granddad?"

"Yes Dylan?"

"What's the smallest bird in the world?"

"Now there's a question."

He thought for a bit.

"I can't say that I know to be quite honest with you. The world's a mighty big place, and I still haven't seen all of it. But the smallest bird that lives round here, hmm, that'd be the Jenny Wren; not much bigger than a ping-pong ball... unless you count the tail that is. They're a rare sight though; quite an elusive little thing. Why, have you spotted one? I should think it's more likely a sparrow in all truth Dylan. They seem to like this garden well enough – probably all the seed I put out. There's plenty about, and they look sort of like wrens, only a tad bigger, and with black markings..."

I can't quite remember what else he said; some more stuff about sparrows I think. Either way, it wasn't exactly what I'd asked him. That's what I mean about old people droning on sometimes. I suppose it was my own fault though, for being too distracted by the bird to keep on asking questions fast enough.

"This isn't a sparrow Granddad. I know what sparrows look like; we have them in our garden too. What does a Jenny Wren look like?"

Now, I know what you might be thinking... but I can tell you for certain I hadn't forgotten about the gate. It's true that I'm not one to get distracted when finding out about a thing, and the gate, or rather, this place beyond it, which my Granddad had talked about, was probably the most interesting thing I'd ever found out about in my entire life. But that didn't change the fact that this tiny bird was sitting there right in front of us, like nothing I'd ever seen before. And experience has taught me (as my mother would say) that one cannot just ignore a thing like that... so I didn't bother trying.

"Well, it's light brown with reddish wings, a bit speckled, and a creamy sort of breast, that shines like satin when it puffs itself up, which is exceedingly often. And it's tail, not very long, sticks straight up and wags about a lot, on account of it being so sure of itself. You see Dylan, the smaller the bird, the bigger the ego. Do you know what that means?"

"Like a celebrity?"

"A what?"

"My mother says that celebrities have the biggest egos; that's why they become celebrities, so they can get paid to be photographed doing nothing all the time."

"Precisely that. I should think Jenny Wren thinks herself a celebrity too."

"This isn't a Jenny Wren though."

"Your bird you mean? Well, no wonder; they're rare little critters lad, just like the real thing."

He chuckled. I've no idea why.

"What real thing?"

"Celebrities."

"Celebrities aren't rare Granddad. There's millions of them."

"Never mind."

I looked at the bird again. Actually, I'm not sure that I'd ever stopped looking at it, but I suddenly became aware of something. It wasn't bobbing around any more, distracted by this and that. It was just sat there, on the edge of that upturned plant pot, watching us.

And then, without any sort of warning, and for the very first time, it made a sound. It wasn't a spectacular kind of bird sound – not like a blackbird or anything. They have the best song of any bird, especially at dawn on a camping trip. I've often wished that my alarm clock could sound like a blackbird singing; it seems to be the only sound that can actually cheer you up at six o'clock in the morning. Someone should invent something like that... or just sell pet blackbirds to people, instead of stupid canaries and budgerigars.

"Dylan?"

I looked back at my Granddad. His expression had

changed. And he'd sort of frozen, I suppose a bit like I had at the gate. I don't know how I knew that he'd frozen, because I don't think he'd moved an inch in the entire time that he'd been sitting there.

"Yes?"

"What does this bird of yours look like?"

His voice had gone quiet, sort of hushed – even more than usual. And he spoke very slowly, like my mother did when she wanted me to shut up about something. Slow words have a sort of warning in them, you see. Though I couldn't think what my Granddad wanted to warn me about.

I looked at the bird. It looked back at me.

"Like a bird. With wings."

I must have panicked.

"Is it green? *Wait*, before you answer that..."

I remember swallowing – you know, like they do in cartoons. I thought that was just a made up thing until then, but it definitely isn't.

"... I want you to look at that bird, very carefully, and think before you speak. All right?"

"All right."

I looked at the bird... very carefully (whatever that meant).

"Yes."

"Yes what?"

"It's green. Not like a leaf though; more like a sort of pear colour."

He gasped. My Granddad actually gasped.

"And does it have a black stripe on its wing?"

"Yes."

"And is it so incredibly small that it looks like it

can't actually be a bird?"

"Yes. That's why I asked you what the smallest—"

"Of course."

I wasn't looking at the bird any more.

"Dylan?"

"What is it Granddad?"

"One last question; does this bird have a golden crown on the very top of its head? Not yellow, like a daffodil, but gold... so gold that it shimmers, as if it might be a real crown?"

It did. I knew that without even looking. It was the first thing I'd noticed about it. But for some reason the words got stuck in my throat.

"Er..."

"Well?"

"Would that be a bad thing Granddad?"

"Does it or doesn't it lad?"

"It does."

He smiled. A kind of long, satisfied smile, that went right up his cheeks and filled his eyes.

"Well I never; I thought I recognised that voice. It's been a long time my old friend – seventy years I should say. By the sounds of it though, you haven't changed a bit."

4

THE CONTEST

Birds can't talk. Everyone knows that. I certainly did. And yet for some reason I half expected this one to reply. When it didn't, I remember being quite surprised.

My Granddad didn't seem at all put off though. He went on talking as if that bird could understand every word he said. And all the while it just sat there, looking at him, sometimes with two eyes, sometimes with just one. It was one of those moments that captures so much of your attention, that you don't seem to be yourself any more, because you sort of forget everything except the thing that's happening. A bit like a dream, only the opposite, because dreams are all hazy, and this was crystal clear.

"Granddad?"

It felt a bit like I was interrupting something.

"Yes lad?"

But he didn't seem to mind; he was too happy I suppose. In fact, I'd say he was sort of *giddy*; which is what my mother calls things that are 'over-happy'. But I don't really see how a thing can be over-happy myself.

"Why are you talking to a bird?"

"Oh, this isn't just a bird."

I looked at the bird. It was definitely bird shaped; though I had to admit, it was far too small, and looked almost too real to be real... like those paintings you see in museums that almost look like photographs, even though they're hundreds of years old and have big cracks all over them.

"It's special you see. Me and it have a bit of a history."

"If it's not a bird Granddad, then what is it?"

"Well, of course it's a *bird* Dylan. The Goldcrest – that's its name – or 'Regulus regulus' for people trying to sound posh – that's its name in Latin. But it's also the rarest bird, and the smallest, that you'll ever meet. So introduce yourself; it's quite an honour to make the acquaintance of a Goldcrest, let me tell you. We've only ever met once before, and that was a very *very* long time ago."

I remember feeling a bit of a tingle on the back of my neck right then, as if I might have been meeting royalty or something, which actually makes perfect sense now I think about it, because I suppose I was.

"Is it obvious – to look at him I mean?"

"Is what obvious Granddad?"

"That he's a *king*, of course."

"What do you mean?"

"Don't you even know that? Gods, what do they teach you kids these days?"

It was probably one of those rhetorical questions;

which means that whatever your answer is, the other person gets to shout at you. I learnt that from my mother.

"Maths."

He seemed to be waiting for something. I couldn't understand what; but at least he hadn't shouted at me.

"Well, anyway... a very long time ago, back in the days of Aristotle – he was a Greek philosopher—"

"What's a philosopher?"

"Never mind what a philosopher is; I'm just trying to set the scene is all."

"Oh."

I didn't really know what 'setting the scene' meant either, but I thought it better not to mention that.

"Anyway, there was a competition, back in ancient times, to find the king of birds. You see, birds have to have kings and queens, just like we do."

He grinned. I don't know why; it sounded very reasonable.

"But not just any bird can be a king; after all, kings have to rule, so they have to be strong, and clever, and charismatic."

"What does that—"

"Charming – it means charming Dylan. Of course, all the greatest birds wanted to be king; who wouldn't? Ravens and condors, pelicans and flamingos, owls and eagles... each thought itself the best, and most fit to rule the others. But the deciding test, which was set by a very wise old albatross – the only bird that didn't actually want to be king – was to see who could fly the highest. Some of the birds thought this was unfair, because it was only really a test of strength, but the wise old albatross knew better. He knew that cleverness and charm were just as important. So he told the birds not to question his wisdom, and because he was almost as old as all the rest of them put together, they immediately agreed."

"Was he just pretending not to want to be king?"

"What?"

"The albatross. I expect he was just pretending, so that he could trick them somehow with this test, and then become king himself."

"Albatrosses do not trick people... or other birds for that matter."

"Why not?"

He seemed a little exasperated then – at least that's what my mother calls it when someone's head starts turning pink because I've asked them too many questions.

"Have you ever met an albatross Dylan?"

"No."

"When you do, you'll know why. That's all."

Albatrosses live mostly in Antarctica. I knew that even when I was seven. And that's an extremely long way away, even for holidays.

"Have you?"

"Have I what?"

"Ever met an albatross?"

"Shut up, and let me finish the story, would you?"

So I did.

"Thank you. Now, like I was saying, because all the birds *respected* the wise old albatross, they agreed to the contest, and all tried to fly as high as they could. Some didn't get very high at all, like the Blue Tit, which is a stupid bird; some got fairly high, like the hawk, because they were strong and fast; and others, like the condor and the raven, got very high indeed... that's because they were clever, and used the hot air currents to carry them up. But it was soon quite obvious to all of them that it was the eagle who would win, because he was the strongest, with the most stamina, and the cleverest at using the air currents."

"That makes sense. And I'm sure my mother once said an eagle was king of the sky."

"Then your mother's a damned fool, who knows about as much about anything as any other fool, which is not a lot, mark my words."

"What do you mean? She's my mother."

"Never mind. I didn't really mean that. It's just that you keep interrupting lad."

"Sorry."

"The point is Dylan; the eagle didn't win the contest. Even when it flew so high that the clouds looked like tiny sheep miles below, and it could see the curve of the world as day became night beneath the stars. *Even then*, it didn't win. Because when it was finally so exhausted, and so out of breath, that it hadn't the energy to beat its wings a single time more, another bird appeared – a tiny bird – from under the eagle's tail feathers, where it had been riding the whole time. The Goldcrest. Regulus regulus."

"So it cheated then?"

I could swear the tiny bird sat on its plant pot in front of my Granddad's deck chair chirped at me with an angry sort of look right after I said that. My Granddad seemed to find this highly amusing.

"Perhaps a bit, but not exactly. You see, the Goldcrest knew that the eagle was the strongest and cleverest of all the birds (apart from maybe the albatross, but he didn't want to be king anyway), so he asked the eagle, rather politely, if he might ride on his tail for a while, and the eagle, being a noble and selfless bird, at once agreed. Not only was the Goldcrest clever, but he was charming too; for he charmed that eagle, didn't he? And just as the albatross knew, to rule, a king must be charismatic, *as well* as clever."

"And strong. What about strong?"

"Ah well, the Goldcrest still had to beat the eagle, and it'd taken just about all his strength even to hang on. Tiny birds, and he was the tiniest of all, aren't designed for great heights, not like eagles, or even condors and ravens. Up so high, the Goldcrest could scarcely even breathe, the air being so thin. And to him, every gust of wind was like a hurricane. But somehow, don't ask me how, he found a strength that astonished even the eagle, and launched himself straight upwards like a golden arrow into the heavens, beating his tiny wings so fast that he clean shook off all the black, and left just a single stripe, like a bullet. He couldn't see, for his eyes were streaming with water; he couldn't breathe, for there was no air left to breathe; and every muscle in his body felt like it was on fire, but still he would not give in, he would not turn back, not until he touched the very moon with his beak, and proved to every bird in the world that he was as strong as them, and stronger."

I looked at the tiny bird, feeling a little in awe. I think it could tell, because it seemed very smug all of a sudden, and cocked its head at a sort of *told you so* angle.

"And did it... touch the moon with its beak?"

"Hard to say. The eagle had passed out by that stage, so the only witness was the moon herself, and despite many attempts, none of the other birds were ever able to get close enough to ask. One thing's for sure though, the Goldcrest had won the contest, and by a considerable way. So from that day forth, he was to be their king.

"But the thing is lad, in spite of his golden crown, which admittedly he wears with pride to this day, as you can see, and the black stripe on his wing, to remind him of the great effort he once endured, the Goldcrest isn't an arrogant bird – quite the opposite in fact. He knew that the eagle had helped him, and so he decided to tell all the other animals, and that included the people, like you and I, that it was the eagle, not him, who was king of the birds. He even gifted the eagle a touch of gold from his crown, which is why the mightiest of all are called *Golden*, and shimmer in the high sun, just like the crown from which they were painted. That way the Goldcrest could get on with ruling, which he knew was what being a king was really all about, while the eagle got all the fame and glory a bird could ever want."

"Granddad?"

"Yes?"

"Do you suppose in a way the Goldcrest was even cleverer than that wise old albatross?"

"Why do you say that?"

"Because he was brave enough to be king."

My Granddad had to think about that for a moment.

"That's very insightful lad. I daresay you do have to be brave to be a king, but I think sometimes..."

He smiled in the direction of the plant pot.

"... you have to be a little bit stupid too."

I expected the Goldcrest to give my Granddad an even angrier sort of look than it had me then. After all, calling a thing stupid, even a little bit, isn't exactly a compliment. But it didn't. Instead it just bobbed its head, flicked its tail once or twice, then flew away, like a golden arrow, back over the gate to goodness knows where.

"Has it gone?"

"Yes. Back over the gate."

I don't know how he knew; it hadn't made a sound when leaving.

"What a treat."

He looked happy, but a bit sad at the same time.

"Just like the first time I met him, all those years ago. It was in that very orchard too. The little charmer; he hasn't changed a bit."

"Do you mean to say that he's been there for seventy years? Beyond the gate, in the magical place?"

He grinned.

"And why not? Do you know how old I am Dylan? Eighty-six."

"Seven."

"What?"

"You're eighty-seven Granddad."

"Am I? Oh yes, I forgot about that. Well, if I can live to be eighty-*seven*, then why shouldn't a king live to be just as old, or even older?"

It was a fair question, and I could only think of one answer.

"Because it's a bird."

He spat out some more air again. I remember

wishing he wouldn't do that; it seemed like he had scarcely enough to talk with without spitting most of it out.

"Even if a bird can't live to be that old – which it can, for the record – it's beside the point anyway, because time's different in magical places. Most things are. And that's where he comes from, the king of birds, just like all the rarest of creatures: otters, owls, green squirrels..."

"You mean red squirrels?"

"I know what I mean lad. Don't you ever get that feeling when you catch a glimpse of a fox, or a badger, or a water vole dashing along the bank of a river into its hole?"

"I've never seen any of those things."

"*You haven't?* Well then, you haven't felt it either... except perhaps just now, when you saw the little Goldcrest."

I had felt something; a tingle, a sort of awe; and something else too, a realness, like suddenly waking from a dream.

"Granddad?"

"I wish you'd stop saying that lad; it makes me feel even older than I am, if it's possible to feel older than eighty-seven. If you've something to say, just say it instead of calling me *Granddad* all the time."

"Sorry."

"Never mind sorrys. What is it?"

"I just thought of something is all."

"Well?"

"It seems to me that the only way you could know all these things – about magical places, and how the rules are different there, and how that's where all the rarest creatures live – is, well..."

"If I'd been beyond the gate?"

"Yes."

"But you already know I have. I told you that I first met the Goldcrest in that very orchard, seventy odd years ago."

"Yes, but then I thought of something else."

"And what might that be?"

"That if you've been there, and you're not there any more, then that means... *you must know how to get back*."

5

A RABBIT, I THINK

I couldn't quite believe it at the time, but we'd been sat there, me and my Granddad, for three hours that April afternoon... it had seemed like less than one to me. Maybe time can work differently in *non*-magical places too.

My mother seemed very pleased with me when we left. She even gave me a handful of sweets from the old pantry – sugared cola bottles, they were my favourite. My Nan never used to give me more than one or two, and even then only ever secretly, and with a little wink which I never understood. I remember looking down into my hand at what must have been twenty then, and wondering why I even liked them so much. They didn't taste nearly as good either. And my mother left the key in the door; the big iron key to the pantry that my Nan had always kept hidden. I suppose it was easier for my Granddad that way; after all, there was a lot more than just sweets in there, but it didn't seem right somehow, just leaving it, right in the keyhole. It's funny how sometimes when a thing you've been dreaming of comes true, but not in a spectacular sort of way, you really just want things to go back to how they were.

"Thank you Dylan."

We were in the car driving home. I already felt a bit sick, but my mother wouldn't let me wind the window down because she said 'the noise brought her migraines on'. I'd sooner have a migraine than feel sick, but there was no point telling her that.

"What for?"

"Sitting with your Granddad. You really seemed to cheer him up somehow. He was almost back to his old self when we left, didn't you notice?"

I hadn't. In fact, it was only then that I even remembered he'd been different that morning. I expect my brain was far too occupied pondering things; like how old albatrosses lived (not to mention Goldcrests); and if a bird really could touch the moon with its beak (after all, Neil Armstrong had walked on it, and that was without even having wings, however strong his arms might have been); and whether that gate, which looked so ordinary, really could lead to a magical place where the rules were somehow different, like my Granddad had said. Most of all though, I couldn't stop thinking about getting back – back through the gate I mean – if I had of gone through. Because if my Granddad could do it, then why couldn't anyone?

"Did we really have to leave so suddenly? He was just about to tell me something."

"Oh really?"

She seemed to find this amusing. Her eyes grinned

at me a bit in the mirror. I looked away on account of feeling more sick; I suppose mirrors mess up your ears or something. That's what makes you sick, when your ears get confused.

"Well I'm glad the two of you were getting on so well, but we had to get home I'm afraid. I've got work in the morning, and your sister has exams to study for."

I didn't see the point of driving such a long way just to drive all the way back again a few hours later. It was inefficient, especially considering how much my mother liked to go on about petrol costs.

"Do you know anything about the gate? I mean, have you ever been..."

It seemed impossible that she hadn't; after all, my mother had grown up in that house, so just think how many hours she must have spent in the garden.

"Ever been what?"

"Nothing."

I can't really explain why, but I decided then not to ask her about any of it: not the gate, nor the place beyond it, not even the Goldcrest. Maybe it was sort of like those sugared cola bottles; I even had to throw the last few away or I might really have been sick. That felt horrible – throwing them away I mean – although I'm sure throwing up wouldn't have felt any better.

I didn't even try to sleep on the way back, not that time; it was hard enough when I was bored, but with my mind trying to puzzle so many things out it would have been just about impossible. I kept staring out of the window, especially to begin with, before we got to the motorway. The roads started off very small and thin, just about wide enough for a tractor, and a whole lot of cars stuck behind it. That happened to us at least three times every journey; my mother seemed to think it made a terrible difference, and was worth shouting about (though never out of the window at the driver of the tractor), but to me, the journey already seemed about as long as a journey can be, even without tractors to get stuck behind, so nothing could really make it any worse. And besides, I felt a bit less sick when we were going slowly.

At first I kept looking out over the fields and hills and wondering if they might be magical places too. We even drove through a bit of a wood, but not like the one in my Granddad's valley – not a proper forest. Still, it suddenly seemed very possible to me, everything he'd said I mean; after all, how much did anyone really know about places? It's not like you see scientists going about in the country wearing white coats and pointing magnifying glasses at everything. Perhaps they might here and there, to examine a particular type of frog or something, but not *everywhere*, and there are so many places, all at least bit different, so why not a lot?

And I had seen the Goldcrest. And it had been no bigger than a hazelnut. And it had had a golden crown, like a king. And I had felt, well... tingly, like I've already said. But I didn't know anything about that back then, except that it was very exciting and made everything sort of glow, like when the sun pops out from behind a cloud and turns the world orange. I remembered my Granddad saying that all the rarest creatures come from magical places, and that sort of made sense too, because it explained why they were so rare. But I'd never seen an otter, or a badger, or even an owl, except in photographs and pictures, which isn't nearly the same, and even in photographs and pictures I'd never seen a green squirrel. I tried to imagine what one might look like... it was actually quite easy.

"Are you all right back there? I expect you're trying to sleep, are you?"

I remember thinking how odd it was that my mother should say that, because if I had been trying to sleep (not that I was) being talked to would have made the whole thing a lot more difficult. But now that I think about it, I expect she'd been watching me in the mirror all along, and could tell that I was thinking about something, and wanted, maybe... *to help*. I didn't know that then. I wish she'd just come out and said it. My mother never seemed to say what she was really thinking – not back then anyway.

"No."

The annoying part is that I must have fallen asleep a bit after that, because the only other thing I can remember about that journey is seeing a dead rabbit in the road, and that was just before we got back. At least, I think it had been a rabbit, it was quite dark by then, and the body was all sort of squashed and bloody. I wondered if that rabbit might have come from a magical place; probably not, because rabbits aren't exactly rare, not like otters, or badgers, or owls. It still made me feel sad though; a bit empty inside. But then everything has to die, doesn't it? That and pay taxes! That's what my mother says... I don't really see how rabbits are supposed to pay taxes though.

MAY

6

THE ORCHARD

It hadn't occurred to me that my Granddad might die, but then it hadn't occurred to me that my Nan might die either, and she had. Perhaps death was just a bit stuck in my brain back then, what with her, and then the rabbit. I expect that's because nobody ever talked about it, and I've noticed the more you don't talk about a thing, the more you can't help but think about it. I asked my mother when we'd next visit – my Granddad that is – and when she told me 'one Saturday next month' in a casual sort of way, I remember suddenly thinking what a long time that was, even more so when I sat down and worked it out in days – about thirty if you're wondering. That really is a long time, especially if you're eighty-seven. Did you know there are some insects that only live for one day? Just imagine only seeing the sun rise and fall a single time.

Not that he had... died I mean. And it was actually twenty-seven days before our next visit, just so you know. By that time it was well into May, and I remember noticing when we arrived how everything smelled different (outside of the house at least). It was sort of fresh and warm at the same time, although that's more a feeling than a smell. It's hard to describe smells. I expect this one was a sort of mixture of grass, and flowers, and *newness*. It smelled alive, as if the world had just woken up and eaten its breakfast (which definitely included lots of jam).

My Granddad was sat outside on his deck chair, which looked a bit less mouldy than last time; I guess he must have worn some of it off, what with all the sitting he liked to do. It did almost seem like he hadn't moved, but he must have, because he was wearing a pink cardigan – I noticed it right away – and he hadn't been before. I suppose when you're blind and live by yourself it doesn't much matter what you wear.

"Hello."

"What?"

"Hello."

I said it a bit louder, just in case he was going deaf too. That happens to a lot of old people for some reason.

"Oh, it's you is it? I didn't hear you arrive. Is your mother here too?"

"She's inside."

"Good."

It's funny how when you haven't seen someone for twenty-seven days, even your own Granddad, you sort of forget how to be yourself, and start acting like they're a stranger. I really couldn't think what to say, except what I really wanted to say, and it seemed like I should say something else before saying that.

"Are you going deaf Granddad?"

Sometimes I wish I knew how to not be quite so direct, but it really is hard. Luckily he smiled, and then laughed. Anyway, it was probably a good thing that I said that, because I suddenly remembered how to be myself, and I think he did too.

"Probably lad. Everything else seems to be shutting down. Except this of course..."

He tapped the side of his head.

"Do you know how old I am Dylan?"

"Yes."

"Eighty-six. And I'll wager there aren't many eighty-six-year-olds as sharp as me."

There probably weren't many eighty-seven-year-olds either.

"Granddad?"

"Yes lad?"

"Do you remember what we were talking about before? About that bird, the Goldcrest, and the orchard where it lives, that you said was a magical place where otters and badgers and owls come from, and that you went through that gate, seventy years ago, but that I shouldn't – go through the gate I mean – because I might not be able to find my way back, but that you did – find your way back that is – because how else would you be sitting here now? Do you remember?"

It all came out a bit too fast I suppose. The time it took him to answer sort of balanced things out though.

"I remember."

"Well?"

"Well what?"

"How did you get back Granddad?

"Now there's a question."

What sort of a thing to say was that? Of course it was a question.

"You said you'd tell me. *Everything*. That's what you said."

"Did I now? Yes, I daresay I did. But only to keep you— You're not thinking about sneaking off in there are you?"

I'd made a promise. He couldn't have forgotten that.

"Are you going to tell me or not?"

"Keep your shirt on lad; I was just checking is all."

I wasn't wearing a shirt, but I suppose he couldn't have known that.

"I'll tell you what; go make me a cup of tea, and when you come back, I'll tell you the whole thing. How's that?"

I might have looked devastated right then, at least that's how I remember feeling, probably for about three seconds, which is a long time to feel something like devastated. Making a cup of tea might take ten or even fifteen minutes, and I had no idea where anything even was, like tea bags for instance. It was sort of like standing in a queue for twenty-seven days to go on that really amazing roller-coaster, only to get right to the front and then be whacked on the head with a measuring stick and told to go and grow another inch.

I had to get my sister's help in the end – that annoyed me. When you're five years younger than someone you always feel like the stupid one who doesn't know anything. Not that she tried to make me feel that way; at least I don't think she did. That's just the way it is I suppose.

He slurped at the tea. I like that sound; it seems to get on most people's nerves, especially my mother, but it always makes me think of hot chocolate.

"Did you have a map?"

"A what?"

"I was thinking about it, just now in the kitchen while I was making that tea, and I thought perhaps you might have had a map – when you went through the gate I mean – because then you could have followed it to find your way back, even if you went deep into that forest."

"Maps aren't much use in forests lad, not when its dark and everything looks just the same. A compass might have helped though... to point the way home."

"I've got a compass. Well, it's not mine exactly, but I could borrow it from my sister."

"And why should you want to do that?"

He stretched his head towards me a bit, and then sort of peered at me over his mug. His eyes were all cloudy and white, but I'm sure he was looking at me. My Granddad really hadn't got the hang of being blind.

"I was just saying... I mean, I *could*."

"Yes, well... it wouldn't do you much use beyond that gate. You can't trust things in magical places – especially compasses. Things work different there; not all the time, and not always in obvious ways, but that just makes things even more confusing... unless you're used to it of course – that takes a lifetime though."

"But you said you had a compass, and that it helped you."

"I said it *might* have helped, but I certainly didn't have one. And even if I had of had one, and it had, by some miracle, gone on working like compasses do out

44

here, I expect the right direction would have been quite the wrong direction anyway."

"What do you mean? How can the right direction be the wrong direction? That doesn't make any sense."

It was like calling your left foot your right, or your right foot your left, or something like that. One can't be the other, can it?

"Because."

"Because what Granddad?"

"Because when you enter a magical place, you're as far away from the gate you stepped through, as you think you are near. And it's only when you think you're as far away as you actually were when you thought you were near, that you might actually be getting somewhere. Understand?"

How could anyone understand that? It was then that I first realised, the only thing worse than people who don't explain things properly, is people who explain things so well that you can't make sense of anything they say.

"Not really."

"You see, it doesn't look the same Dylan, on this side and on that. Oh sure, there's an orchard, and a forest in a valley, but it's a different shape, and much, much bigger. It's like I told you lad, everything's different beyond that gate. And if you want to get back, well, first you have to find the right way, and most often the right way is where you least expect it to be."

"Granddad?"

"Yes?"

"Can't you just start at the beginning?"

"What beginning?"

"When you went through the gate. Seventy years ago. And saw the Goldcrest. Can't you just tell me the whole story – I mean, exactly as it happened, without any sort of explaining?"

"Oh, *that* beginning. Hmm."

His eyes twinkled a bit. I suppose he must have liked the idea.

"Well, I daresay I could... with some sugar that is."

"Sugar?"

"I like my tea sweet Dylan. And this..."

He handed me the mug.

"... isn't."

I looked down at the tea. It was a runny sort of brown colour. I don't know why people drink tea, or coffee for that matter, not unless they've run out of hot chocolate anyway.

"But you've already drunk half of it?"

"I was thirsty."

"It's going cold Granddad."

"All the more reason to make it sweet."

At least he had an answer for things. My mother would have just told me to shut up and get on with it.

"Next to the bread bin. In the round pot, shaped like a— um, melon; a smallish melon. I'm sure you'll find it."

Isn't it strange that I remember things like that? You wouldn't think making cups of tea, or going to find sugar pots shaped like melons was all that interesting. Maybe it's like that last breath you take before diving under at the swimming pool. There's nothing more boring than breathing; even watching paint dry (which I tried once, mostly just to spite my mother, but actually found slightly interesting, because I started seeing shapes as it went from wet to dry); but breathing, well... we do that every second of every day without even thinking about it. That last big breath though, at the pool, right before you enter a different world, far too interesting for a thing like breathing, *that* you remember.

"Much better. Thank you Dylan."

I wonder if tea exists in magical places. Hopefully not.

"Well now; the beginning. Let's see..."

He smiled.

"Yes, of course. It began with the second most beautiful thing that I've ever seen."

"You mean the Goldcrest?"

"Gods, no. Kings are majestic, but not beautiful."

"Then what?"

"You should know lad, you're looking at it. Or at least you might be if you weren't gawping at an old man. *The orchard* Dylan, bursting with colour and life. There's nothing like a wild orchard in May. Of course I'm lucky, that's what I see every time I come out here, even in winter."

"But you're blind Granddad."

"You don't say."

Sometimes it seemed like he needed reminding.

"Go on, take a look. A good long look."

It wasn't like I hadn't seen it already, but it's funny how you can see a thing, without always feeling it, especially as my Granddad could somehow feel it, without even seeing it at all.

I felt it then though. Every tree, and there must have been hundreds, was covered in flowers; so thick that you could only see the odd dot of branch beneath. And they weren't just white; they were a million shades of white. I don't even know how that's possible, because I always thought white was only one colour, but it's definitely not. It sort of looked like those trees were covered in snow, but not how they would be in winter, without leaves to catch it all... more like they'd reached out and grabbed every last flake from the air, and then, somehow, painted it all with honey.

What made it look even more beautiful, was that nothing else was white; not even the little glades and meadows that had been back in April. They were yellow now, filled with dandelions I suppose. I remember wishing that I was there, lazing in the sunshine, hidden in some little glade where no one could find me.

"I don't see it."

"You don't?"

I realised that that had come out a bit wrong.

"What I mean Granddad, is that I don't see how it can be the *second* most beautiful thing you've ever seen. What was the first?"

His eyes went a bit sad then, but only for a second, as if the sadness sort of exploded, like a firework, and let out a whole lot of colour. I've often noticed that about people; maybe sadness and happiness are kind of the same thing.

He smiled a bit secretly.

"That'd be the thing I found there, beyond the gate."

"I thought you said the Goldcrest wasn't beautiful."

"Don't be daft lad. I didn't go in there looking for the bird. I just sort of met him. In fact it was he that tempted me in. I followed him you see, into that magical place, until I was quite lost in a sea of flowers, drowning in the heady perfume of summer. Deary me, I've come over all poetic. I daresay it is though... love."

"What's love got to do with it?"

I wasn't trying to sound like Tina Turner – that's just what came out.

My Granddad looked up to the sky in a serious sort of way.

"Oh, nothing much. It was... the bird. Yes, the king. He told me that there was a girl, in the orchard."

"What sort of a girl?"

"What do you mean what sort of a girl?"

"The sort of girl that likes to climb trees, and make catapults, and keep on eating apple crumble until she's actually eaten more than me, which I really didn't think was possible... or the *other* sort?"

"What's the other sort?"

"All the rest, I suppose."

He grinned.

"Definitely the first, except more beautiful even than the orchard. If you can imagine such a thing."

I could. But only just.

"And magical of course, like all things that come from magical places."

"So that's why you went through the gate? To find a magical girl, even more beautiful than the orchard, who the Goldcrest told you about?"

"Yes. But he wouldn't like it if you called him that, especially not beyond the gate. He really is the king there. And that bit of gold on his head; it really is a crown."

"You mean... he looks different too?"

My Granddad laughed.

"No lad. He looks different here, in our world. The same is true of all things from that place. When they're there, they look just how they're supposed to, however bizarre that might seem to you or I, but when they're here, on our side of the gate, they look more or less how we expect them to look, except, well... with a sort of spark. Like you saw in the king. A little spark of something *extra*."

So that's what it was. That tingle. That extra realness that sort of looked like a painting. I had seen it.

"Sometimes things get passed over, from their side to ours. And we see them, once in a while, without even knowing what they really are. Unusual things, that are somehow strange, or seem to stand out; like that one pebble you find on a beach that doesn't look like any of the others, and seems to glow a bit in your hand; or that peculiar leaf that looks more like a little person than a leaf, with arms and legs, and a twisted sort of neck, until you look again that is, and then all you see is a leaf; or that shadow you half notice out of your window late at night, which doesn't seem to fit where a shadow ought to, and is perhaps a bit too black for any ordinary shadow... you might even feel a shiver down the back of your spine, but then you just draw the curtains, go to bed, and forget all about it. These things, and a lot more besides, were all born in magical places, but each, somehow, found its way into this world – our world. Perhaps forever, or perhaps just now and again, when it suits them.

"Of course, in our world they can't be magical any more, not on the surface at least, but if you were to take such a thing back to its home, the place it was born, through that gate for instance, well... you'd probably think yourself a loony and go quite mad. It's a wonder I didn't, I tell you."

I remember remembering so many things after he said that: collections of pebbles and shells buried on my window sill; leaves and conkers and other strange natural things I'd found when exploring; branches that looked like arms, or even faces. There was even this wild egg that I'd found when I was seven. It was a sort of luminous green, speckled white. But it was stone cold, and tiny. I kept it for weeks, thinking it might hatch, but it never did. I'd often wondered what happened to that egg – more than ever right then. I suppose I thought my mother must have thrown it out or something. Sometimes she really couldn't see the things that were important.

"Granddad?"

"Dylan?"

"That shadow you talked about; what does it turn into, when it goes home I mean... beyond the gate?"

7

GIRLS

We had ham sandwiches for lunch, out in the garden; my mother had brought the ham and bread from home. She didn't much like my Granddad's food, most of which came in tins. She said it was unhealthy to eat things that had last seen daylight before you were born. We had some of his tinned peaches for afters though – at least me and my Granddad did. I remember how delicious they were.

Of course, we didn't talk about the gate, or anything like that, not while they were there. My sister might have understood, but then again, she might not have, not with my mother there too. In fact, my Granddad seemed very different when we were all together, sort of like I remember him being before my Nan had died. He complained a lot, mostly about ordinary things, like 'the excremental rubbish they put out on the wireless these days' and how 'the country's gone to pot since privatisation' (whatever that meant). My mother didn't say a whole lot, sort of like my Nan, except without all the grinning and laughing. Did I tell you my Nan had the heartiest laugh I've ever heard?

I suppose it's a good thing he got the chance to get a bit of complaining in, even with mouthfuls of ham sandwich; after all, there was no one else to listen any more, and I expect he wouldn't enjoy complaining nearly as much by himself – at least not without looking in a mirror, but then he couldn't have done that anyway.

Not that I was really paying much attention to any of it; there were so many new questions all sort of bubbling up in my brain: about pebbles, and leaves, and green eggs, and girls... only the magical type of course. I remember lining them all up in order, so I could try to interrogate my Granddad a bit more efficiently that afternoon. My mother was always telling me to plan things better; she had an entire notepad for doing just that. I don't think having a notepad makes any difference though. She just made things fit how she wanted them to, and when they didn't fit, she ignored them, or kept on squeezing until they did. I used to wish I could do that.

"A darkling grub – most often at least, unless it's an especially rare one."

We were alone again, my mother and sister had just left to go 'organize the pantry'.

"That's what they turn into lad... the shadows that don't quite fit. You didn't think I'd forgotten did you?"

"I..."

"Except it's the other way round of course. It's the darkling grub that becomes the shadow when it pays us a visit."

"What's that?"

"What's what?"

"That thing you said."

"A darkling grub?"

"Yes, that."

"Well... it's a big black creature, naturally, except sometimes it can be tiny, or even a medium sort of size, and it's not exactly black, more transparent really, like a thin mist at night. And that's when it comes out – at night – and spends all of its time in the very darkest places that it can find. That's why you only ever see its eyes – red, like fire opals they are."

I don't think I even knew what an opal was at first (it's like a glass stone if you're wondering), because I remember imagining eyes made of actual fire, burning red and orange.

"There are lots of eyes beyond that gate Dylan; mostly watching you, especially at night, or in the depths of that forest. And you can see them all, not like here where you just think you can, but when you look closely they're not there any more. In magical places those eyes look right back into you."

"Do they eat things... like people?"

"I daresay some of them might, if you're not careful. But it's generally teeth that eat things, not eyes."

"Not the eyes Granddad, the darkling grubs... do they hunt people from those dark places so they can eat them?"

He looked at me as if I was stupid. But it wasn't my fault. How was I to know he'd met one?

"Just because a thing might *seem* scary, it does not necessarily follow that it *is* lad. That's one thing I learned beyond the gate. And of course the opposite."

"What opposite?"

"That there are things out there which don't seem scary at all... until you get to know them a bit that is. As for darkling grubs, well, the only thing they eat is light, which is a curious thing, because they're quite terrified of it."

I remember trying to imagine how a living creature might eat light. It seemed very odd, because how could it swallow it? And when you turn the light on, or go stand in the sun, there isn't exactly something obvious that you can stick a fork into, or shove in your mouth. But then I remembered that plants eat light; we'd learned a bit about that at school. And they grow into trees so big, that some of them are bigger even than blue whales; so light must be quite a good thing to eat really. It made me wonder why everything doesn't eat light, like people for example? Then we wouldn't have to waste so much time chewing things.

"If they eat light Granddad, then why are they so terrified of it? It's not like we're terrified of ham sandwiches, or tinned peaches."

I must have forgotten about marzipan.

"Isn't it obvious lad? What's every shadow's worst enemy?"

It hadn't occurred to me that shadows could have enemies.

"The one thing that can swallow them whole."

"Oh. You mean..."

Light.

He grinned, a sort of toothy grin.

"It eats *them*... right out of existence. Except for their eyes, but they just fall to the ground and turn into ordinary opals."

"But if light eats them, then how do they eat light?"

"With great difficulty I should think. But then I never really asked – it seemed impolite."

"Do you mean to say... you actually met one Granddad?"

He seemed to grow a few inches when I asked that, or at least his back straightened up a notch or two. He looked very proud. But then I suppose there can't be many people who've actually *met* a darkling grub.

"That's right lad. Seen hundreds of course, at least their eyes, in the forest mostly, where it's dark and there are places to hide. But they're terribly shy creatures. Won't let you get close. Except for this one..."

"What one? How did you meet it? What happened – exactly I mean?"

And then I remembered the plan. At least the bit about starting at the beginning.

"Wait. I want to know everything Granddad."

"Yes, I'd gathered that lad."

"No, I mean from the start. You said you went in the gate looking for a girl... a magical girl?"

"Yes, I suppose I did. Not that I was really expecting to find her."

"Why not?"

"Because, well... when you're a young man you don't ever really expect to find girls – especially not ones like that."

He shuffled a bit, awkwardly.

"Besides, would you believe a talking bird Dylan? A talking bird claiming to be a king? I didn't know everything I've told you remember, not back then. Back then I didn't know anything much about anything, truth be known."

I couldn't see what was so hard to believe about a magical girl... at least not when it's a talking bird that tells you about her.

"You mean to say the king tricked you somehow?"

"No, not at all. But I was just minding my own business, admiring the orchard from afar, much like you I imagine, when he appeared out of nowhere."

"Like he did to me. When he sat right there, on that upturned plant pot."

"That's it lad, except I followed him you see. And when he got beyond the gate, well, that was when he suddenly changed. Of course, I couldn't quite believe it at first. You see, his wings had grown little hands right at the end, and with one of them, his left I think it was, he reached up to his beak, and adjusted a little pair of spectacles – they can't have been any bigger than pinheads. Then he looked right at me, sort of peering through those tiny glasses, and started talking... in a voice deep as thunder too.

"Well, I near swooned; you know, passed out, like you read about in Dickens and such. I thought I must be losing my mind. But, after a time, I just became accustomed to it, and I could tell he was a decent sort of fellow."

"Because he was a king you mean?"

"Yes, I expect that was it. And that crown, well... you can't much argue with someone wearing a thing like that, even if they are about an inch tall. I daresay it's the finest crown I've ever seen."

"What about the Queen's? I mean *our* Queen's, in

the tower of London?"

He spat out some air, and then coughed, as if he'd accidentally swallowed some at the same time.

"Not a patch lad. Crowns forged in magical places, and I doubt there are many at that, are like nothing you've ever seen. Come to think of it, you more feel them than see them."

I remember being even more impressed by this than I might otherwise have been, because as he said it, tears were rolling down his face and his voice was all broken. I had to remind myself that it was only because he went on spitting out air all the time.

"Then what happened?"

"He told me about the girl. She was just like me, he said... except a girl, obviously."

"What do you mean 'just like you' – because she was a person? I thought you said she was somehow magical?"

"And she *was* Dylan. Oh, like nothing else too. But the king, well, he could tell, that her and I were... a good sort of match I suppose. She was a bit of a dreamer too you see – that's what he told me – and an outdoor type. The sort of girl that likes to climb trees, and make catapults, and keep on eating... what was it?"

"Apple crumble."

He grinned.

"And make it too; with rhubarb and blackberries mixed in so it's extra sweet. I like things that are extra sweet lad."

I wonder if tea might actually taste nice with all that sugar my Granddad put in. My mother never let me try it with sugar; she said it tasted just the same without, you just had to get used to it, and that because it had taken her about twenty years to 'get used to it', she was going to spare me and my sister the same effort.

"But how did he know all that Granddad – about you and the girl?"

"Kings know things... just like people who do a lot of watching know things. And he was both."

"But you didn't believe him? That's what you said."

"I didn't exactly know what to believe, standing there, looking over that gate, talking to a king. But then I daresay I didn't have a whole lot to lose, and when he told me the girl was even more beautiful than that orchard, and better smelling too, well... that settled it."

I remember wondering what a girl could possibly smell of that was so nice. I knew about perfume of course, but I've never really liked perfume, especially not the way my sister used to put it on. Whenever I told her that she smelled like acid she always use to laugh, and tell me that was the whole point, to make my eyes bleed (which I'm sure it did sometimes). But now that I think about it, girls do have a sort of smell, at least I know of one that does. Perhaps its only the magical sort.

"Granddad?"

"Yes Dylan?"

"What about Nan... wasn't she the most beautiful thing you've ever seen?"

He didn't answer.

"Before she was all wrinkly I mean."

The silence was somehow much louder than any words.

"And old."

I wish I hadn't said that. Any of it.

8

EIGHTY-SIX BEAMER

My Granddad was gone for what seemed to me like a very long time.

He just got up and left. Back into the house. I didn't say anything of course. Sometimes you just sort of know when you've already said too much, and that saying something else would just make things worse. My mother was always telling me to think before I spoke. I remember wishing more than ever right then that I could have been better at doing that.

The strange thing is, I didn't really miss my Nan back then. I do now, especially when I think about stuff like rubber bands, and sugared cola bottles, and invisible drafts; even thinking of marzipan makes me remember her in a good way. But back then, I don't know, I suppose she hadn't been dead long enough for me to miss her, or maybe I just didn't know what it meant to miss someone. You're supposed to grieve when a person in your family dies; that's when you think about them a lot, and it makes you cry. I did a fair bit of crying when I was nine, but never about my Nan. It was always about something stupid or selfish, like being forced to go to bed early, or not being allowed to get a pet guinea pig. I don't know why I even wanted a pet guinea pig; all they do is eat grass and make honking sounds when you poke them a bit.

"Here. This is for you."

I didn't even notice him come back... not until he was standing right next to me. I suppose I must have been thinking about things. It's funny how sometimes you can concentrate so hard it's like the world stops existing around you, but other times, like when you *have* to concentrate, you can't help but notice every little thing there is to notice, except the one thing you're supposed to be concentrating on. It's almost as if brains have a miniature brain of their own, and when you tell them to do something they don't want, they act a bit like I did when my mother refused to let me have a guinea pig. Sometimes I wished mine would just grow up and learn to do exactly what I told it.

"What is it?"

My Granddad's eyes were a bit red and puffy, but he seemed better somehow. He was even smiling a bit.

"What's it look like lad?"

It looked like a stone, except made of glass, and with an entire galaxy trapped inside, like those pictures you see of space, with impossibly bright colours – stars I expect – all swirling about to make shapes. I wonder if our sun looks like that from the other side of the universe, and there are aliens somewhere with photographs of us, shrunk down to just one tiny dot of light on a page of millions.

He sat down again on the deck chair. It took him a while. I hadn't realised that sitting could be such a complicated business.

That stone... it was different somehow. As if it might have been alive.

"It was your Nan's, but she'd have wanted you to have it Dylan. It's not like I've much use of it any more, and besides, something tells me you'll treasure it better than, well... anyone else."

But what it looked like most of all, when I stopped thinking about it so hard, was an eye.

"It's a fire opal lad."

I think my jaw really must have dropped. I remember my mouth being so open that I'm sure something flew inside – probably some sort of beetle. It tasted like burnt chicken.

"But Granddad, this is—"

"Now don't get all soppy on me lad. It's just a little memento is all."

I've still got no idea why he said that, because I had no intention of getting even a little bit soppy.

"These little chats of ours, well, they cheer me up no end, in case it wasn't obvious. And I didn't mean to, you know... storm off like that."

I suppose it might have been a storm, if storms didn't have any thunder, or lightning, or rain, and were just very overcast.

"Anyway lad, I got to thinking, back in the house, what with all our talk about, well... everything, and then I remembered *that*."

He nodded at my hand.

I still couldn't quite believe it.

"But Granddad; how did it die?"

"How did what die?"

"The darkling grub – the one you met? You said that when they die, all that's left are their eyes, and they just sort of, fall to the ground, and become..."

I looked down again at the eye; I could swear it was glowing in my hand.

"Fire opals. Yes I did, didn't I?"

"Did the light swallow it whole, like you said?"

I'm not sure he really wanted to tell me, because he seemed to ponder for an awfully long time before finally answering.

"I daresay it was the first creature I met, excepting the king that is, but you already know about him. I'd just stepped through the gate, and suddenly it appeared in place of a shadow. I must have seen it from this side, just not for what it really was. Two fiery red eyes looked straight at me from a wispy sort of body, so thin that you could see right through it. And there was nothing else: no arms or legs, no ears, no mouth. But I'm sure it gave me a smile all the same; it could see I think, just how shocked I was, and scared. Until I looked into its eyes that is – there wasn't a lot else to focus on – and I saw that they were warm, and gentle... not scary at all.

"Of course, I asked the king what it was, and he told me right out, but he seemed to think I should just ignore it and go on looking for this girl he talked of. I daresay he was used to things like darkling grubs, being from there and all, but I certainly wasn't. And how could I ignore a thing like that? A mysterious creature with eyes like fire opals and a body made of black mist. Well, I walked for a bit, not really paying any attention to where I was going of course, but it just followed me, and every time I turned around, there it was, looking right at me, as silent as if it were a real shadow."

"I thought you said they only came out at night, and lived in the darkest of dark places, away from the light?"

"That's right lad... but not this one. I told you it was a bit different, didn't I?"

I stared at the eye. The colours were incredible; they seemed to dance and twinkle just like a real flame.

"What was its name?"

"Darkling grubs don't have names lad. How can a thing without a mouth have a name? It could never tell you what it was."

"Nor can babies."

"What?"

"Babies can't tell you what their name is, but they still have one. So do guinea pigs... at least mine would have."

He smirked, sort of like my sister did when she thought she was about to beat me at chess even though it was still my turn; which was usually about the time that I'd accidentally knock the board over, or suddenly feel so ill that my mother would say we had to 'call it a draw'.

"Ah, but both babies *and* guinea pigs – not that I see what they have to do with anything – do have mouths, now don't they lad?"

"Mole End."

It was the name of my Nan and Granddad's house – *his* house. I've no idea why they called it that, because as houses go, it was really quite pretty; made of wonky old stones and covered in ivy and flowers. My mother always described it as 'a tumbledown cottage, likely to tumble down at any moment'. She seemed to find this hilarious; I could never understand why, because that could have been quite inconvenient when you think about it. Anyway, whatever it was, I'm sure it looked a lot better than a mole's end. I expect my Granddad only called it that to scare people off.

He wasn't smirking any more.

"What about the door? That's sort of like a mouth."

"No it isn't."

"No, I daresay it isn't."

"This house isn't even alive, not like the darkling grub, and yet you still gave *it* a name Granddad."

"Oh well, of course the darkling grub had a name that someone *else* had given it – that's different."

I remember trying to think of something which had a name that it had called itself. For some reason all I could think of was Elton John, because my mother had once told me that that wasn't his real name – his *first* real name I mean.

"What was it then?"

I don't know why he didn't just tell me in the first place.

"Eighty-six."

"What's *eighty-six*?"

"Beamer. Eighty-six Beamer – that was her name."

I considered this for a moment. It was definitely a very strange name, but then it would probably have been wrong to imagine that something like a darkling grub could have a name that *wasn't* very strange.

"Why's there a number in it?"

"Because... there's a lot of them, darkling grubs."

There's a lot of people too, but for some reason it didn't occur to me to point that out.

"Oh."

"And Beamer, because, well... this one had a particular knack for beaming, like I told you, even without a mouth."

That made sense, I suppose.

"How did you find out – its name I mean?"

"I asked the king. And he knew everything, naturally."

"Did he tell you who gave it it?"

"Who gave what what?"

"Who gave Eighty-six Beamer her name?"

I probably wouldn't have thought to ask that, not if my Granddad hadn't reminded me that it hadn't named itself. It's not the sort of thing you think about really.

"Well... whoever made her I suppose."

"You mean her mother?"

"Not necessarily; things in magical places aren't always made in the same way that things here are."

"What do you mean?"

"Never mind what I mean lad. Don't you want to know what happened, to Eighty-six Beamer that is? I was in the middle of telling you her story, or did you forget?"

"No."

"You don't want to know what happened?"

"Of course I do."

"Then why did you say 'No'?"

I remember his voice being a little louder as he said that; I didn't know why at first, but it was quite convenient, because normally his voice was so quiet that

I had to strain my ears just to hear what he was saying.

"Because you asked me if I forgot. And I didn't."

"It was a rhetorical question lad – the one about forgetting I mean. Don't you even know about rhetorical questions? Wait, there's another for you."

Of course. That explained why his voice had got louder. Just like I said.

"Yes."

For some reason it didn't work a second time. He just smiled.

"Do you remember I told you that darkling grubs were terrified of light?"

I nodded... sometimes I forgot he was blind too.

"Because it eats them. I remember."

"Well not this one lad – not Eighty-six Beamer. You see, she wasn't afraid any more. I daresay she'd lived too long to be afraid of anything much. They get like that sometimes... when they're very old. The king told me so."

"What do?"

"Darkling—"

He paused.

"People, Dylan."

I suppose that made sense too. After all, my Granddad was eighty-seven at the time, and he didn't even seem to be afraid of my mother.

"Anyway, as I was walking, deeper into that orchard, surrounded by flowers and the sweet smell of summer bonfires..."

"Bonfires?"

"Yes, well, the king was hopping about on my shoulder smoking a pipe, and that's what it smelled of."

"I thought smoking was a bad thing. My mother says it gives you cancer."

"Pipes are different... especially the ones that come from magical places and are smoked by the king of birds."

"Oh."

"Anyway, I kept looking back at the darkling grub – at Beamer. But I told you that already, didn't I? Wait, don't answer that lad. I know that I did. But I didn't tell you what I saw. You see, she was changing, each time I looked; getting smaller, and thinner, and fainter."

"Because of the sun?"

"There was enough shade beneath those leafy fruit trees to keep her going for quite a while, and it wasn't like she was unhappy; every time I looked, that beaming smile of hers grew a little stronger... even as she slowly faded away.

"I didn't know at the time, about them being eaten by light that is. I just thought it seemed very strange. And it is a queer sort of thing, when you think about it, being followed by a smiling shadow into an orchard."

I looked down again at the fire opal – at the eye. I'm sure it looked right back into me. My own eyes started to throb a bit, and my throat went all tight. I know this is going to sound ridiculous, but I felt like crying. I'd never even met Eighty-six Beamer, and had only found out about her that very day, and yet for some reason – I think it was the way my Granddad explained it all – I felt as if I missed her.

And then I remembered my Nan, who I didn't really miss at all – not back then.

"So it died?"

"Yes, I daresay it did lad. We came out into a glade – a parting in the trees – and that's when I heard two little thuds. It was the eyes, you see."

"Good."

My Granddad didn't look nearly as shocked as I felt; not that I showed it.

"Why do you say that Dylan?"

"If a thing is so stupid as to walk about in sunlight, even when it knows that sunlight kills it, eats it right up, then it deserves to die. That's what I think anyway."

I felt angry, but not really at Eighty-six Beamer.

My Granddad leaned over the side of his deck chair and smiled at me in a secret sort of way.

"Do you know what I like best about you lad?"

I didn't answer. I think I preferred his quiet voice right then.

"You've got more common sense than the rest of this family put together. It's a rare thing, that."

I swallowed hard. The tears never came.

JUNE

9

THE TELEPHONE CALL

There was one question – one vitally important question, as I saw it – which for some reason hadn't occurred to me that Saturday afternoon in May.

My mother is always telling me that I 'can't see the forest for the trees'; it's one of those silly proverb things which people say to try and sound more clever than they really are. Anyway, I think it's a lot of nonsense, because it's really the other way round, isn't it? Seeing the forest is easy, because that's the obvious part; it's seeing each tree, and noticing what makes it different that's really tricky.

The details don't always stand out, not unless you think really hard about a thing. And that's what I did when I got home. I stopped feeling, sad and angry, which left plenty of room in my brain for puzzling stuff out. And then it just appeared... the question, I mean.

What had happened to the other eye?

My Granddad hadn't mentioned the second one. In

fact it hadn't even seemed like he had it, not from the way he talked. It nagged at my brain that question, like a sort of worm, crawling about in my ear tubes, always whispering the same old thing – if worms had mouths to whisper with that is. But it wasn't like I could ring him to ask; of course, there *was* a telephone there, but it was only my Nan who would ever use it. My Granddad outright refused to even acknowledge it existed, let alone answer a call. The most baffling part about that was that when my mother once asked him why, he said that he preferred to look a person in the eye when he was talking to them, instead of staring into thin air. Sometimes I could swear he was just pretending to be blind.

One very good thing did happen a day or two after that visit though: I found the egg. You know, the little green egg with white speckles that I'd first found abandoned when I was seven. My mother hadn't thrown it out at all. I should have known she wouldn't do a thing like that – she was far too clever. She'd just put it somewhere safe when tidying my room up, which is probably a good thing, because I might have lost it otherwise.

So I had the egg, and the fire opal, which was really the eye of a darkling grub called Eighty-six Beamer. I knew that came from a magical place, and I was fairly certain the egg did too, even though I couldn't really say for sure, unless... no, I'd made a promise. Perhaps if I just showed it to my Granddad though, he might be able to tell. The funny thing was, I remembered that fire opal almost filling my hand back at my Granddad's house, and the little egg, well... that had once seemed exceedingly little, even for an egg. But now, or rather *then*, they were both sort of the same size – not exactly, exactly, but near enough.

So I hid them both together; in an empty jam jar with a lot of toilet roll shoved in the bottom for protection. I think I might have even punctured some air holes in the lid, just in case. Then I buried it in our back garden, which was the only sure way to stop my mother from tidying it up again; not that that was a bad thing, it just might have been very inconvenient is all. I think that was the third deepest whole I'd ever dug, and probably the only one I ever filled in again. I even planted the grass back on the top to add an element of disguise. I remember it being tremendously exciting when I dug it back up though, especially the moment my spade scraped the top of the jam jar. But that wasn't for another four weeks; not until the Friday evening before the Saturday morning when we were next supposed to visit my Granddad. Except we didn't... and it was all my sister's fault.

"She's sick Dylan. And that's the end of it."

"But she doesn't look sick."

And she hadn't, at least not any more than usual.

"She's not even in bed."

"That's irrelevant."

Whenever I was sick my mother made me stay in bed – actually, that's not quite right; she didn't exactly *make* me. You see, she told me that if I had the energy to get out of bed, and walk down the stairs (to get a packet of salt and vinegar crisps for instance) that my body was obviously not so sick that it couldn't walk about at school. And if I could watch television in the lounge, even if it was lying down on the settee wrapped in the eider-down, that my mind was obviously not so sick that it couldn't concentrate on school work just as well. She said the best cure for the kind of sickness I seemed to get was doing things (as long as it wasn't watching television or eating crisps). And there was never any point trying to reason with her when she said a thing like that; she'd only have started asking me rhetorical questions.

"But can't we just go without her? It's not like she even talks to Granddad. She might as well not be there at all."

My mother stopped what she was doing and glared at me, tight-lipped. That was never a good sign.

"Well maybe she wants to Dylan. Maybe she just doesn't know how. I seem to remember there was a time when you didn't either. Or have you forgotten that?"

"Yes, well... then I just *did*."

"And whose to say she won't too?"

I remember thinking how unlikely that seemed.

"Besides, she helps me with the cleaning, and that's just as important. It'd be infested if we didn't clean that place, and then where would he be? In hospital no doubt, with food poisoning, or something far worse. Not that he ever says thank you – not once. And he hasn't smiled at me in years."

She looked right at me then, as if she might have somehow forgotten I was there. Just for a second though.

"We'll go next Saturday, all right? Now don't keep going on about it. I've things to do."

And that was the end of that.

My sister was standing in the doorway, listening in. I gave her a look – probably not one of my nicest looks.

I think I might even have snarled a bit, come to think of it. I expected her to laugh at me, or suddenly come over all smug, like just about every other time she got her own way (which was practically always). But not this time; this time she just walked away without even looking at me. Maybe she really had been sick. That's not what I remember though. What I remember is how sad she suddenly looked. I've no idea why.

I couldn't quite believe it when he called that Sunday morning – my Granddad that is, on the telephone, just like a normal person might.

Unfortunately it was at 7:37 in the morning; I know that because the first thing I did when my mother pulled the duvet off my bed (which she called 'the last resort') was look at the time on my alarm clock... and then throw it at the wall. It was one of those alarm clocks shaped liked a football that you're supposed to throw at the wall. Normally that's how you turn it off, so I suppose I must have mistook my mother's voice for the siren or something.

"For the last time Dylan, get up! Your Granddad's on the telephone and he wants to talk to you."

I'd say it was probably about the twelfth or thirteenth time she'd said it, but it was only then that the words actually sounded like words, instead of just a lot of noise that my brain couldn't understand.

I got up and followed my mother out of the room. She led me to the kitchen and handed me the telephone.

"Yes?"

"Hello."

"Hello."

"Who's that?"

76

"Dylan."

"Dylan?"

"Yes."

"Oh, good."

I remember thinking the whole thing must have been a dream, and trying to work out if I was actually awake. They say you're supposed to pinch yourself, but I'm sure I've done that plenty of times in dreams, and it hurts just as much.

"Your voice is all squeaky lad. Must be the telephone; makes you sound like a girl."

I tried to levitate instead.

"Um... okay."

That's when you sort of will yourself to start flying, and your body begins to float up off the ground. Usually it works in dreams – at least it does in mine.

"What in God's name is that noise? Is this thing even working?"

I must have been straining a bit too hard, not that it made any difference.

"Nothing."

I definitely wasn't dreaming.

"Can you hear me lad? *Hello*?"

"Hello. Yes."

"Well then... you couldn't visit yesterday Dylan. Your mother told me."

"I know."

"Apparently your sister's sick, and it's none of my business what's wrong with her."

I think he must have forgotten that we all lived in the same house.

"But your mother's going to drive you here next

weekend. Next Saturday. In the morning. Arriving sometime between ten and eleven."

I knew that too.

"Yes."

"So... how are you Dylan?"

You know how sometimes when a person yawns it makes everyone else yawn too? Well that's because yawning is infectious. I always used to think that was because a 'yawn' was actually some invisible creature which lives in mouths, and has to keep making them open all the time, probably when it runs out of bits of food stuck between teeth (which obviously it eats), so that it can leave one mouth and enter another to find more bits of food stuck between teeth. Anyway, that's what I *used* to think, like I said, until, that is, I watched a nature documentary about chimpanzees. Apparently chimpanzees catch yawns off each other too, and it has nothing to do with some invisible creature. It's actually because people (and chimpanzees) like to copy each other, without even knowing they're doing it, so they feel more like they're the same. And if you feel more like you're the same as someone, that's supposed to 'strengthen your bonds' with them... according to David Attenborough at least – it was him that said it on the documentary. The point is, I expect it's the same with everything: like being happy, or sad, or smiling, or picking your nose, or... getting nervous.

And I think that's what must have happened; my Granddad was nervous because it was probably the first time he'd ever used a telephone, and so I caught it off him without knowing it to try and 'strengthen our bonds' and got all nervous too.

"Fine. I'm fine."

Saying all that, it was the first and only time my Granddad had ever asked me how I was, which certainly threw me a bit.

"Excellent. So am I."

I can't believe I didn't ask him – about the other eye I mean. I'd been thinking about nothing else for weeks. I'd even spent that entire Saturday staring at the egg and fire opal (having just dug them up again) and trying to plan out my next set of questions for the following weekend. There was so much to find out.

I think that was when he coughed down the phone; except not quite *down* the phone, sort of more like *away* from the phone, only so loud that he might as well not have bothered. I wasn't worried though; my Granddad coughed all the time, though admittedly not often like that. I just sort of moved the telephone a bit further away from my ear-hole.

"Right then Dylan, I'll be off. Things to do lad. Can't stand around here all day chatting to the likes of you on this contraption."

"Goodbye Granddad."

I don't think he'd got the hang of Goodbyes yet. He just hung up.

I'll never forget that call. It took me weeks not to get at least a little bit nervous every time the telephone started ringing. It didn't occur to me until much later that day to ask my mother why he'd called us so early.

"Because he's old."

I suppose that explained it perfectly well; after all, he was eighty-seven. And blind. I wonder what he did all day, apart from sitting down, and then getting up again to go to the toilet, or to make a cup of extra sweet tea, and then sitting down again. He couldn't even do jigsaws, but then I expect I mentioned that already, didn't I?

10

INSPECTING THINGS

"He's not in the garden."

It was the following Saturday, at just before ten o'clock in the morning. We'd arrived early, having set off even more early, on account of my mother hoping to avoid the 'mid-morning tractor rush'. It hadn't worked though; apparently the early morning tractor rush is even worse than the mid-morning one.

"Of course he is Dylan. He's never not in that garden, you know that."

She didn't seem the least bit concerned – my mother I mean – but there was something about that deck chair without my Granddad sitting in it that I didn't like. I remember noticing an empty mug on its side underneath the chair. Then I looked a bit harder through the kitchen window and noticed five or six more. It wasn't that he was lazy, more that he forgot about things, and then couldn't spot them later, like most people would have – at least that's what my mother kept saying... mostly to herself.

"He really isn't. *Look*."

She sighed. I don't think she considered finding my Granddad half as important as cleaning out his fridge. Apparently it smelled 'like a toilet' in there, which I found hard to believe, because even rotten vegetables don't smell like a toilet. But then I suppose my Granddad didn't really eat vegetables. I remember briefly wondering what was in that fridge. And then backing away a bit. More or less all the way to the window.

"*See*. He's right there."

I turned around.

And there he was. At the very end of the garden. Close to the gate, as if he might have just come through it in fact; not that it was open or anything.

I remember looking around to see where else he could have come from. There really wasn't anywhere obvious, unless he'd been hiding behind a bush, but that seemed unlikely, because it would have required him to crouch down, or at least lean over quite a bit, and it took my Granddad ten minutes just to sit on a chair. Then again, he did seem to enjoy sitting on chairs, so maybe he did that on purpose to drag the whole thing out, in which case, who's to say he didn't like crouching, or leaning over too? But anyway, that's beside the point, because what could he have been hiding from? It's not like he knew we were there or anything.

"Did you go through the gate?"

I was already half way down the garden, and might have accidentally shouted a bit.

"What the bloody hell—"

He definitely hadn't known we were there.

"Sorry Granddad."

"Oh, it's you lad."

My Granddad used a walking stick some of the time; not like one of those fold-up white ones which most blind people use to stab you with on pavements. More like an ordinary walking stick, made of wood, and with a big thick handle. He had it right then, and I remember noticing that he'd lifted the end about twenty centimetres off the ground. I suppose he must have thought I was an intruder about to mug him or something. It's funny how a person can seem so powerful when sitting down and talking, and yet look so weak when standing up and trying to seem powerful. It even trembled a bit in his hand.

"Early aren't you?"

"We were avoiding tractors."

He smiled.

"Were you in the orchard? Do you still go in there Granddad... to the magical place beyond the gate? Can I come with you – I mean not sneaking off, but *with* you?"

"No. Stay out of there. I told you about that, didn't I?"

His voice was a bit sharper than usual. It almost felt as if I was being told off for doing something that I hadn't even done.

"I was only asking..."

"Yes, I know. Sorry Dylan. You caught me a bit off guard is all lad."

"What were you doing then, if you weren't in the orchard I mean?"

"Oh, just... inspecting... things."

"What things?"

"Trees mostly. Especially that one."

He nodded towards a large tree at the far end of the garden, covered in a thick layer of leaves. There were quite a few medium-sized trees dotted about too, but that was the only giant, this side of the gate I mean.

"What with?"

"Eh?"

"What were you inspecting it *with* Granddad?"

Well he was blind.

He glared at me for a second or two, as if I'd gone mad.

"Bring that deck chair over would you. And get one for yourself, from the shed there."

I'd forgotten about the other deck chair. It was blue and purple with a flower design, unlike his, which was a sort of faded orange mixed with browny-green (probably on account of the mould). I think that flowery chair must have been my Nan's; I remembered it the moment I saw it, without *actually* remembering it, if you see what I mean.

"Now then lad. Put them here under the tree."

It wouldn't unfold at first – the second chair. Then my Granddad kicked at it... and it still wouldn't unfold.

"Why are we sitting under this tree?"

"It'll be a hot one today Dylan. No clouds, see?"

I looked up. He was right. And it had been very hot the last few days, but then it was nearly July, and that's the hottest month of the year. I used to think it was August, the hottest month of the year, until we did this school project on weather. Did you know October is five degrees hotter than April? It makes you wonder if Nature's got it a bit wrong; you know, springing to life when it's still cold, and then dying off when it's still hot. You'd think someone would say something really.

"Best stay in the shade. Don't want to get frazzled by that sun now do we lad?"

I looked at the bright red bald spot on the top of his head, and wondered how more 'frazzled' it would have been possible for him to get. Then I thought about all those hats sat on the dresser that he could have worn. And then I realised that a tree *was* a sort of hat if you sit under it, but one that doesn't make your head itch, unlike the regular sort (especially the ones on that dresser).

I'd finally got the blue and purple deck chair unfolded and was just about to sit down on it when something made me stop.

I had the little green egg in my pocket – my back pocket.

"I've got something to show you Granddad."

"Oh?"

"Do you remember how you told me about things that are born in magical places, but somehow end up on our side, in this world? Things that we can sort of see are different, but can't really explain how, like pebbles and funnily shaped leaves?"

"And shadows."

"What happened to the other eye?"

The question just sort of came out; I hadn't meant for it to, especially not when I was about to ask about the egg, but it was as if the word 'shadow' had suddenly woken up that worm crawling about inside my brain. And you know when you wake someone suddenly, like by shouting right in their ear for example, they make an uncontrollable noise, or say something they hadn't meant to? Well that's sort of what happened with the question. It woke up all startled, and then just fell out of my mouth without bothering to tell me first.

My Granddad seemed a little confused.

"The other fire opal Granddad? When Eighty-six Beamer died in that glade, and you heard two little thuds as her eyes fell to the ground. You gave me one, but what happened to the other? You never told me. And I can't understand why, because it's obviously very important, so I've been thinking about it an awful lot. And I meant to ask you on the phone last week, but then you started asking me how I was all of a sudden, and I couldn't think straight. So that question's been in my head for an entire month, and then an extra week on top of that because of my stupid sister. Which is why it just came out like that, because it was so desperate I mean; sort of like when you're bursting for the toilet, and then you accidentally imagine what it looks like – a toilet I mean – and that's when it just—"

"Yes... yes. I get the picture lad."

It was as if that worm had left a hole in my brain, and all those words had suddenly rushed in to fill it. I felt a bit embarrassed.

"Do you still have it – the other eye?"

"Certainly not. It's a wonder I even had one of them."

"What do you mean?"

"What do you mean *what do I mean*? Isn't it obvious?"

It wasn't.

"You can't just go about *taking* things from magical places and moving them to different worlds where they don't belong. Things are different there; everything has a will of its own Dylan, however big or small, complicated or simple – none of that matters."

"But you said things from magical places end up here all the time, in our world I mean."

I looked down at the little green egg now in my hand.

"And they do... but not because some fool like me goes in there and steals them out. Rather, because they *want* to be here, because they choose to: for a day, or a week, or a lifetime even. And not for some grand purpose; the things beyond that gate don't hold with *destiny* and all that rot. Mayhap they just fancy a change of scene, or a bit of a holiday. You see, nothing's controlled over there, or told what it can and cannot be, so things more or less do what they want to do, occasionally for big reasons, but more often than not just because that's what they feel like doing."

"So the first eye – the one you gave me – it *wanted* to come here?"

"Precisely! Except it wasn't an eye any more. Because things are only what they are, when that's what they are. When the darkling grub—"

"Eighty-six Beamer."

"Yes, Eighty-six Beamer; when she died in that glade, the eye became something different – no less important of course, but certainly different."

"A fire opal?"

"No lad. That's just a name, and names are mostly a lot of nonsense, because they don't tell you what a thing really is. Take yours for instance. *Dylan*. If that was all I knew about you, then I certainly wouldn't have the first clue who you really were, or even *what* you were, let alone *why* you were. And Eighty-six Beamer; well, I should think that sounds more like some type of car than a darkling grub. So what's in a name?"

He was right. What *was* in a name after all?

"A whole lot of letters?"

My Granddad seemed to consider this by scratching his chin a bit. It made a bristly sort of sound, like those wiry old brushes people used to sweep footpaths with before leaf blowers were invented. I think I might have been slightly jealous, because my chin didn't sound nearly as impressive when I scratched it.

"That's it lad. Very profound indeed."

I wonder if having a bristly chin makes you wiser, or if people who are wiser just naturally have bristly chins... probably because they're too busy thinking about things to bother with the likes of shaving.

"So what *did* happen to the other, um... *thing* that used to be Eighty-six Beamer's eye?"

My Granddad grinned.

"Ah well, it became something else of course. A thing as important as that, can't go about *not* being a thing – not for very long anyway."

"How?"

He grinned even wider. I think he must have been remembering something.

"Well now, there's a story in that lad... if you're interested."

11

ENERGY

The garden was alive with life that June – new life. Insects and birds; I even saw a baby squirrel, the ordinary grey sort, being carried about by a much bigger one, its mother I expect, high up in the tree above us. It was pink, and soggy looking, just like human babies are.

Everything sort of hummed, like one big choir all singing different parts of the same song, much like it had in May, except there was no secret to it any more. The birds flapped about all over the place, young ones mostly, just out of their nests I expect, chasing bugs or just trying their wings out for the first time. The older ones, with brighter colours and fatter bellies, mostly just watched, sitting idly on twigs or fence posts, sort of like mothers do at theme parks.

The longer we sat there, me and my Granddad, not really *doing* anything, the better everything got at ignoring us. I suppose that's why crocodiles are so good at catching things in rivers, because they just lie there pretending to not be doing anything for about ten hours, until everything forgets that they're even there, and then they just open their mouths and things practically walk right in. Not that I had any intention of catching anything of course, and I made sure to keep my mouth firmly shut after what happened last time. I'm not sure my Granddad felt the same way about those squirrels though; when I told him what I'd seen he started going on about 'digging up bulbs' and 'bird seed' and 'twelve boars in the shed', which didn't make any sense, because I'd just come out of the shed and there wasn't even one boar in it, never mind twelve.

Not that I paid much attention to any of that; my brain was too busy thinking about the Life Turner, and what he might make out of my little green egg. But then I haven't quite got to that bit yet, so I better go back to where my Granddad began.

"You see, it all started when I picked them up – the eyes that is."

"Didn't you say they weren't eyes any more Granddad... not after Eighty-six Beamer had died?"

"Yes Dylan, I did. And they weren't. Only, she had still been alive the last time I'd looked back, so when I heard those two little thuds, turned round, and saw them, shining there in the long grass, well, I didn't much think about what they might have turned into, not yet awhile, particularly as they looked much the same as they had when they *were* eyes.

"It was the king who explained it all of course. But only after I'd picked them up. They were just so beautiful, and the colours, well, you've seen yourself lad; it was like a rainbow had caught fire and then been trapped in a prism for all eternity, except even more vivid than that. How could I *not* have picked them up? But I didn't know..."

"Know what Granddad?"

"That when you pick up a thing like that, a thing that's unique, made of *Life* itself, well, you can't just put it down again, or put it away somewhere and try to forget that you ever picked it up in the first place. No. The king told me. It was my responsibility you see. I had to find a particular sort of person; one who could *turn* those little fire opals—"

"Didn't you say—"

"Let's just call them that for the time being lad, elsewise things get confusing."

I suppose names can't have been entirely 'a lot of nonsense' after all.

"I had to find a person who could turn them into just what they wanted to be. *A Life Turner*. That's what the king told me they were called. A special sort of person who knows how to listen to things – not words or sounds, they can't always be trusted, even by the thing making them – but what's on the inside, the part that you can't see or hear in normal ways."

"And then?"

"And then... well, he helps them *turn* – the Life Turner that is – from being one thing, into being another thing... the thing they want to be. Don't ask me how of course."

I remember him chuckling then, as if saying a thing like *that*, so amazing that I nearly fell off the blue and purple deck chair, and then refusing to tell me how it worked, was somehow slightly funny.

"Why not?"

"Because..."

"Yes?"

"Because it would complicate the story unnecessarily."

"You mean like when you can't see the forest for the trees?"

He thought about that for a moment.

"Yes, I daresay I do."

"That's alright Granddad; I prefer the trees anyway."

I should probably have explained what I meant by that; it might have prevented my Granddad from staring at me with a very bemused sort of look on his face for about the next seventeen seconds.

"Fine. But I don't expect you'll understand, being... what are you, seven?"

"Nine."

He sighed.

"It has to do with *Energy*, you see."

"What sort of Energy?"

"Well that's the point, isn't it?"

"What is?"

"That Energy isn't always the same; it's changing all the time, from one sort into another sort."

"Like what?"

"Like when a star explodes."

I almost wish he hadn't said that, because it sort of blew my mind a little bit (actually quite a lot). I remember trying to imagine a star exploding. The sun is a star, and quite small compared to a lot of them – we learnt that in a school project on stars. Anyway, it's still over a million times bigger than the earth – the sun that is – we learnt that too. And the earth is probably about a million times bigger than the orchard, and forest, and valley, even with all the little meadows and glades, all put together. So I tried to imagine something about a million *million* times bigger than all that, which was about as far as I could see, suddenly exploding, right in front of me.

"You see Dylan, when a star explodes—"

"Just a minute please, I'm trying to imagine it."

I'm sure my brain was actually beginning to heat up with all the strain.

"Imagine what?"

And then it occurred to me... all you have to do is imagine that the star is a million million miles away, and then it's just like a little rocket exploding in the black sky. Easy.

"A star exploding, like you said."

The only trouble was, I couldn't imagine how far a million million miles was.

"Never mind imagining things lad. I'm trying to explain something to you here. You see, when a star explodes, all the Energy stored inside it suddenly wakes up and decides to become something different, like light for instance, that's what you'd see, or heat, what you'd feel, or even sound, if you were close enough to hear it. That's all made by Energy, transferring from one thing into another thing."

I hadn't known that. It seemed like the sort of thing everyone should know, but I hadn't. I remember thinking that it should have been a crime to go on teaching children about stupid grammar rules, and forcing them to spend hours memorizing times tables, when there were things as amazing as that to learn. And it wasn't even hard. He just said it, and then it got stuck in my brain, where it has been ever since.

"Are you sure you wouldn't rather I just tell you about the Life Turner lad?"

"You are."

"Well, yes, I mean... without all the details."

"I like details. Can't you just tell me everything?"

He smiled, probably because he was imagining all the talking he'd have to do, and like I said, there's nothing old people like more than talking... except perhaps sitting, but then my Granddad was talking *and* sitting, so it's really no wonder he was smiling. In fact, it's quite surprising he ever didn't smile when I was around.

"Right you are Dylan. Well now, do you know what the most remarkable thing about Energy is?"

I thought about electricity – that was a type of Energy.

"That you can't see it?"

"I daresay that is quite remarkable, although you can see what it does, just not what it *is* exactly. But I don't think that's quite the *most* remarkable thing about Energy."

"Then what is?"

He leaned over a bit closer then, as if what he was about to tell me needed to be whispered, like it was a secret. I couldn't see who from though, unless the birds and the insects couldn't be trusted; or the trees and plants, not that they did much talking, unless you count leaf rustling of course, but that was more the wind than the trees. Perhaps it was those squirrels he didn't trust;

they might have been listening I suppose – listening and making plans. I wonder if that's what he needed all those boars for.

"It's immortal lad. Energy never dies; it just goes from being one thing, to being another thing. And when they die, as things will, it becomes something else. Stars become heat and light, and that very same heat and light becomes trees and flowers, which turns into the insects and animals that eat them. It's all Energy, because Energy is the spark of life. And it lives forever."

"But when they die, the insects and animals, what happens to the Energy then?"

He smiled.

"Well now, that's just the point isn't it lad? For a time it might be trapped inside something, like, say... a fire opal, or something that looks like one at any rate. But Energy doesn't much hold with being trapped inside things, it's more of a *doer* than a *sitter*, if you take my meaning."

"Sort of like the opposite of you Granddad?"

He glared at me for a second.

"I see you're getting the hang of those rhetorical questions Dylan."

I don't know why he said that. I had no intention of shouting at him.

"Yes, well... that's what Life Turners are for anyway; turning the things, like fire opals, with all sorts of Energy whirring about inside them, perhaps even a bit from the very heart of a star, into *other* things."

He leaned back and sort of smirked. I expect he was quite proud of being able to explain all that. And I had to admit, it was a very good explanation, and I'm very glad he told me it... it just wasn't the right one.

"Well?"

"Well what lad?"

"Well *how*? That's what you were refusing to tell me wasn't it Granddad? *How* those Life Turners go about turning one thing into another. Not that I don't appreciate you telling me the *what* part – about Energy I mean – but *what* isn't exactly the same as *how*, is it?"

There's something very satisfying about watching smirks turn into looks like the one he gave me right then; it was sort of like how my mother looked when she'd just overtaken twelve tractors, sped down the road a bit, and then got stuck behind a flock of sheep travelling at about one mile an hour, only for the twelve tractors to catch up again. That actually happened once.

"*How*? You want to know *how*, do you?"

"Yes."

Obviously.

"Well how the bloody hell am *I* supposed to know how?"

"You refused to tell me – at first I mean. You wouldn't have done that if you didn't know."

"I didn't exactly..."

He sighed.

And then scratched his chin again.

"It's really quite simple; they *listen* is all, like I said. Life Turners just have a knack, a talent I suppose, for *hearing* Energy. Not just a buzz or a hum or something like that, but actual words – words that aren't spoken, but felt."

That didn't make any sense at first.

"Granddad?"

"Yes Dylan?"

"Do you mean to say, that in magical places, Energy is actually *alive* somehow? Not like in a battery or a light bulb or something, but like a person, which thinks and feels for itself?"

His cloudy white eyes grinned at me then.

"That my boy, is *precisely* what I mean. In magical places Energy isn't controlled like it is here; you can't go about harnessing it in batteries or light bulbs, which is why there aren't any things like that beyond that gate. They just wouldn't work, much like that compass we were talking about.

"No. In magical places, Energy does more or less what it wants to do, just like everything else, because there aren't any laws to tell it what it *must* and must *not* do. Well, there *are*, but sometimes, not always, not even most of the time, just *sometimes*, it doesn't listen to them is all. It does what it wants instead, because, well, that's what living things do. Being alive makes a thing unpredictable, doesn't it?

"Energy here, in our world, is like a machine, always doing what those laws tell it to do, but in magical places it's more like a person, and a whimsical one ta boot, mostly doing what it's told, but not always, because where's the fun in that? And even when it *does* do what it's told, which like I said is quite often, it doesn't necessarily do it in quite the way you might expect."

"What does whimsical mean?"

"It means like you lad... and me, I daresay. But probably not like your mother – least not the way she is now."

"Oh."

I couldn't imagine my mother ever having been different, not back then.

Granddad?"

"Really Dylan, don't start all that Granddading business again."

"Is it like a sort of god – Energy I mean?"

"Good God, no. I don't hold with gods lad; lot of nonsense they are. Energy is nothing like a sort of god. For a start, it's not one big thing, with one set of thoughts. It's millions and millions of little things, divided up all over the place, like I told you. Some in stars, others in light, in heat, in sound, in fire opals... each with its own memories, and thoughts, and desires, and even its own unique voice to express them with. Much like us people, really.

"And unlike gods, Energy isn't a judgmental sort of thing, always sticking its nose into other people's affairs and saying what's right and what's wrong. No. Energy is quite satisfied doing its own thing, like everyone else. Of course, what it does may seem extraordinary to you or I, but then I expect what we do probably seems just as extraordinary to it.

"Certainly, Energy has its quirks, like all living things, which makes magical places somewhat peculiar, even dangerous at times as I've told you, but for the most part, the *very* most part, it doesn't wish anyone harm, or go about wilfully causing it; in fact, it sometimes even tries to do a little good, in its own sort of way."

"So there isn't a dark type of Energy then – doing bad I mean?"

"That, Dylan, remains entirely to be seen."

I don't know why he said that. I wouldn't have

asked if it *didn't* 'remain entirely to be seen'.

I was just about to tell him that when my sister arrived carrying a tray with three glasses of lemonade on – the home-made sort. It smelled incredible, of real lemons mixed with sugar; probably because that's exactly what it was. She even started smiling – my sister I mean – mostly at my Granddad. I've no idea why; it's not like she normally went about smiling.

My Granddad seemed delighted. He started talking about how it reminded him of summer holidays as a lad, and how it was probably the finest home-made lemonade he'd ever tasted, and how he once made about two 'shillings' by selling home-made lemonade which wasn't even half as good as the lemonade my sister had made, and how 'times were different back then of course'. It was when he said that that I pretty much lost all hope of finding out any more about Energy, or the Life Turner, or even of asking about that little green egg, which I still had hold of.

My sister was completely useless. I don't think she asked a single question, which, as I think I might have mentioned, is essential when it comes to very old people. She just sat there smiling at him, pretending to be interested I suppose. She even looked happy for some reason – not that that would last, I was sure of it. Anyway, that's when I decided to go inside for a bit; I was hungry too.

My mother was standing there looking out at us through the kitchen window. Even *she* was smiling – not like the usual fake sort either.

I asked her for another glass of lemonade.

It had been quite nice, after all.

12

THE RIGHT WAY

"What happened to that girl Granddad?"

I was in the garden again. We'd eaten lunch – some sort of salad thing which wasn't nearly as good as ham sandwiches – and my sister had finally gone back inside to 'suck out some pipes'. I think that just meant using a plunger to unblock plugholes (instead of throwing it at walls and trying to make it stick like I always did).

"What girl?"

"That girl beyond the gate. The one the king of birds told you to find; you know, that liked to climb trees and make apple crumble."

He smiled.

"Don't forget the rhubarb and blackberries that make it extra sweet."

I hadn't.

"Well Dylan, nothing happened to her. She was still out there, somewhere, beyond that gate, living her life, perhaps even waiting for me in a way. I just got a bit distracted is all, what with those fire opals I'd picked up, and the king harping on about responsibilities and 'doing the right thing'. He really was quite a bossy sort of fellow that king."

"I expect kings have to be Granddad – to rule I mean."

"Quite right lad, quite right. But I hadn't forgotten about her; that's why I'd gone through that gate after all."

"Was she anything like my sister, the magical girl?"

I really have no idea why I bothered to ask that. It seemed like a stupid question, even right after I'd said it. Whenever I asked my mother stupid questions she always gave me a disappointed look, and told me to 'think before you speak Dylan'. Come to think of it, she often did that even when the questions weren't stupid. My Granddad didn't though. Even then, and that really *had* been a stupid question. He just grinned, and tickled his chin a bit.

"Yes. Quite a lot actually."

"So you did find her then – in the end I mean?"

"Oh yes, I found her all right. But I wouldn't say 'in the end' exactly; it was more like a beginning."

"A beginning of what?"

He laughed a bit then, as if he knew something that I didn't. I hate that sort of laugh.

"Well now lad, never mind all that; we'll get to it, I'm sure. Don't you want to find out what happened to that other fire opal?"

I'd forgotten. I'd *actually* forgotten. I bet it was that salad; vegetables definitely seem to make my brain slower. And that's logical too. I mean look at cows, and sheep, and rabbits: they all eat nothing *but* salad. I expect they wouldn't be nearly as stupid if they ate ham sandwiches all day.

"The Life Turner... you found him too?"

"That I did."

"But how did you know where to look, without a map, or a compass, or anything?"

"Oh, I had *something* lad. The king of birds. And that's a handy sort of thing to have in a magical place, I tell you."

"You mean he led the way?"

"Not exactly *led*, more like... *corrected*. You see, he wasn't best pleased is the truth of it; kept telling me what a fool I must be to pick things up without even knowing what they are. I expect he had some sort of *grand plan* did that king. He really was a clever sort, as you well know Dylan. He wanted me to find the girl you see, and I daresay he wouldn't have tempted me beyond that gate if he didn't think it important.

"But he knew all the same... when a thing was *right* and when a thing was *wrong*. And to leave them there, those fire opals, fit to bursting with life as they were, only to be forgotten in the long grass of that glade, well... that certainly would have been wrong. We had to find that Life Turner. Of course, I hadn't the first clue what one looked like, let alone where to find him. In fact, the whole business quite boggled my mind to be honest, which is why I didn't exactly, um... cooperate, at least not to begin with."

"What do you mean?"

"Well, put yourself in my place lad. If you'd been led through a gate on the guise of finding a magical girl, more beautiful and better smelling even than an orchard in bloom – which, let's face it, no young man could have resisted – only to *not* find a girl, at least not right off like you'd expected to, and then been told you had to go find someone else, who you'd never even heard of, but certainly *wasn't* a magical girl as beautiful and better smelling than an orchard in bloom, well... what would you do?"

"Go and find him."

Apparently that wasn't the right answer, because my Granddad spat out a whole lot of air again. He sounded a bit like a horse chewing on a balloon.

"You're too young to understand lad."

My mother often said that, except without the 'lad' bit. I think it really means that the person saying it is too old.

"Anyway, I turned back, is what I did. Tried to find that gate. Tried to leave. Got scared I expect."

"But Granddad, when you step through a magical gate you're as far away from the gate you stepped through as you think you are near. You told me that."

He looked suddenly surprised. I couldn't think why at first.

"I did, didn't I? You've some memory on you lad, particularly for, what are you... eight?"

Isn't it strange that you can remember things from months earlier, clear as if they'd just happened, but important things, like the answer to questions that you've been waiting five weeks to find out, can just, sort of, disappear? I think it all comes down to that extra brain that your brain's got – you know, the miniature one, like I talked about? It probably finds it funny or something – making you forget things I mean – and then when you remember something that you probably shouldn't, I expect that's just it showing off. Then again, perhaps all that salad had just worn off.

"Nine."

"Yes, well, the fact is, I didn't know any of that at the time, now did I?"

The king might have told him. That's what I'd thought.

"So naturally, it seemed no more difficult than turning round and walking back the very same way that I'd come. Of course... things didn't quite pan out as I'd expected."

"You mean you got lost?"

"In a manner of speaking."

"What manner of speaking?"

He had to think about that for a second.

"An accurate one."

Sometimes words confuse me.

"Is that the same way as saying 'Yes'?"

He sighed.

"I suppose... in a round about sort of way?"

"What round about sort of—"

"YES."

I like that word though. People usually say it when something good is about to happen.

"Anyway Dylan, that's when the king took to *correcting* me, as it were, after each wrong turn. Of course, I ignored him at first, trusting more to my own memory of the route. But it did me not a jot of good is the truth of it. So after an hour or two of walking through that orchard, between trees and across glades, up hills and down, I finally stopped walking, and started listening.

"Why, it certainly was a queer sort of adventure I'd found myself on, and with the king of birds for companion no less; I even recall thinking the whole bizarre business must have been a dream. I mean it's not every day you meet a talking bird that wears a crown, and see a shadow come to life only to, well... leave it again. I even pinched myself a few times to make sure, but sure enough, it hurt like mad every time."

"You should have tried levitating."

"Say what lad?"

I was about to explain how levitating only worked in dreams, and that it was better than pinching yourself, when it suddenly occurred to me that in magical places things probably went about levitating all the time, so you'd think you were never *not* dreaming.

"Dylan?"

"Oh, nothing Granddad."

He squinted at me a bit.

"Yes, well anyway... I walked, and he flew; sometimes up high, to get a better look about, other times far away into that valley. And I tell you lad, it wasn't the best of feelings when he left me like that, even if it was only ever for a little while. It sends a chill right down your spine being lost in a place like that, strange and unfamiliar. I felt quite alone when the king wasn't there, twittering away in my ear, or just smoking his little clay pipe. It may be hard to believe, but it lifted my very heart whenever I saw him flying back to me, even if he was no bigger than my thumbnail."

I once got lost in a supermarket because my mother kept rushing off to get things and I got distracted trying to work out what oddly shaped carrots most looked like. They had to make an announcement on that tannoy thing for her to come and collect me. I thought she'd be angry, but I don't think I've ever seen her look more happy. She even gave me a hug.

"It's not."

"It's not what?"

"Hard to believe."

He nodded in a grim sort of way.

"And then night finally came. By George, was that ever an experience. We slept under a tree... at least I did. His majesty preferred the penthouse suite."

"What's that?"

"It means he slept in the tree lad. Above my head."

"The tree had a house in it?"

He squinted at me again.

Building a tree-house was my number one life goal back then, and not some sort of poncy propped up one, like you see 'professional tree-house builders' make (I've done a lot of research). If it touches the ground it's not a proper tree-house, that's what I think. Mine would be at least five times my own height, more like twenty if possible (I'd measure it out to be sure), that you could only get in to by climbing up a rope ladder, which would require immense skill and expertise, on account of being extremely wobbly (to keep people out). It would have a bed inside, and a window or two, and even a door that locked. You could stand up of course, and I'd likely have some sort of pet that would live in there and guard the entrance from intruders – definitely not a guinea pig though. The only trouble was, the tallest tree in our garden back home was still in a plant pot. It was a horse chestnut that I'd started growing myself from a prize-winning conker a year or two earlier; not that it had actually won any prizes, but that's only because prizes don't exist for prize-winning conkers. I had to admit though, it was taking a bit longer than I'd expected to reach tree-house height... probably because I hadn't been feeding it enough vitamin tablets. Apparently you have to take one every day or you won't grow straight – that's what my mother keeps telling me anyway.

"No."

"But you said—"

"Yes, I know what I said thank you Dylan. It's an expression is all."

"What does it mean?"

Expressions are when people try to sound clever by saying one thing when they want to say something else, instead of just saying the thing they wanted to say in the first place. It's like a sort of secret code, except completely pointless.

"I've told you what it bloody means... the bird slept in the tree, and I slept under it. Shall I continue now?"

His face went a bit pink as he said that.

"So 'penthouse suite' means when a bird sleeps in a tree, with a person sleeping underneath the tree at the same time?"

More or less the same shade of pink as that baby squirrel come to think of it.

"Yes Dylan. Exactly that."

He said it very slowly, as if I was foreign or stupid or something.

"Oh."

But then maybe I was. Nobody else seemed to have

trouble with that sort of thing.

I remember deciding not to say anything for a while, even if my Granddad started trying to be clever again.

"Now, where was I? Oh yes, sleeping under a tree in that orchard. Except it can't have been in the orchard, not any more; we'd been walking for half a day. It's like I once told you lad, it's much bigger than it looks beyond that gate. Anyway, I've never heard such noises in all my life. It sounded like a circus was playing the whole night through: laughter and singing, trumpets blaring, drums beating, fiddles... fiddling. I didn't say a word of course, I just curled up under that tree, eyes closed, pretending to be asleep. I didn't want them to know I was there you see, whatever *they* were that is."

We once went to a circus. On the way out I saw a clown throwing up against a tree behind the tent. He still had a big red smile painted over his mouth. It was probably the most disturbing thing I've ever seen in my life.

"I must have fallen asleep eventually though, because I'll never forget what happened when I woke up. It was well past dawn when I opened my eyes; the sun was already half way up the sky. And there was no sound; the din of that night had been replaced by something far worse... an unnatural silence. Except you don't exactly notice unnatural silences while you're asleep, so the waking up part felt rather pleasant at first, what with the sunlight poking through the leaves above; much like Sunday mornings, when you just drift back into the world without really noticing it."

Unless your Granddad happens to call you on the

telephone at 7:37 AM that is.

"And then I saw them. Hundreds of them. All looking down at me at the same time. Perched on every branch and twig and leaf of that tree. Not moving a muscle. It was unnerving I'll tell you that much lad, especially as not a sound could be heard."

"What was?"

"The procession of course. Hundreds of little people, each no bigger than my hand, and every one of them, to a man, dressed in royal green from head to toe. I swear to you lad, I've never seen the like of it, before or since. And all staring at me; waiting, expecting..."

I remember wondering how a colour could possibly be royal. That didn't make any sense. But it was a different question that came out of my mouth.

"Why did you call it a... *procession*?"

"Because that's what it was, though I didn't know it at the time. They'd come for a reason you see, just like Him they followed."

"Who?"

"Why, The Life Turner of course. Who else?"

13

COURAGE

It had never really occurred to me that courage was something that one person could *give* to another person. But now I think it's probably the most important thing that a person *can* give. Sometimes it's sort of disguised as something else, like three glasses of lemonade, but most often it's just a lot of words. And words should be easy to give, because they just come right out of your mouth, and don't cost a thing to say. Except that they're not... easy to give I mean. It's much harder to say the right words to someone than it is to just hand them something and pretend to smile.

"You mean the Life Turner was right there Granddad?"

"Certainly he was."

"But how? I mean, how did he find you under that tree?"

"Oh, I expect he knew we'd be there somehow. Life Turners have a knack for knowing things lad, much like kings."

"What did he look like?"

"The king? Oh, mighty pleased with himself. He was in on the whole thing, no doubt."

"Not the king Granddad; the Life Turner?"

"The Life Turner? Well, he was..."

He seemed to need to think about that. I've no idea why.

"No bigger than your hand? Like the hundreds of little people in that *procession* thing?"

"Yes, only... tall, and thin."

I tried to imagine how a man about as big as a hand could possibly be 'tall'. And then I remembered picking runner beans. There's always one or two that sort of stand out for being extra tall. Of course, not if you stand them up next to a marrow, even a small one. Next to a marrow the very tallest of runner beans wouldn't seem very tall at all. It would definitely seem thin though.

"And dressed in green too?"

"Indeed. From head to toe."

"That *royal* sort again?"

He gave me another one of those looks, which really wasn't fair, because it was *him* that'd said the whole *royal* thing in the first place.

"I'll tell you just what he looked like lad..."

"Yes?"

"A Funeral Director."

I think I probably looked right back at him in just the same way after he said that.

"A Funeral Director?"

"A Funeral Director."

It wasn't that I didn't know what a Funeral Director

was. My Nan had had one. I remembered him well. He'd been tall, and thin, and very kind – at least that's what my mother had said. My Granddad hadn't said much at all... not to anyone I don't think.

"Only green."

"A *green* Funeral Director Granddad?"

"That's right. Dressed in green, just like the rest. But smart mind you. He wore a suit. Made of leaves it was. And stitched together with spider's silk; with a waistcoat, green velvet shoes, and even a top hat made from a pine-cone, but not in a crude, roundabout sort of way. It was a work of art that top hat. In fact, I'd say it was probably the finest little ensemble I've ever seen."

"What's an *ensemble*?"

"The suit Dylan. It was much better than the usual black sort. I even felt a little awed just looking at him, come to think of it. He seemed somehow different did that Life Turner. Special."

"I thought all things beyond that gate were *different* Granddad?"

He smiled.

"Yes, but He was even more different than the rest."

The trouble with words like *different* is that for the most part they don't exactly mean something. And that's the whole point of words, to *mean* things, otherwise people might as well just go about honking like guinea pigs, or even trumpeting like elephants... whatever takes their fancy really. I'm sure that'd be more fun too. Besides, I bet elephants don't go about trumpeting things that don't mean anything. I bet every time an elephant trumpets something, it knows *just* what it means, and so do all the other elephants that hear it, because otherwise it wouldn't bother. Unless it happened to be singing or something.

"What were they doing there – all the rest I mean?"

"The procession lad?"

That's what he'd called them... all those hundreds of little people in the tree.

"Yes, *that*."

"Well they were following Him, like I said."

"Yes, but *why*? And why were they making all those noises in the night? It was them, wasn't it?"

"It was. And they were celebrating Dylan. Of course, I had no way of knowing that in the darkness. And being on the outside of a celebration isn't nearly the same as being on the inside of one."

"Celebrating what?"

I remembered the Funeral Director; the one *not* dressed in a green suit made of leaves with a top hat carved out of a pine-cone; the one my Nan had had. People hadn't been celebrating then. They'd been doing the opposite of celebrating. The funny thing was, I think half of them, including me, were only doing the opposite of celebrating because that's what everyone else was doing. I wonder what it's called, the opposite of celebrating? Oh yes... *grieving*. That's the thing I hadn't really got the hang of back then.

"Have you forgotten everything I told you lad? The Life Turner *turns* life."

"I remember. He listens to the Energy inside a thing, and helps it become something new; the thing that it wants to be."

"Well then... do you mean to say you don't think a thing as spectacular as *that* reason enough to celebrate?"

"But the darkling grub... Eighty-Six Beamer? *She'd just died.*"

He looked at me a bit sternly then. As if I shouldn't have even said that. But it was true, wasn't it? Shouldn't they have been *grieving* instead?

"Yes. I daresay you're right Dylan."

And then he just sort of sunk back a bit in that orangey-browny-mouldy-green deck chair and stared up at the sky.

"It's getting late. The day's almost over. You'll be heading home soon."

"I don't think so."

"What?"

"About being right Granddad."

It's funny how sometimes you only realise that you're wrong about a thing when someone first agrees with what you thought was right.

"It *is* spectacular, one thing *turning* into another I mean. And if I'd been there, I think I'd have wanted to celebrate too. Besides, Energy lives forever. So Eighty-Six Beamer hadn't really died... not really."

His mouth, *and* his eyes, in fact just about every part of his face, grinned at me when I said that.

It felt very good.

And hadn't really been hard to say at all.

"I still haven't told you what it turned into, have I lad? That other fire opal."

"What?"

"Well now, first I should say, it didn't exactly happen right off – the *turning* that is. There were a lot of formalities to take care of before he'd even look at them: introductions, hand-shaking, even the odd disclaimer to sign, written in a language I couldn't understand of course. Still, the king reassured me all would be fine."

"How?"

"How what?"

"How did the Life Turner shake your hand?"

I tried to imagine shaking hands with someone whose hand was bigger than I was. I suppose you could pretend your whole body was a hand, and your arms and legs were fingers, and your head and neck was a thumb, then sort of twist yourself into a hand shape. That seemed a bit undignified for a Funeral Director though, even one wearing a pine-cone for a hat.

"The usual way lad, only... more vigorously."

I never did find out what that meant.

"But that's not the interesting part Dylan. All those formalities were just, well... *formalities*, even if they did take half the morning. The really interesting part was what happened next."

Unfortunately what happened next for me and my Granddad was more annoying than interesting.

"DYLAN?"

It was my mother.

"IT'S GETTING DARK. WE'RE LEAVING SOON. DO YOU HEAR ME?"

She was shouting from the back door, a little bit louder than she really needed to. At least that's how it seemed.

"FIVE MINUTES, ALL RIGHT?"

We heard the door close.

I remember suddenly panicking. It *was* getting dark, so there was no point trying to reason with her or anything. And five minutes really *wasn't* very long at all.

But I had to find out what happened to that other fire opal. I just *had* to. Otherwise I was sure that that question would squirm back up into my brain (probably through my ear-hole or something) and start on whispering at me again, and I didn't think I could live with that. It'd probably drive me so mad that I'd have to run away from home and join the circus just to get distracted from it. Because what could be more distracting that joining a circus? Especially one where clowns throw up against trees.

"*Courage* lad."

"What?"

For some reason that came out even squeakier than usual.

"We all need it, even your old Granddad sometimes. And I daresay that's why the monster was born."

The panic sort of rose up in my stomach every time he said something. It seemed like instead of answering questions my Granddad was just trying to make more.

"What are you talking about? What monster?"

"That's what it turned into Dylan – the other fire opal, the one from her left eye."

"It turned into a monster?"

I couldn't quite believe it.

"Not just *any* monster..."

What other type of monster was there?

"... a *Courage* Monster."

I didn't say anything at first. I think all that panic had got stuck in my throat and didn't quite know what to do next. And the more I sat there thinking about it, the less those two words seemed to fit together.

"You mean a monster that you needed courage *from*

Granddad?"

"No lad. I mean a monster that *gives* courage. A Courage Monster, like I said."

"But how can a monster *give* you courage?"

"TIME TO LEAVE DYLAN."

My mother's voice was even louder this time. Arguing with her would have been like a guinea pig trying to argue with an elephant by honking at it.

I suddenly felt like I was about to burst. I expect all that panic must have turned into a lot of Energy, because I remember leaping right out of that blue and purple flowery deck chair in an uncontrollable sort of fit. Probably a bit like when a star explodes come to think of it. Except I don't think my Energy turned into much light, like it does with stars, and there wasn't a lot of heat either, apart from some concentrated bits at the ends of my ears. It was more the *normal* sort of Energy, where things just move about a lot – mostly my arms and legs.

And then I remembered the egg. The little green one that I'd wanted to ask about. The one that I was sure must have come from a magical place. It had been in my hand all that time. And now there wasn't any left... time I mean.

"Granddad?"

"Yes lad?"

"Do you have to live here by yourself? I mean, wouldn't it be easier if you just came and lived with us? That way I wouldn't have to keep waiting entire months just to find out the answer to questions only for a whole load more questions to spring up in my brain because you never answer things properly in the first place."

Well, it was true.

"DYLAN? DON'T MAKE ME COME DOWN THERE AND GET YOU."

"Something tells me that wouldn't work lad. And besides, how could I ever leave this?"

"Leave what?"

"*This*."

He opened up his hands, as if the moon was about to fall right out of the sky and he meant to catch it.

"You mean the garden, and the house?"

"It's my home."

"Oh."

Perhaps homes give you a sort of courage too.

"What sort of questions anyway?"

"Every sort."

Like what did a Courage Monster look like exactly? And how had the fire opal turned into it; had it grown like a tree, or just sort of... climbed out, like a butterfly from a chrysalis? And how big was a Courage Monster? And could it talk? And were there other Courage Monsters or was that the only one ever to have existed? And what happened to it next? And *why* had all that Energy in the fire opal wanted to become a Courage Monster in the first place?

"Well then lad, what's the most important question of all? We've only time for one more answer. So you better choose. Quickly now."

I thought.

"DYLAN? DO YOU WANT LEAVING BEHIND; IS THAT IT?"

It wasn't easy.

"What's it to be lad?"

And then I knew. There was one question more

important than all the others put together.

"The first fire opal – the one you gave me – why didn't the Life Turner turn that too?"

He smiled.

"Because it wasn't ready yet, that's what he told me. That it was waiting."

"Waiting for what?"

My mother appeared. She took me by the hand, and without really knowing it, I just started going with her.

"Isn't it obvious lad?"

My Granddad turned his head as we left.

"Waiting for *you*."

JULY

14

CATCHING A STORM

I wonder if people can catch storms from the sky, just like they catch yawns off each other (and being nervous). That would explain it – what happened that July I mean. It was the worst storm I'd ever seen, and in the hottest month of the year too. Each droplet of rain sounded like a bullet being shot into the world. My mother must have caught it first, right out of the sky. And that's why the argument began. She had to let it out I expect, otherwise she might have been split in two or something. Except instead of thunder and lightning, it was *words* and *looks* that she let out... they both did.

There are two types of argument: the type where you know everything will be all right in the morning, because no one really wants anything to change, however much they shout; and the *other* type... the type that breaks things. Forever.

But that's not what happened first. What happened first, after we left my Granddad that June evening, was three of the hottest, most joyous weeks of my life. It was the last three weeks of school before the summer holidays, and all I can really remember is the *back field* – that's what they called it, the teachers. But it was more than just a field, because there was a huge oak tree at one end, the type you could climb, if you were good enough that is; a nature reserve at the other, with actual frogs and tadpoles; and a great long hedge, about three times my height, right the way down one side, which we used to make dens in and collect caterpillars from. But the thing was, they only ever let us out on that field when the weather was so terrifically hot that even the stupidest of mothers, with the sickliest of children, couldn't possibly have accused the school of infecting them with 'the sniffles'. I only say that because of how annoyed I used to get whenever they *didn't* let us out on that field because of 'a dark cloud on the horizon' or 'a bit of dew on the grass' or some other stupid reason. I suppose the good thing about that though, was that when they *did* let us out on it, like every day for three weeks straight that July, it was sort of like eating an entire five litre tub of ice-cream after being force fed Brussel Sprouts for a year, except without the feeling sick part after about the twentieth spoonful.

I hadn't forgotten about my Granddad though, nor any of those things he'd told me about: like the Life Turner who wore a green suit made of leaves with a pine-cone for a hat; or the procession of tiny people no bigger than hands that followed him about playing little instruments; or the fire opal that had been a left eye until he'd turned it into a Courage Monster – not that I knew what a Courage Monster really *was*, not back then anyway; or the other fire opal, the one that my Granddad had given to me, the one that had been Eighty-Six Beamer's right eye. That's what I remembered most of all, and thought about all the time, even when I was doing things, like watching tadpoles turn into frogs, and hunting for caterpillars, and climbing that oak tree. The *remembering* never went away... not that I wanted it to or anything.

'*Waiting for you*' – that's what he'd said. But why? Sometimes I just stared at it for hours – the fire opal I mean – watching that galaxy trapped inside, wondering what it was, and more to the point, what it might become back *there*, if it returned somehow to the place it was born. But then it had been a very long time. Seventy years in fact. Perhaps it'd forgotten how to even be anything other than what it was now. That sort of blew my mind a bit when I thought about it. *Seventy years*. Everything he'd told me had happened *seventy whole years* ago. That didn't seem like much less than forever to me.

I suppose it was sort of like when you learn about ancient kings at school; you know, the ones that pulled swords out of stones, or got shot in the eye with arrows, or chopped the heads off their wives. It seems so different when written in books, or told by teachers. Maybe it had all changed – in that seventy years I mean. After all, it wasn't like there were kings going about pulling swords out of stones any more, never mind getting shot in the eye with arrows, or chopping the heads off their wives. That's just history. And I couldn't help but wonder, gazing into that fire opal, if magical places might somehow have become history too.

One thing was for sure; I had to go back. I had to hear the whole story. There was so much more to find out. Like about that magical girl.

"I don't think you should come this time Dylan."

School had ended. And with it, so had the heat wave.

It was the very last day in July.

"It's raining for one. You won't be able to go outside, and there's nothing else to do. Apart from get in the way. You'll be bored Dylan."

I remember wanting to cry when my mother had said that. My chest got all tight and it felt like I could hardly breathe. I didn't want her to see though. She always looked away when I cried, like she was ashamed or something.

"Yes, but it might not be raining there, and I can sit in the house anyway, as long as me and Granddad can talk. I don't mind. And I won't get bored. Not if we're talking."

"I think I'll be doing most of the talking this time Dylan."

"What do you mean?"

She sighed, in a sad sort of way.

"I know you're only trying to help, but this whole thing with your Granddad... it can't go on. Don't you see that?"

Trying to help? I hadn't been trying to help at all. It wasn't like I did any of the cleaning. What could she have meant by that? And why couldn't it go on? I got this horrible feeling then, probably the worst feeling that I'd ever had, that the world was about to change, and there was nothing I could do about it. I couldn't stop them after that – the tears. I didn't exactly cry... but I'm pretty sure my eyes started leaking.

"Is it because I didn't come when you shouted me? Only I will this time – *every time* from now on. I was just very distracted. I didn't mean to—"

"No, Dylan. That's not what I meant. It's got nothing to do with you."

She'd only ever said that once before. I hated those words.

"Then why can't things go on any more? I don't want *anything* to change. Please. I *have* to go. It's not fair."

It all came out together; half words, half sobs.

My mother looked away.

"Fine."

I hadn't expected that.

"But you need to let me talk to him first. It's important."

I couldn't see how I'd ever stopped her from talking to him.

"And..."

She hesitated.

I waited.

"Just remember that... that I love you. You do know that, don't you?"

I suppose you might think I'd have felt better when she said that; after all, it wasn't like she said it very often. But I didn't. I felt worse, because it made that horrible feeling I talked about come back, only much stronger. Why is it that people only tell you they love you when something bad is about to happen?

That was when the rain became a storm, getting

heavier and heavier, until the sky was so black that it felt like night, and the wind so strong that I'm sure it nearly picked up our car and threw it right over, as if it might have been a toy. It took us longer than usual to reach my Granddad's house, even without a single tractor to get stuck behind. I counted seven lightning bolts out of the window (and that was just on the left side), most of them just before we arrived. My mother must have been used to storms; I kept looking at her in the mirror, but she never once seemed afraid.

I was though.

When next my mother spoke, it wasn't to me, but to my Granddad.

"I can't keep doing this. I won't. Not any more. Do you hear me?"

It was the first and only time since my Nan had died that my Granddad had been inside the house when we'd arrived. He was sat in the lounge right next to the window. It looked like he was looking out, but I suppose he can't have been.

"I hear you."

He didn't turn to face her.

"It's not fair, what you expect of me. I've got my own house and family to look after without driving half way across the country just to spend the whole day cleaning up after you. It's just not *fair* Dad."

"So you keep saying. You always have."

"HOW DARE YOU?"

I've never heard my mother shout like that. It felt like the whole house shook.

"I'm not some child that you can patronise any more. It's *you* who's dependent on *me* now, not the other way round. Not that you ever thank me for anything. You don't even look at me half the time. *This isn't my fault Dad.* None of it is."

He didn't speak.

"Why can't you just face up to what's happened, deal with it, and move the hell on?"

"Like you did, you mean? That's 'moving the hell on' is it?"

I expect the house was still being showered with bullets, but I can't say for sure, because that was probably the loudest silence I've ever heard. I'm only glad I was standing in the corner, and couldn't see my mother's face.

When finally she replied, it was quietly, almost in a whisper. I don't know why, or how, but that scared me even more than when she'd just been shouting.

"I'm done. You can stay here and die for all I care. Go rot in that precious garden of yours. *Alone.*"

"Don't worry... I intend to."

That was only the second time I'd ever seen my mother cry. She hadn't needed to at my Nan's funeral – not like everyone else. It didn't last very long, and she didn't make any sound, like I would have. She just wiped her eyes, and that was it. I can't explain why, but it felt like a relief somehow. Just to see her do it I mean.

She turned and looked at my sister, and then at me.

"We're leaving."

My sister didn't say a thing, but I couldn't help it. I didn't want to leave. Not like *that*. It didn't seem right. If only they'd have kept talking. That was the trouble; they did the bit where you shout, and then say things you don't really mean, but not the bit after that, where you say sorry, or even just sit there for a while, drinking a cup of tea or something. It was just like the storm outside; when that ended, the world didn't end with it. The rain stopped, and the sun came out, and the birds started to sing again. That's what was *supposed* to happen.

"But..."

"*We're leaving Dylan. Right now.*"

I just stood there. It wasn't that I meant to. That's just what I did.

She stared at me from the hallway. But there wasn't even a second warning, let alone a third or fourth. Not this time.

I heard the front door close. It hadn't been slammed. The storm was over – at least my mother's was – I could still hear the rain pouring outside.

A second or two must have passed, perhaps even longer. And then I just sort of... woke up.

I remember running to the front door. It had a blurry glass bit from about half way up. I looked through it. I even looked again. But it was no use...

She'd gone.

My mother had left me.

15

DRIPPING

It's funny how I'd been so desperate to talk to my Granddad, and thought so much about what I might say, only to sit there with him for that whole day, hardly saying a word. Not that he did much talking either. I suppose we were both too distracted with thinking about things. The only thing I really remember, apart from my own thoughts, is the sound of the rain outside, and the ticking of a clock somewhere in the house. I'm sure I'd never heard that ticking before. Maybe it was just filling the silence... so me and my Granddad didn't have to I mean.

I don't know what he was thinking about – he didn't look at me very much, not like he always had in the garden – but the only thought stuck in my head was whether or not my mother would ever come back. My Granddad had said that she would; that he'd known her for a very long time, and that I wasn't to worry. I can't remember him saying much else, not until after the phone call that is, but that wasn't for hours and hours, when the rain had finally stopped, and that clock must have ticked a million times.

She'd never left me before... except in that supermarket, like I told you. That had been an accident though, not like this. This had been on purpose, and without even saying goodbye. It wasn't that I was scared to be without her or anything, certainly not in my Granddad's house; it was just that, well... it was one of those things that you never really imagine happening. *No matter what.* I suppose that's a bit stupid though really, because mothers are just people too, and all people make mistakes, don't they? The trouble was, I didn't really know if that's what it had been – a mistake I mean. I expect if I'd known that I wouldn't have felt like I did, but it really hadn't seemed like one, not at first anyway. And for some reason, just *thinking* that made me as scared as I can ever remember being.

The instant the phone started ringing my Granddad rose from his chair, not saying a word, walked into the hall, closing the lounge door behind him, and answered it. I'd never seen him do that before.

I didn't move all the while. I just sat there waiting, listening without really trying to, but all I could hear was the odd grunt and mumble of my Granddad's voice. The words weren't clear; I think I was glad of that. And the call was over as suddenly as it had begun.

"She'll collect you tomorrow."

I just looked at him.

"So you'll have to stay here tonight. It's all right, there's a spare room upstairs. The one in the gable-end, where your mother used to sleep. I haven't been in there for years, but your Nan always, well... it should be clean enough, and the bed made up. I'm sure you'll be fine in there."

I don't know why I didn't say anything, but I didn't.

"Are you all right lad?"

"Okay."

He wasn't gazing out of the window any more.

"She's sorry Dylan, for leaving you that is. And so am I, for what it's worth, for, well... *everything*."

His voice went a bit trembley when he said that. I just wish he'd said it to my mother instead of me.

"Don't take it to heart lad. This has got nothing to do with you, I promise."

There it was again – that horrible sentence. And it wasn't true. It had *everything* to do with me, because if it hadn't, then why was I sat there feeling like that? People shouldn't ever be allowed to say those words. It's just a way for them to pretend that you're not getting hurt by something. Why couldn't people just tell the truth, about feelings and stuff, instead of saying stupid things that don't mean anything just to make *themselves* feel better?

I felt angry, but I didn't tell my Granddad.

"The rain's finally stopped."

It's not often that feeling angry is actually a good thing, but it was so much better than what I *had* been feeling that I almost started laughing.

"Dylan?"

"I know it has. I've got ears too Granddad."

He smiled at me then. It was the first smile I'd seen all day. I couldn't help but smile back.

"It'll be fun lad; like a sleepover. And we shan't bother with cleaning up, or eating salads, or anything like that. I've a good stash of goodies hidden away, don't you worry."

"Granddad?"

"Yes Dylan?"

"Did you mean it... about wanting to die?"

He looked shocked. I don't know why – that *was* what he'd said, wasn't it?

"Of course not lad. Things get said, that's all. I'll live forever me."

"You're not... *sad* then?"

"*Sad*?"

"Since Nan died I mean?"

He took a deep breath.

"A bit... I should think. But life goes on, doesn't it Dylan?"

I had to think about that.

"Not if you go and die it doesn't."

He laughed. Out loud I mean. It was a good sound, even though I didn't know why he was doing it. So good in fact that I started laughing too – laughing without having the first idea why I was doing it. I must have just caught it off him I suppose. I wonder if there's anything you *can't* catch off a person.

"To hell with rhetorical questions lad; you just go on saying things like that and the world will be a better place for it."

I couldn't see how it would... not unless I went about shouting all the time, or got everything I said published in a newspaper or something. How else would the world hear what I was saying?

"Fancy a cup of tea?"

"I don't like tea."

"No, that's right."

He thought for a second.

"I might have a bottle or two of dandelion and burdock stashed away if you fancy it?"

I couldn't tell if he was being serious or not.

"That's *weeds* Granddad. Nobody makes drinks out of weeds."

I once ate a dandelion. It tasted like grass, only yellower. I was sure any drink made of it would have been even worse than tea.

"So you've never tried it then, eh?"

"Of course not Granddad. People don't go about drinking weeds."

"Is that so?"

He left the room, grinning.

Have you ever noticed that when it stops raining, it doesn't exactly *stop* raining? Not after a storm at least. I think the sound of things dripping was even louder than the rain had been. Everything from branches, to leaves, to drainpipes, to things on the roof; even the unused washing line covered in rusty clothes pegs seemed to add a few notes. It was different from that storm though – the dripping I mean... *safer*, somehow, almost like it might have been protecting us a bit. From what I don't know.

"Here. Try this lad."

He handed me a half-filled glass of something browny-black coloured and fizzing.

"What is it?"

"What do you think it is nitwit? Dandelion and burdock of course."

I'm sure my Granddad used to invent words.

"But it's not green..."

"What of it?"

"Or yellow."

"And?"

I'd only ever seen browny-black weeds once before, and that was when my mother had sprayed half our garden in something called 'Deathall Total Kill'. She said it was to get rid of them – the weeds I mean – but it seemed to get rid of everything else too, like all the insects and birds. Apart from the neighbour's cat that is, which liked to sniff on the dead weeds and then lie there like it was asleep but with its eyes wide open and sort of twitching a bit. It wasn't dead though; every time I poked it with a stick it started running round in circles for about an hour.

"Go on lad, give it a sip."

I sniffed at the drink. It smelled all right – better than I'd expected actually. Sort of like a *normal* drink might have.

I hesitated.

"*Here.*"

He took the glass right out of my hand – don't ask me how he knew where it was – pressed it to his lips and took a huge gulp. Then he started coughing and nearly choked to death – at least that's what it looked like to me.

"Wrong hole."

His eyes were watering a bit; quite a lot actually.

"Went down the wrong hole is all. Quite safe."

He handed the glass back to me, took a slightly less huge gulp of tea, and then hurried back to his chair by the window, breathing a bit strange.

"Are you all right Granddad?"

"Look, if you don't want it..."

I took a sip, avoiding the greasy lip mark which now covered half the glass.

It tasted a bit like Coca-Cola, only stronger, and more ancient somehow. Very sweet though; not like tea at all. I think I even liked it.

"Thanks."

He smiled a bit and wiped his eyes on the curtain.

We just sort of sat for a while then; him slurping on his mug of tea, and me wishing I had more of that dandelion and burdock (there'd only been about two mouthfuls left) and wondering, at the same time, if I was about to start running round in circles like that cat had. I didn't though.

"There's nothing like a good dousing of rain to wake the world up, don't you think lad?"

"I suppose."

It hadn't really seemed asleep to me.

"Yes, and I daresay we were long overdue a storm."

That didn't make any sense, because it wasn't like the weather had a schedule or anything. Then again, maybe it did, because those ladies who looked a bit too perfect to be real and had the sort of smile that you couldn't look away from were always saying what it was about to do – on the television I mean.

"Don't you hate the rain Granddad?"

"Hate it? Why would I?"

"Because it stops you going in your garden. And that's where you like to live, isn't it?"

He smiled.

"True enough, but it also makes me appreciate it all

the more when the sun comes out again. Anticipation is half the pleasure of a thing lad, but I expect you're a bit too young to understand that just yet. Anyway, the rain has its uses."

"Like what?"

"Like feeding the plants and trees, which in turn feed the insects and animals."

How can water feed anything? I've never understood that. I'm sure if I drank nothing but water I'd starve to death in about two days.

"Oh, yeah."

"Then of course, there's the *umbrella*."

"What do you mean?"

"Well lad, people don't invent things unless there's a use for them. So without any rain, there wouldn't be any umbrellas, would there?"

Up until that day – well, more *evening* I suppose – I hadn't much liked umbrellas. Not that I'd even thought about them a great deal, but the thinking I had done was focused on the fact that my mother never let me carry ours, because I wasn't tall enough to hold it over her head, which meant she'd get poked in the eye all the time, even if I was standing on tip toes (we tried it once). That annoyed me, because it meant I always had to stand under the edge part of the umbrella, which is where all the water drips off. And the drips that fall off umbrellas are far worse than ordinary rain drops, especially when they keep running down the back of your neck all the time. But like I said, that was only *until* that day – now I know better of course.

"Did I ever tell you about umbrella trees lad?"

He had a distant, remembering sort of look about

him as he said that.

"You mean trees shaped like umbrellas that you stand under to keep dry?"

"That's what I told you is it?"

"No."

"Good. And I should think not, because that's not what umbrella trees are at all."

"What are they then?"

He slurped up the last dregs of his tea and then sighed in a smug sort of way.

"Well now lad, it's a complicated business is umbrella trees. Not sure if you're quite ready for it yet. Didn't believe a word of it when the king told me... not until I saw it for myself at any rate."

The king? Beyond the gate. The magical place. The Life Turner. The Courage Monster. The other fire opal. *Waiting for me.*

"What happened next?"

"Next?"

"You were sat under that tree when the Life Turner and his *progression* thing of little people found you and then he turned the fire opal – Eighty-Six Beamer's left eye I mean – into a Courage Monster, but you didn't say what a Courage Monster was exactly, and then you said the other fire opal – the one you gave to me I mean, that I've kept safe by burying a second time even though my mother complained about holes in the garden – was waiting for me somehow. But that doesn't make any sense, none of it does really, because you keep saying things and then not explaining them properly, which isn't very fair when you think about it, because I don't see you for months on end, so it's probably some sort of mental torture actually, but anyway can't you just tell me what happened next? That's what I mean, I mean."

I don't know why I kept doing that. I either said too little or too much, but never just the right amount. Sometimes I wish words would just cooperate a bit more.

"*Procession* lad. Not progression."

"That's what I meant."

"I know you did."

He grinned.

"And I was just about to tell you Dylan, if you'd let me that is."

"Tell me what?"

"What happened next of course."

"I thought you were about to tell me about umbrella trees?"

"You shouldn't assume the two are mutually exclusive lad."

"What does *mutually exclusive*—"

"It means try listening for a while and you might discover why."

"Why what?"

"*Dylan!*"

"Sorry Granddad."

16

THE MONSTER

"So there I was... somewhere in a magical place, that much I knew, though I had no clue where exactly; with a Courage Monster, determined it seemed to follow my every step; one remaining fire opal, the Life Turner having returned it to me with strict orders to keep it safe and then disappeared as mysteriously as he'd arrived, procession and all; and the king of birds, who I'd begun to think of as the normal one, if you can believe that lad. And that's probably why I got down on one knee and begged him not to go."

"Begged who not to go?"

"The *king* of course; for it was then that he decided we should part company. But for all my attempts to persuade him not to, even the getting down on one knee part, he just wouldn't listen: 'important business in the hills', 'pressing engagements to meet', 'urgent enquiries to make'. There was no hope of changing his mind. It was like being shipwrecked in the middle of the ocean only to have your life raft suddenly decide it wants to fly off."

"Couldn't he just tell you how to get back – the king I mean?"

"That, Dylan, is precisely what I kept asking him. But he was insistent that there was no way back; that the way *back* was in fact the way *forward*, which of course didn't make any sense, but what choice had I except to take him at his word? And that, lad, is where umbrella trees come in... well, one umbrella tree at least. You see, the king told me—"

"What did it look like Granddad?"

"What did *what* look like?"

I'd given up on the idea of lining questions up; it didn't seem to work. They just got stuck in a great long queue that kept getting longer and longer. Sort of like weeds I expect. If you let one grow up then it's not long before your whole garden is so infested that you have to spray it all with 'Deathall Total Kill'. I wonder if there's some sort of weed killer for brains... for when they get infested with questions I mean – not with weeds, because that would be silly.

"The Courage Monster, Granddad; you never told me what it looked like."

Unless of course you start drinking them.

"Big."

"Big?"

"Yes, big. *Extremely* big."

"How big exactly?"

"You want exact measurements do you lad?"

My Granddad seemed to like talking in yards and feet, which never made any sense to me, so there wasn't much point in 'exact measurements'. Fortunately I had a better idea.

"Bigger than, say... a cat? A very *big* cat I mean."

"Of course bigger than a cat."

"Bigger than... *you*?"

"Yes, much."

"Bigger even than a tree?"

He scowled at me a bit.

"It's not like trees come in one size Dylan; some are big, some are small, some are somewhere in-between. So how the bloody hell am I supposed to answer that?"

I suppose he had a point.

"Bigger than a tree that's about as big as an elephant?"

He looked at me as if he wanted to start making up words again.

"Why not just say *bigger than an elephant*? What do trees have to do with any of it?"

I'd once seen an elephant – at a zoo I mean. It turned out to be much bigger than they'd looked on the television, and that had annoyed me, because it made me realise that I'd lived my entire life (I was about six at the time) thinking that an elephant was about the same size as a very big cow. And it's not. Because it's actually about *three times* the size of a very big cow. I remember asking my mother why she hadn't bothered to tell me that, but she just said 'the thought never occurred to me' and then asked me if I wanted an ice-cream.

"I was just trying to make it easier for you to understand Granddad. Not everyone knows how big elephants are."

The scowl got even worse then.

"If I don't know how big an elephant is, then how on earth am I supposed to know how big a *tree* that's about as big as an elephant is... *is*?"

I remember wishing he'd just get on and answer the question.

"Never mind – don't answer that Dylan. I shall try and be as exact as possible, but bear in mind it has been seventy years since I last saw him."

"*Him*?"

"Yes, at least I think so... didn't really ask, but it's

hard not to think of a monster as a Him, even one that exists solely to give others courage when they most need it. As for his size, well, I should say about twice as tall as an elephant, but more in the shape of a person; only with a smaller head, and larger stomach, on account of being pleasantly rotund."

"You mean he was fat?"

He sighed.

"I daresay he was, yes. But only to begin with."

"What do you mean? Did he go on a diet or something?"

My mother once told me that diets are when fat people trick their body into thinking its starving, so that when they go back to eating normally again it makes them even fatter than they were in the first place, just to make sure they don't *actually* starve to death if it happens again, which of course it will (according to my mother) because fat people keep going on more diets all the time. At least I think that's what she said; it was probably more my sister she was telling, and I just happened to be listening in.

"No of course he didn't go on a diet. What's got into you today Dylan?"

Come to think of it, I expect that's why my mother never got fat, unlike most mothers seemed to. Because she just ate salad all the time and never went on diets. I think that's a bit boring though... sort of like having the same hair cut for your entire life. I'd rather have it long sometimes, and then short for a bit until it grows long again. Change is more interesting, isn't it? So why shouldn't the same be true of getting fat? And besides, animals get fat all the time, like grizzly bears for instance. They catch so many fish in summer that the only part they bother eating is the brains – probably to try and make themselves smarter or something – and then when they're so fat from eating fish brains that they

143

can hardly walk, they just collapse in a hole and sleep for the entire winter. And the best part is, when they wake up again in spring, their body has eaten up all the fat just by sleeping, so they can do it all over again. I quite fancy trying that myself... except with ice-cream instead of fish brains.

"Then how is it that he was only fat 'to begin with'? That's what you said."

"I would have got to that if you'd let me tell the story..."

"Can't you just get to it now instead?"

Asking questions right out seemed to be working well.

My Granddad groaned a bit.

"What do you suppose Courage Monsters are made of Dylan?"

I had to think about that, but I remembered once learning that people are made of about seventy percent water, which is quite shocking really, because you'd think the slightest prick and they'd burst all over the place like water balloons or something.

"Courage."

He looked at bit surprised when I said that.

"I thought you might say blood or water or something obvious like that."

"Things are different in magical places Granddad."

It wasn't like he hadn't told me enough times.

"Yes, well, you're quite right Dylan. Courage Monsters are made of concentrated courage. And so it stands to reason that by *giving* courage to someone, which is what they do, like I told you, they... well, *shrink* a bit, or indeed a lot, depending on how much courage they have to give. Why, it might even be the case that a Courage Monster gives a person so much of its courage that it becomes so small it simply ceases to exist."

"How does it get it back – the courage I mean –

after its given some out?"

"Well, by eating things of course. Just like when you eat food, all the Energy trapped inside becomes other things, like, well..."

"*Brainwaves*?"

"Precisely lad. And heat, to keep you warm, and electricity, to make your muscles work. It's all just different types of Energy, like we talked about."

"I remember."

"Anyway, when a Courage Monster eats, it turns all that Energy into pure *courage*."

"And that's how it gets bigger again? Until it's taller than an elephant?"

"That's right. The more it eats, the bigger it gets, and the greater store of courage it has to give. But equally, the more courage it gives, the smaller it becomes, and the more it must eat just to stay alive. Quite simple really, as remarkable as it is. Of course, I knew none of that at the time lad. I had to find it out, and I daresay you can guess how that happened?"

There was only one answer to that.

"It gave you some of its courage?"

"More than just *some* Dylan; for it was bound to me, that Courage Monster. I can't say why, not to this day, but it mirrored my every step, and would have given its life for me, if it ever needed to. But I shan't tell you a thing more about it – not yet awhile anyway. It was the king leaving, and the journey to that umbrella tree which came first. And that, my lad, is *not* the occasion upon which I was gifted courage, though no doubt I could have used a little. Or indeed, quite a lot."

That was when my Granddad got up to close the curtains. I remember it well, because he seemed to take about five times longer doing it than I'm sure I would have, even though his chair was right next to the window. It was completely dark outside, at least that's how it looked from the inside. I've often noticed that darkness is a lot less dark when you're standing in the middle of it, than when you're looking out on it. Anyway, I couldn't look out on it any more, not with the curtains being closed. And I don't know quite why, but I'm sure the room felt a bit smaller then, and the dripping from outside sounded a bit louder. It was odd to think I'd be staying there the whole night, with the gate, and magical place beyond it, right outside my window.

"Fancy a top up lad, before I sit down again? And a bit of food perhaps?"

I must have forgotten to be hungry, because I don't think I'd thought much about food all day, apart from at breakfast, but that was before we'd even left home. When he mentioned it though, it suddenly occurred to me that I was actually starving – well, not *actually*, because that'd probably take at least two days or something, but it definitely felt like it.

"Why do you like sitting down so much Granddad? Is it just because you're so old?"

He stared at me for a second. I expect he just had to think about it a bit.

"*Yes*."

"Oh."

That's what I'd thought.

"Now do you want some food or not?"

"Yes please."

"Right then."

When he returned, it wasn't with a plate, or a bowl, or a tray or something, like how ordinary people give you food; it was with a cardboard box, so big that he had to carry it in both arms, which he just dropped on the settee, right next to me.

"Take what you like lad. There's plenty more where that came from."

He went off again. And when he next came back,

about eight minutes later, it was with a bottle in one hand, a tin opener in the other, and a second cardboard box under his arm, a bit smaller than the one he'd given me.

"Here. This should last you."

He handed me the entire three litre bottle of Dandelion and Burdock. It even had a label, which I read after wiping off a few cobwebs.

"And you'll be wanting this. Don't worry, I've one of me own."

He held out the tin opener.

"What for?"

"Haven't you looked in the box yet?"

"It's closed."

"Then open it you ninny."

He dropped the tin opener on my lap and took the second cardboard box back to his chair, where he sat down again, making the usual sort of sound to indicate how much he liked it – sitting down I mean.

"Nothing stopping us now, is there lad?"

"Stopping us what?"

He pulled out a tin of something. It didn't seem to have a label – that worried me for some reason.

"Well, *going on living*, I should think."

That puzzled me a bit, because I couldn't see anything that had been stopping us from 'going on living' *before*, but it seemed like eating the contents of those boxes might have stopped us *then*.

"What do you do Granddad, when you're not busy sitting down I mean, and there's nobody to talk at?"

"Talk *at*! What's that supposed to mean?"

That seemed like a stupid question. I'm usually the one who asks them, so I tried to show a bit of sympathy.

"It means when you keep on endlessly talking and talking at someone because you've got nothing better to do and the person you're talking at is too stupid or polite or whatever to interrogate you properly."

I think his jaw might have dropped a bit then; I wish it hadn't though, because he was chewing some sort of fishy thing that he'd got out of that tin. A bit of jelly even fell out of his mouth and landed on his trousers, but I don't think he noticed.

"Never you mind what I do lad. That's my business. Now get on and eat your dinner or I won't tell you about that umbrella tree."

I opened the box.

Dinner didn't seem like the right word for it somehow.

17

A KING'S PATH

"There were two choices – according to the king that is: the first, was to *not* do precisely what he told me, and ended with me probably getting skinned alive, or eaten by something, if I was lucky; the second, was to follow his every instruction, and ended with me probably *not* getting skinned alive, or indeed, eaten by something, unless I was particularly *unlucky*. Not much of a choice really, was it?"

"So what did you do Granddad?"

"What the bloody hell do you think I did... wander off and get skinned alive?"

It hadn't been *all* tins in that cardboard box. There were some packets of things too; mostly dried up biscuits that tasted a bit like scabs, except more salty. The trouble with the tins was that none of them had any proper labels, but then I suppose labels are a bit pointless when you're blind. My Granddad must have just kept picking them at random and gobbling up whatever he found inside. Not that he seemed to mind. I expect that's because when a person gets very old they just stop tasting things properly, you know, like how they always go a bit deaf I mean. Everything probably tastes the same once you get to about fifty, and my Granddad was eighty-seven at the time, so I doubt he could even tell the difference between rotten fish, like the kind he was eating, and say... sugared cola bottles. I wonder if not being able to taste anything makes horrible foods taste better, or delicious foods taste worse, or everything taste somewhere in the middle?

"You might have."

He gave me a funny sort of look.

"How could I possibly be sitting here now if I'd been skinned alive Dylan?"

I think it was then that he started drinking cold baked beans straight out of the tin.

"Skin regrows Granddad. It has to because it's falling off all the time. I learnt about that in a school project on skin."

"You don't say."

I've no idea why he bothered saying that, because I obviously *did* say.

"And there are millions of little bugs that live in beds and carpets and things, which eat the dead bits of skin that drop off you; so it might have just regrown, mightn't it? If you'd been skinned alive I mean."

He took a deep breath and then shook his head a bit whilst sighing; I expect he hadn't been taking in enough air what with swallowing all those baked beans. My mother's always telling me not to eat so fast. She says eating too fast gives you wind, because you gulp down all the air that you're supposed to be breathing. I think that's just nonsense though, because I once took three hours just to eat some disgusting cabbage soup thing that she'd made, and I still got wind afterwards.

"What I did Dylan, to answer that question of yours, is precisely what the king told me to do, because knowing that skin regrows wasn't, surprisingly enough, much of an incentive to have mine ripped off."

"What's an *incentive*?"

"Promising not to lock someone in the pantry if they shut up for a bit."

For some reason my Granddad raised his eyebrows when he said that – well, not eye*brows* exactly, because he only really had one. I expect it used to be two, before the bit in the middle grew I mean. I wonder what it was for... the middle bit? It looked a bit like those caterpillars that are all hairy, except not quite as green.

"What's this... no wisecrack reply lad? I see you're not as witless as you look."

He grinned.

"Granddad?"

"What?"

"Why've you got a middle eyebrow? Is it because when all the hair fell off your head it got stuck there... you know, because you're bald I mean?"

The grin disappeared.

"This is what he told me Dylan..."

"Who told you?"

"The king, right before he left."

"Oh."

"Head north, up beyond the orchard and meadow, until reaching the very edge of the forest – the *real* forest that is. There you'll find a *direction tree*, whose job it is to give directions to weary travellers. Ignore everything that lying scoundrel says or face certain death. In fact, never listen to a tree unless it can't talk, in which case it's probably trustworthy."

"If a tree can't talk then how are you supposed to listen—"

"I'm just telling you what he said lad, and that wasn't even the best of it. Next he wanted me to follow a path, except not one on the ground that you can see. This was the sort of path, or so he claimed, that was made of *sound*."

"Why?"

"Why what?"

"Why was the path made of sound?"

"Don't you mean *how*?"

"How what?"

"*How* was the path made of sound?"

"I've no idea, but if you tell me *why* then I'll probably be able to work it out Granddad."

He took an extra long time to chew on a mouthful of what had been tinned sponge cake before next saying anything.

"Because in magical places, such as beyond that gate, things move about a lot, even things like umbrella trees, so paths on the ground, the ordinary sort that is, can't be relied upon, as they don't necessarily move at the same time. Furthermore, being *things* themselves, the paths are just as likely to move as the thing that they're leading to is."

"But why sound instead?"

"Hold your horses lad, I was just getting to that."

The tinned sponge cake actually looked quite nice, even the stodgy bit he kept chewing. I remember deciding to keep opening tins until I found one for myself.

"Paths that are made of sound keep getting *remade* you see. Because sound, which as you know is a type of Energy, doesn't hang about for very long – not one to dawdle like other types of Energy, gets bored easily I expect – so you have to keep making more of it all the time. And that means that when a thing moves, like say, an umbrella tree, or indeed the world around it, any paths that are made of sound get automatically moved too, just as soon as they're remade, which is all the time, like I said lad."

"But what makes the sound that makes the path?"

"Ah, now that would be *a path-maker* – met one of them once, nice enough chap he was."

"You mean some man runs about shouting all the time to tell people where things are?"

"Don't be ridiculous Dylan; he plants Soundposts is all."

"*Soundposts*?"

"That's right. Like signposts only... *Soundposts.* They make the sounds."

"But doesn't that mean they're stuck in one place, just like all those other *things*?"

"Well of course *they* are, but the sounds they make aren't, are they? Sounds aren't stuck in things. They can go wherever they want in the blink of an eye, just like my voice is going from over here, where I'm sitting, to over there, where you're sitting, so quickly that you probably can't even tell that my lips are moving first."

"Only because you're too close."

I remembered sitting in the car that very morning counting the seconds between lightning bolts and the claps of thunder that they made. Each second is supposed to be a mile, so if you count seven seconds between what you see and what you hear, it means the lightning hit the earth about seven miles away. I expect it's impossible to ever count nought seconds... without dying I mean.

"It works with thunder and lightning."

He smiled.

"Quite right lad. Now then, the king told me that if I followed the sound path I'd eventually reach—"

"But what did they sound like – the sounds made by the Soundposts I mean?"

I tried to imagine what sound an ordinary sort of post might make; for some reason my brain kept thinking of hitting a tent peg with a big wooden mallet, except hitting it so hard that the tent peg snaps in two, and then someone screams at you for hitting it too hard. And then I tried to imagine a post screaming... with the voice of my mother I mean.

"Why, anything and everything lad. Soundposts make sounds, and that's *all* they do, for hundreds, or even thousands of years, so as you might expect, they're rather good at it. Trees creaking, leaves blowing, birds singing, frogs ribbiting; you name it, they can copy it. *Any* sound. Some of them even sound like people, when they've a mind to that is. I believe one or two even dabble in poetry, written on the wind of course."

"How can you write something on the wind?"

"How should I know? You'd have to ask the Soundposts."

The first tin I opened contained whole tomatoes in a sloppy sort of vinegar syrup. I ate one but bits of tomato skin got stuck in my teeth so I didn't bother with the rest. The second tin had those little fish in, like the type my Granddad had just eaten. I've no idea what they tasted like because I felt too sick to even try one – it was the smell. The trouble is, when a lot of fish get sealed up in a tin, there has to be a someone who *opens* that tin, and whoever that someone is gets too much smell all at once, like a sort of overdose I suppose. And fish smell is one of those things that you have to notice sort of... *gradually*, so your nostrils have a chance to get used to it I mean. That's why in supermarkets they always put the fish isle as far away from the entrance as possible, because if they didn't people wouldn't ever buy any fish.

"Granddad?"

"Yes Dylan?"

"If Soundposts can make any sound – I mean *any* sound at all – then how did you know which sounds made up the path that you were supposed to follow, and which were just ordinary sounds in that forest, like frogs ribbiting or something?"

"Well that's obvious isn't it lad? The king told me."

"Told you what?"

"That there were three Soundposts which made up that path, sometimes four, but the fourth was a very long way away, deep in the forest, and could only be heard on the rare occasions it chose to play the bagpipes, and even then only by the keenest of listeners and on an especially still morning. The other three were much closer though, and easy to hear, providing you knew the particular sounds each preferred to make."

"You mean like Scottish people play?"

"What?"

My mother hated bagpipes. She said they sounded like squeezing the stomach of an old cat which has been inflated with air using a bicycle pump – actually, she didn't mention the bicycle pump part, but how else would a cat get inflated with air?

"Yes, more or less exactly like Scottish people play."

That definitely didn't make any sense.

"*More or less* and *exactly* don't fit together Granddad."

"Well, I daresay there were *some* differences..."

"What sort of *differences*?"

I think my Granddad must have had enough of eating rotten fish, cold baked beans, and sponge pudding, because he didn't bother opening any more tins after that. He just leaned back a bit in his chair and belched a few times whilst rubbing his stomach. I was on to the my third though – tin I mean – not that I'd exactly eaten what was in the first two, well, except for one tomato. The third tin contained a sort of spaghetti, only shaped like hula hoops. That might even have been nice if it was hot, but I just couldn't bring myself to eat *cold* spaghetti, so I decided to put it on the radiator for later... in case I didn't find any sponge pudding I mean.

"For one thing lad, the Soundpost was only *imitating* the sound of bagpipes, having the extraordinary ability to make any sort of sound it wanted, like I already told you. But for the record—"

"What record?"

"Never mind what record, it's just an expression."

"Oh."

Did I mention that I hated expressions?

"*For the record*, bagpipes made in magical places do have certain... *qualities*, which those made in our world—"

"By Scottish people?"

"Would you bloody well stop interrupting? It doesn't matter who made them; it could be Scottish people, or Irish people, or..."

"Welsh people?"

"Well, no, because Welsh people don't play bagpipes."

"Why not?"

"Never mind why not! They don't play them and that's *that*."

"Oh."

I remember my Granddad's mouth opening very wide then, as if he wanted to say something. Except he didn't. Instead he just stared out into nothing with a blank sort of expression. It lasted for four seconds (I was counting), but seemed a lot longer.

"You once told me that I never explain things properly Dylan. Well in case you hadn't worked it out, there's a reason for that lad."

"It's alright Granddad; sometimes I forget what I'm saying too."

"That's not what I..."

He looked at me for a second, and then suddenly started laughing. It was the sort of laugh that made his

156

whole face crease up in a lot of little wrinkles.

"Not what you *what*?"

"Just a minute lad..."

He got to his feet.

"I need the bloody toilet."

18

SOUND

The dripping had mostly stopped by then... apart from the occasional big one from the drainpipe. And that's probably why I remember noticing how loud the wind had suddenly become. It was even howling a bit; you know, like how people say it does sometimes, mostly in stories. I suppose it sounded like a Jack Russell or something – the howling I mean. Definitely not a proper wolf, because that'd be much louder... unless it was a *dwarf* wolf. I wonder if it's only people that can be dwarfs?

"Just promise me you won't interrupt for a while, or my old head might explode, all right lad?"

My Granddad had returned from the toilet. He'd been an awfully long time, but then I expect that's what happens when you eat things straight out of tins, especially cold baked beans.

"All right."

"Splendid. Now then, where was I? Ah yes, there are two types of instrument you see: those made in magical places, and those *not* made in magical places.

158

Instruments *not* made in magical places, like say... pianos, and recorders, and even guitars, wouldn't work if you tried to play one beyond that gate. The sound just wouldn't cooperate you see – I mean why should it? Sound is just a type of Energy, and in magical places Energy doesn't always follow the rules, like I keep telling you, particularly not when it comes to music, because, well, music's a *special* sort of thing – a truly *magical* thing, I daresay.

"Of course, instruments that *are* made in magical places, like bagpipes, and lutes, and tin whistles, well, the reason they *do* work beyond that gate, is because they've been made in a very clever way. Instead of just trying to turn Energy into sound, like our instruments do, instruments in magical places do something a bit different; they try to make the Energy *dance*. And if there's one thing Energy loves above all else, it's dancing. So, naturally, it can't resist the temptation, and does just what it's told to by the instrument, which in turn, does just what it's told by the person playing it.

"But don't you ask me *how* instruments in magical places make Energy dance, because I haven't the first idea lad. All I know is that only the most skilled and gifted of master craftsman are able to make them play even a single note, but when they do, why... there's nothing in the world quite like hearing sound truly dance. It might have scared me witless sitting under a tree that first night, when the Life Turner's procession played right above my head, but that was only because it was dark, and I didn't know quite what I was hearing. The sound of a lute, or a harp, or a set of bagpipes when played in a magical place, for an audience whose ears are ready and willing to listen, is quite possibly the most beautiful sound that a person could ever hear. Apart from the *Tranquilium* of course, but that's just a thing of legend, even in magical places; heard only by the very oldest of trees in the very dawn of their youth, or so they claim.

"Anyway, that just about explains that lad. Now, what were we talking about before instruments?"

I think that was the first time in my life that my brain got so overloaded with questions that I actually felt like being sick – I mean *properly* sick – and I'm sure it wasn't just because of those rotten smelling fish. Speaking of which, that was when I opened the *seventh* tin; it was sponge pudding; the fourth, fifth, and sixth having contained mushy peas, black cherries with the stones still inside, and a lump of meat that looked like cat food.

"Ah yes, I was trying to tell you about those *Soundposts*; the ones that made the path the king instructed me to follow through the forest. I already said there were three of them close enough to hear, didn't I lad?"

I couldn't really speak. I didn't want to open my mouth in case anything accidentally flew out, like that tomato in my stomach.

"Dylan?"

"Mmm."

"Cat got your tongue has it lad?"

That didn't make a whole lot of sense, because my Granddad didn't even have a cat. But then I suppose if he had, it would probably have preferred eating *tongues* to the stuff in that tin.

"Oh, that's right, I told you not to interrupt. Well then, I better make the most of this while it lasts, eh?"

I think he might have winked at me then.

"I was instructed to listen carefully for three very particular sounds, possibly four, though the king seemed doubtful I had the right sort of ears for hearing those distant bagpipes, even if the fourth Soundpost *had* been playing them, unlikely as that was.

"The first sound, made by the youngest and nearest of the three Soundposts, planted in a glade beneath the midday sun, would begin with the gentle buzzing of insects, on account of that glade being awash with flowers which attracted them every summer. The buzzing would steadily intensify – get louder that is – until the listener might think himself surrounded by an angry swarm of killer bees. This, the king reassured me, was only because the Soundpost was still young, and slightly mischievous of nature, so were I to return in a hundred years or so, I'd probably be slightly less traumatized, by virtue of it having 'grown up a bit'. I should also expect to hear the low crackling of a summer fire, and occasional merriment of a mildly drunken sort, which the Soundpost often heard, as its little glade was a favourite meeting place of forest travellers.

"The second sound, made by the least pleasant of the Soundposts, planted on the edge of a wooded bog, would certainly commence with the squelching of trotters – that's feet of a sort – in deep leafy mud. This is because a family of hogs lived in that bog, the patriarch of which – that's the head of the family – had an uncanny love of theoretical mathematics; don't ask me why, because I never met the fellow, but folks do say, even in our world, that pigs are smarter than we give them credit for. Anyway, that's why the Soundpost could also be heard screaming mathematical formulae in an exasperated, high pitched voice, quite unlike the hog, which it was in fact attempting to discombobulate – *put off* that is. Obviously it didn't share the hog's love of numbers.

"The third sound, made by the most creatively gifted of the three Soundposts, planted in the shadow of an ancient oak tree deep in the bowels of the forest, was the singing of Leafling Stars; a curious little creature which fallen leaves sometimes turn into, particularly those from old oak trees. And the thing about Leafling Stars, well... *one* of the things at least, is that they have a wonderful talent for choral singing. That's like in a church choir; all singing different parts at the same time but in perfect harmony. And the Soundpost had learnt to imitate this, though admittedly not nearly as well as the real thing, or so the king seemed to think; I can't say I ever actually heard Leafling Stars sing myself. That third Soundpost could also be heard, though not as often, calling like a loon – that's a type of bird, not a crazy person – on account of there being a hidden lake nearby, swathed in permanent mist, which is just the sort of place that loons like to haunt with their lonesome call.

"And there you have it; that was just about everything the king told me. I was to listen for each sound in turn, then speak my destination, that being the umbrella tree, and simply let the sound, well, guide me in the right direction. It might seem a bit wishy-washy, I'll grant you, but then things beyond that gate often do, at least until they go from being just *sayings* to actual *doings*, if you catch my drift."

Perhaps it was a good thing my Granddad gave me that box of tins, because otherwise I might never have felt sick enough to stop asking questions for a bit. And then he might never have told me all that. I'm glad that he did though.

"Granddad?"

"Yes Dylan?"

"Have you got a spoon?"

"What do you want a spoon for?"

"To eat a sponge pudding with."

The sick feeling had sort of turned back into hunger by then.

"Use your fingers lad; that's what they were made for isn't it? Cavemen didn't bother with spoons, so why should you?"

I used my fingers.

"Granddad?"

"And don't talk with your mouth full, it's *undignified*."

"Sort of like a caveman you mean?"

He didn't answer.

I swallowed the first bite of sponge pudding. It was actually quite nice, though would have been a bit too dry if I hadn't of had all that dandelion and burdock to wash it down with.

"Did it work?"

"Did what work lad?"

"The king's instructions. Did you make it to the forest, and then hear the sound of the Soundposts, and then get guided to the umbrella tree, like how he told you?"

"Well... *yes*, in a round about sort of way."

"What does that mean?"

"It means that I might have taken a somewhat, well... *indirect* route."

"How indirect?"

He mumbled something too quietly for me to hear.

"Pardon?"

"I said *three days*, that's how indirect. Three wretched days wandering about trying not to get skinned alive. Not that it was my fault mind you; that great lump of a Courage Monster was afraid of just about *everything and anything*. And it took us the whole day just to reach to the edge of the forest. He kept insisting we stop so that he could eat things. Said he couldn't help it, that it was important, and just pleaded with me to wait for him every time... which I daresay I did.

"By the time we finally got there – to the forest that is – it was nearly nightfall, and I must admit, staring into the darkness of those trees, whispering as they were in the gloom, I felt a little afraid myself. But I would have kept going, unlike that Courage Monster, who out and out refused to take another step, or indeed to let me, what with him clinging to my arm like an elephant-sized leech.

"When I did finally set off again the next morning, having, I should add, slept in a ditch the entire night, with his ugly mug snoring away next to me, it was near impossible to hear those Soundposts properly, because the Courage Monster wouldn't stop talking. Everything seemed to terrify him: from the trees, which he was sure might fall on him at any second; to the cracking of twigs beneath his feet; to the innocent twittering of birds, conversing in the canopy above. Every time I began to feel like the sounds were guiding me in the right direction, he'd start waffling on about something, or whimpering, or worse even than that, wailing in terror; how can anyone be expected to concentrate with a kerfuffle like that in their ear-hole?"

"Then how did you get there – to that umbrella tree I mean?"

"One word lad; *perseverance*."

"What does that mean?"

"It means your old Granddad can be quite determined when he needs to be, as you should well know."

"It wasn't the thought of being skinned alive then?"

He gave me a funny sort of look, and then replied without bothering to unclench his teeth, like he was pretending to be a ventriloquist or something.

"I daresay that might have helped, yes."

It wasn't a Jack Russell any more – the wind I mean. It was howling like a proper wolf by then, so much so that I kept hearing something rattle and bang on the roof. I never did find out what that was, but I remember it lasting the whole night, or at least the part until I fell asleep.

"Good God, is that the time already? I'd no idea it was so late."

I looked at my watch. It was one of those calculator watches with a hundred buttons that you couldn't press properly because they were too small even though the watch was so big that it weighed your whole arm down and stopped your wrist working.

"It's not even nine o'clock yet Granddad."

The funny thing is, I think calculators are just about the most boring invention in the entire world... unless, for some reason, which I can't understand, they're put into a watch.

"It most certainly is; I just heard the clock chime."

My watch beeped twice – that meant the hour had changed. It *had* been 8:59 though.

"Now it is."

He got up.

"Bed time lad."

"Bed time? But it's holidays."

My tin of spaghetti hula hoops wasn't even lukewarm yet, and there were still at least two glasses of dandelion and burdock left in that bottle (I think I'd had six already at that point).

"Not for me it's not."

He walked to the door.

"Yes it is."

"Bloody isn't."

Surely if you don't do anything, like a job or school I mean, then *every* day is a holiday? That's how it works, doesn't it?

"You can stay up if you want lad – doesn't bother me – but I've to get to sleep; got some dreaming to do."

It was funny the way he said that, as if dreaming was a sort of *task* or something, which I think is why I said what I said next.

"What about?"

He stopped in the doorway and looked down at me.

"Oh... flying I should think."

"*Flying*?"

I never had dreams about flying, except when I started levitating to test if I was awake or not. But that's not the same, because as soon as you start levitating in a dream, the brain of your brain (that miniature one) knows that you're dreaming and wakes you right up, which means you don't *actually* get to do any flying at all, apart from about three centimetres off the ground.

"Yes lad; *flying*."

"But... how do you know?"

"Oh, just a guess. I expect it's on my mind, what with all this talk of umbrella trees."

And then I suddenly realised.

"*You haven't told me yet*."

"Told you what Dylan?"

"What an umbrella tree actually is..."

All I knew was that it wasn't a tree shaped like an umbrella that you stand under to keep dry, because that much he had told me. But it's no good knowing what a thing *isn't*; what's the use in that? Just think how many things the average sort of thing *isn't*? Like an elephant for instance. An elephant *isn't* every thing that there ever has been *except* for what it is, which is an elephant. If someone told me that an elephant *isn't*, say... a spoon, then it wouldn't help me know what it actually *is*, apart from knowing that you couldn't use one to eat sponge pudding with I mean. And even that's probably not true, because I expect you could use their trunk like a sort of straw, or just train them to squirt the sponge pudding straight into your mouth.

"You don't say. *I wonder why that is*."

He gave me another one of those raised eyebrow looks, and then turned to leave.

"Wait. Granddad?"

"Tomorrow lad. We'll have time in the morning."

"But..."

"But nothing. You wouldn't deny a blind old man the chance to dream about flying would you?"

That was just it. He *had* to tell me.

"But what have umbrella trees got to do with flying?"

He was in the hall now. I couldn't see him any more.

"Oh, just about *everything* I should think. Goodnight."

I think that's the only time in my life that I've ever *heard* someone grin. It doesn't seem possible when you think about it, but I'd swear that I did.

By the time he'd got to the top of the stairs, which took about six minutes because he was so old and had to hold the banister with both hands whilst breathing extra heavily, the only sound left to hear was that rattle and bang the wind kept making on the roof.

I suddenly felt very alone.

And then I remembered my mother: the storm, the argument, everything that had happened that day. It seemed like a lifetime ago, a distant sort of memory... but it wasn't. *She'd left me.*

I stuck my finger in the spaghetti hula hoops. They were still cold.

My Granddad had been right... it *was* time for bed.

AUGUST

19

THE SLEEPOVER

There are three reasons why that was probably the worst night's sleep of my entire life – no wait, I've just thought of a fourth one. And thinking of that has made me remember another one, so actually; there are *five* reasons why that was probably the worst night's sleep of my entire life. That makes sense too, because I'm a pretty good sleeper most of the time (at least in beds) so if there had only been three reasons, I might have been okay, but five was just too many. Sort of like in movies when the hero keeps getting shot with arrows; you know to ignore the first two or three, because they're just to try and make stupid people (like my sister) *think* he's about to die, even though they only hit him in the leg or the shoulder, where there aren't even any organs. Five arrows is different though; that means he really *is* about to die, unless they all happen to land in his foot or something, like if it was extremely large and he used it as a shield, but that never happens for some reason. Anyway, the point is, I doubt even Conan the barbarian could have got any sleep that night, not with five reasons not to, and not even one of them landing in his foot.

The first was that I had to keep getting up to go to the toilet, which might have been because I'd just drunk about three litres of dandelion and burdock. But the annoying thing about that, is that I never *once* needed to go to the toilet before I started *thinking* about needing to go to the toilet, which I only started doing when I was lying in bed.

I'm not really sure, but I suspect the second reason might also have been down to that dandelion and burdock. My whole body felt tingly, and my eyes wouldn't stay shut, and I had a strange sort of urge to start jumping up and down on the bed, or running round in circles singing made up songs about as loud as I could. I've since learned that that's what happens when you have too much sugar and your body isn't used to it, which definitely makes it my mother's fault, because if she'd have given me tea with sugar in all those years then my body *would* have been used to it, wouldn't it?

The third reason was because that room, which probably hadn't even been slept in for about twenty years, didn't smell of Imperial Leather soap, like all the other rooms in my Granddad's house. There was a *bit* of that I suppose, but mostly it just smelled of my mother (because it used to be her bedroom) only dustier. And I think that's why I couldn't stop thinking about her, even when I did finally fall asleep and start dreaming. I wish that room had smelled of soap though, because I'd much rather have had dreams about flying.

The fourth reason was actually lots of little reasons all sort of adding up to make a big one. Things kept waking me up all the time – noises I mean. Mostly it was the wind howling and that thing on the roof which it kept making rattle and bang. And the trouble was, about every hundred or so *rattle and bangs*, the *rattle and bang* turned into a *bang and rattle*. If only it had stayed a *rattle and bang* all the time I expect my stupid brain could have just ignored it. It wasn't only that though; once I'm sure I heard something actually *land* on the roof. I couldn't tell what it was, but I definitely remember the sound of feet walking about up there, and in the dead of night too. If only that room had had a proper ceiling, instead of just big beams with the roof right on top like it was made in the attic or something, I might not have heard any of those things.

I suppose you might find it hard to believe after all that, but the fifth reason was even *more* annoying than all the rest put together. Just when the wind had finally stopped howling, and the rattle and bang had finally stopped rattling and banging, and I'd got up so many times to go to the toilet that I don't even think *dreaming* about toilets could have woken me up – even if they somehow involved my mother, which I'd rather not think about – *just then*, when the very first ray of sunlight poked a bit of gold through my window, was when my Granddad decided it was time to get up.

It wasn't that he *tried* to wake me exactly; he just completely forgot that doing things, especially things that involve making a lot of noise, like for instance, coughing up about three sink-fulls of snot, or shouting at the stairs for not being where they were supposed to be, wakes people up whether you mean them to or not. I stayed in bed for as long as I could, even though I knew that getting to sleep again was hopeless. It wasn't until I actually got up, and sat on my bed watching the dawn out of that little window, that I finally started to feel a bit better, even though it was only 5:24 AM (according to my calculator watch that is).

My Granddad had once told me that the second most beautiful thing in the world, behind only a magical girl whom he wouldn't talk about yet, was that orchard in May, when every tree was covered in white flowers. But seeing it *then*, at dawn on the first day in August, as the sun slowly rose over the edge of that faraway mountain, made me think he'd got it a bit wrong. The flower blossom had all gone, but it didn't matter, because the whole world glistened, every leaf and bit of grass, as if it was alive somehow, and not just in an ordinary sort of way. The strange thing is, I can't exactly remember it now – not like a photograph I mean – even when I close my eyes and concentrate *really* hard. But I can remember the feeling it made me feel, just as if I'd been sat there gazing through that tiny window only yesterday. And remembering that feeling makes me smile without even trying to. I only wish I could go back now and see it all again.

"Good morning my sweet."

It was my Granddad's voice, but not in the house; the sound was too far away for that. And it was a bit different somehow, almost like he was actually *happy* or something. I'd never heard him say 'my sweet' before either; I expect that's like 'darling' or 'love' or something, but it was very strange to hear him say it. I wonder if on the outside he was mostly just pretending – when people were around I mean. I can't think why though, because the inside part seemed a lot nicer to me.

Not that it was me he'd said it to of course. I don't think he even knew that I was awake, which was probably a bit stupid of him, because how could I *not* have been awake after all that noise he'd been making? Anyway, when I saw a pink blob at the end of the garden I knew it was him, even though it was quite a long way away from my window. For one thing, the blob was moving, which blobs don't often do (even that slowly), and for another, the only thing *that* pink was that pink cardigan he kept wearing. None of that matters though... in fact it's not even very interesting. But what *did* matter and *was* very interesting, was what I remember seeing that pink blob do next. And I definitely hadn't been mistaken, not that time...

My Granddad went through the gate.

If I hadn't been properly awake before that moment, then seeing what I'd just seen had definitely changed that. I think my eyes opened so wide that they almost popped right out of my head. I wonder if that's even possible? Like if you saw the most amazing thing in the entire universe I mean. I expect we'll never even find out, not with the universe being so big. What's the point in that anyway? It's like the opposite of something being so small that you can't ever see it. I wish things would just stick to being somewhere in the middle; not too big and not too small. That way we might be able to reach alien worlds and discover things that make our eyes pop out, not to mention the fact that nobody would ever catch a cold (because you'd always see them coming).

Not that I thought about any of that back then of course. I was too busy rushing to put on my clothes so that I could run down to the garden and find my Granddad. Unfortunately I tripped on one of the stairs (it hadn't been where I'd expected) and so slightly fell over and stubbed my left big toe, which delayed me by a whole minute. The worst thing about stubbing toes is that first few seconds when you don't feel anything, but know you're *about* to... and it'll be agony. I think it always hurts a bit more because of that.

It wasn't until I got into the garden that I realised how wet everything still was, largely because I'd forgotten to put any shoes on, and socks aren't made to be waterproof (they should be though). Anyway, even though I think having wet socks is probably the most uncomfortable feeling in the world, I somehow managed to ignore it, and run all the way to the gate. And that's where I stopped, not quite knowing what to do next. I couldn't see my Granddad, but he must have been out there somewhere. I wanted to go through – to open the gate and go after him – but I *couldn't*. I'd made a promise, and breaking a promise makes it a lie, and the *worst* kind of lie too. It wasn't just that though... I think I felt a bit afraid as well. After all, it wasn't like that first time I'd nearly gone through back in April, which seemed like a lifetime ago, even then. I knew so much more: about the king of birds, and darkling grubs, and life turners, and processions that aren't progressions, and courage monsters, and soundposts, and bagpipes that make Energy dance, and umbrella trees... well, maybe not umbrella trees, apart from that you don't stand under them to keep out of the rain, oh, and that they have something to do with flying – no wait, *everything* to do with flying, that's what he'd said. The point is, I knew that beyond that gate was a magical place, and that magical places were strange and wonderful and exciting. But I also knew that just because skin regrows that's 'not an incentive to have mine ripped off'... because he'd said that too, and not knowing what an *incentive* was didn't make the words any less scary. *Magical places are dangerous Dylan* – I could hear him saying it in my head, and not in that 'Good morning my sweet' voice either.

The wind from the night before had completely stopped; it wasn't until I was standing there, not knowing what to do, that I even noticed. All I could hear was the sound of my own breathing. The air was still and silent, but tasted brand new, like it had been put there for the very first time that morning. Even the birds weren't awake yet. I looked up, but there were no squirrels in that tree either, unless they were hiding somewhere, still asleep. The deck chairs were still there though, just how we'd left them that June evening... only slightly more covered in bird pooh. I poked at some of it with a stick, but it didn't come off and looked to be dried on, so I decided to sit down and take my socks off. At least that'd give me chance to think.

There were only two choices: the first was to stay sitting on that blue and purple (and white) deck chair, waiting for my Granddad to come back; and the second was to break my promise, and go through that gate to find him. That was unthinkable, but sitting there doing nothing was unbearable (except for my wet feet, which were in favour of the idea). It just wasn't fair; if only there was a third choice.

And then it occurred to me.

Perhaps there was.

20

THE LITTLE RED BOX

There's something about trees that makes me want to climb them, especially giants, like that one at the bottom of my Granddad's garden. It's not *just* that they're high though, because so are buildings, and lamp-posts, and I don't go about wanting to climb them. I think it's the standing under them part – trees I mean – and looking up at the branches, all different shapes and sizes, and then seeing that bit of light at the very top, poking through the leaves, and imagining what it might be like to be there, looking out on the world, in a secret sort of place.

It was a sycamore tree, that giant, not that I had any way of knowing that at time, on account of it not having grown proper helicopters yet; those are the flying seeds which spin like helicopter blades when you drop them. Sometimes we used to have *slow races* at school, where we'd all drop one at the same time, and the winner was whoever's helicopter took the longest to reach the ground. The trick was to flick it up a bit with your finger (without anyone noticing of course) to get an extra few seconds of height. But even then, my record was only

4.23 seconds, which isn't all that long when you think about it. I wonder how long one could stay up if it fell from the very top of that tree though? I think if it was a windy day, and it was carried in the direction of the valley, it might fly for miles, perhaps even all the way to the other side.

Anyway, *that* was the third option – climbing the tree I mean, not jumping off the top and trying to fly over the valley. It wasn't nearly as good as going through that gate and searching for my Granddad of course, but at least I didn't have to break my promise that way, or risk getting skinned alive. And if I could make it to the top-most branch, I'd have a much better chance of seeing him, wherever he was in that magical place, and everything else there too, which was a lot better than just sitting there on dried bird pooh not doing anything (apart from drying my feet).

I remember looking up at the branches, and planning a sort of... *strategy*, like how you're supposed to in chess; imagining one move after the next. I probably didn't need to though, because it was the sort of tree that seemed to be *made* for climbing. Most of the bigger branches had smaller ones attached to them (perfect for hands and feet), and the trunk seemed to twist all the way to the very top, where it split into three, like a sort of upside down stool, and opened up beneath the sky. I couldn't see that bit clearly though, not from down on the ground, because it was mostly hidden behind leaves.

The first part was the hardest. I had to leap just to reach the lowest branch. And even then it was so wide that I could barely hold on long enough to wrap my legs around. Having eventually managed to though, I just hung there for a few seconds, upside down, like those sloths you see on nature documentaries, to let myself recover a bit before the next manoeuvre. That wasn't as difficult, but it was extremely uncomfortable, because it involved wriggling for about three minutes, in a way that I can't possibly describe (not like a worm though), until my body went from being under the branch, to on top of it. Still, once I'd made it that far, the tree was as good as conquered... except for it being about twice as tall as my Granddad's house I mean. But I just kept going. And tried not to look down very often.

By the time I finally made it to that upside down stool my legs were trembling a bit, and my hands felt weak, because I couldn't help but hold on much tighter than I needed to. I remember thinking how much harder the way back down looked than the way up had from the ground, which doesn't make a whole lot of sense, because things going *down* have gravity to help them, whereas things going *up* have to fight against it all the time. But then I expect it was the being helped by gravity part that I was most afraid of. And that's probably why I didn't notice... not at first anyway. I just sat there, on the top of that upside down stool, surrounded by leaves, which made me feel oddly safe somehow. No one could see or hear me up there; I was invisible. Just like *it* had been, forgotten in that hidden place, or left there, for someone to find again.

The top of the trunk was flat, just like the bottom of a real upside down stool would have been, and smooth, as if it had been sat on by a thousand bottoms before mine, or perhaps by just one bottom but a thousand times. In the middle though, where it split to make those final three branches, was a deep hole – so deep that when reaching in I could barely touch the bottom. Nobody could have ever seen that from the ground, not even in winter when that sycamore tree was bare of leaves (and helicopters). Inside the hole was a layer of moss and dead leaves, some so old that they'd turned into soil in which little white sprouts were growing, like baby mushrooms. But beneath the moss and dead leaves was something else... something that didn't quite fit in, because instead of being green or brown or black like moss and dead leaves and soil, it was *red* – not *very* red, but just red enough to catch a bit of sunlight, and make me wonder what it was.

The thing I finally pulled out looked almost as ancient as the tree in which it seemed to live, but it can't have been, because when I scraped the layers away I finally realised what it was. A little box; made of metal but painted red, with a tiny keyhole in the front, and definitely heavy enough to not be empty. Someone had put it there... a very *very* long time ago.

"I see you're *up* then lad... in more ways than one."

I nearly dropped the box when I heard those words. It's lucky I didn't though, because it would have landed right on my Granddad's head, and without any hair to cushion the blow I expect it would have knocked him clean out. Not that I thought that at the time; I was too busy panicking I suppose. I could just about see him through a gap in the leaves. He was standing at the foot of the tree looking up, as if he could actually see me, but that was impossible, because even someone who *wasn't* almost completely blind couldn't have seen through all those leaves and branches. But I didn't really think about that either, at least not to begin with, because I suddenly felt very guilty, like I'd been caught in the act doing something wrong, and feelings come before thoughts whether you want them to or not. Perhaps it was holding that little red box that did it, like I was a master criminal robbing the crown jewels from the tower of London or something. I remember putting it back in that hole a lot quicker than I'd taken it out.

"Dylan? That is you I take it, because otherwise I shall have to go get the twelve-boar."

I was sure boars couldn't climb trees, but then my

mother was always telling me that pigs could fly, and that hog in the magical place could even do theoretical mathematics, which was almost as impressive as doing *real* mathematics, so I suppose climbing trees wouldn't be any effort at all when you think about it. Anyway, I *didn't* think about it, like I said, because I just started sweating and panicked a bit more. I couldn't work out what to say, apart from the truth, which was that I'd been spying on him, or at least trying to. Except of course it was *him* that had ended up spying on *me*. That annoyed me somehow.

"Could be a squirrel I suppose... bloody huge one mind you."

I could tell then, that he was sort of *joking* I mean; you know, the sort that isn't even slightly funny.

"*What*?"

"And a talking one at that..."

"It's *me* Granddad."

"Really? You don't say."

I remember wishing he'd stop saying that I didn't say all the time. It made me wonder if he was more deaf than he really let on. More deaf and less blind, maybe that was it.

"Yes I do."

"Eh?"

"I *do* say."

"Say what?"

"That it's *me*."

"Well of course it's *you*; I didn't seriously think you were a giant squirrel lad."

I knew that.

"How did you know I was here?"

"Never mind how I knew you were there. I've spent more hours in this garden just *listening* than you've spent living, or even than your mother has for that matter. I know what I hear when I hear it, and what I heard was someone climbing that there tree. It's a sound I've heard before, *many times* lad. The real question, is what were you doing up there?"

I could see him grinning at me down below, but that wasn't what I really noticed, because what I really noticed was something else – something that didn't make any sense.

"And, of course, have you the skill to get down again?"

He started walking back to the house.

"Because I sure as hell won't be climbing up there to fetch you."

He wasn't wearing the pink cardigan any more. And it wasn't anywhere nearby; on the ground, or the deck chairs, or even the gate."

"Granddad?"

"Yes lad?"

He was almost back at the house by the time I finally asked.

"You just came through the gate, didn't you?"

He stopped.

Not turning round.

"Yes... I daresay I did."

21

TIGER LILY

I remember being quite astonished when my Granddad offered to make me fried sausages for breakfast, mostly because fried sausages didn't come in a tin, and *had* to be cooked... in a pan... on the stove. At least that's what I'd thought before he gave me a plate of cold hot dogs.

"Pre-cooked lad. Saves you the effort."

No wonder he drunk so much tea. I expect it was the only hot thing that ever went in his mouth.

Still, they weren't exactly horrible... apart from the green one, but I mostly just spat that out.

"You got down all right then?"

It hadn't been as hard to climb down that giant sycamore tree as I'd expected it to be, but I think that's because I was so distracted by what he'd said, and whenever my brain gets distracted by thinking about something – *really hard* I mean – the *doing* part of things gets left to that other brain, the miniature one. And it's really very good at doing things, unlike my main brain, which doesn't get much practice I suppose. I've learnt that you can tell which brain does something by whether or not you can remember it; like for example brushing your teeth. I can never remember doing that, which means it must be the brain of my brain that gets stuck doing it every day. I wonder if that's why it doesn't always cooperate with me – because I keep giving it all the boring jobs I mean. Perhaps if I concentrate really hard from now on whenever I brush my teeth I might even start having dreams about flying, you know... as a sort of thank you.

"You told me you hadn't been through that gate in seventy years Granddad. But you have, haven't you? Before today I mean."

We were sat in the kitchen eating our cold hot dogs.

He looked at me from across the table.

"I know what you're going to say lad, but there's no real answer for it."

He dipped an entire hot dog in tomato ketchup and then took such a huge bite of it that the bit left in his fingers was so small he might as well have just shoved it in whole. I expect he just wanted a lot to chew on... so he had time to think I mean. I did that with my mother sometimes, but then she was always telling me not to talk with my mouth full, whereas I didn't much care if my Granddad did. Anyway, he looked like a hamster.

"Answer for what?"

He finally swallowed.

"For not telling you."

"Not telling me what?"

"My God Dylan, don't be so bloody obtuse. You *know* what."

"What does obtuse—"

"And you shouldn't have been spying on me. This is *my* house, and that's *my* garden, and it's entirely *my* business what I do in it. I've never had to explain myself to anyone else, so I don't see why I should start now to an eight-year-old boy."

"Nine."

"Oh, for pity's sake!"

I remember him standing up quite sharply then; it almost made me jump, probably because I was so used to seeing him move about like a tortoise all the time... only less green and more bright pink. I couldn't understand what the problem was. Why hadn't he just admitted it in the first place? It was almost like he was ashamed that he'd even been there – beyond the gate I mean, to the magical place. But why?

And then I suddenly realised. The bits all came together like those last few pieces in a jigsaw.

"She's still alive isn't she Granddad?"

He looked at me then, in a way that he'd never looked at me before, or did since. His face was sad, but serious too, and there was something else, a sort of... desperation I think.

I knew I must have been right.

"That magical girl; the one beyond the gate who liked to climb trees, and make catapults, and bake apple crumble, except with rhubarb and blackberries to make it extra sweet, and who you said was the most beautiful thing you'd ever seen, even though you won't tell me about her, not properly anyway..."

It was then that his eyes went sort of glassy, which made them look like ginormous pearls, because they were white and cloudy instead of black like ordinary eyes. I couldn't tell if he was angry, or upset, or just something else which I didn't understand.

But I do remember wishing he'd say something... something from that *inside part* that he seemed to keep hidden.

"It's because of the pink cardigan – that I worked it out I mean. I saw you this morning through my window – not that it's not morning any more. I just mean even *earlier* this morning, at about 5:24 AM. Anyway, you were wearing it then, when I saw you go through the gate... and I *did* see you go through the gate because I remember it perfectly Granddad even though it was 5:24 AM, so don't try and pretend or anything. But then you didn't have it when you came back, when you were under the tree and I was on top of it. And that's why I asked you... if you'd just come through the gate. And you said yes, which meant you must have left it there. But why would you leave it there? That's what I couldn't understand... and then I remembered that magical girl. It's *hers* isn't it? Her cardigan I mean. Because it's pink and human-sized, just like girls are – their *clothes* I mean, not the underneath part... although I suppose that is too, and so are boys' underneath parts come to think of it; but the point is, boys don't go about wearing pink cardigans – except of course you Granddad, but that's only because you're blind... and so old I mean."

It's strange that sometimes a lot of words can take away sadness, or anger, or whatever it was my Granddad had been feeling. Words are supposed to *mean* things, I've always thought that, but sometimes what they mean doesn't have anything to do with how they make a person feel; sometimes they just have to be words, and you just have to keep on saying them.

My Granddad smiled. It wasn't much of a smile, and it was mostly just on one side, but it still made me smile back all the same.

"Well now... there's no keeping secrets from you is there lad?"

"It's *true* then? That *was* her pink cardigan? She *is* still alive beyond that gate somewhere?"

He thought about that for a second. I think he just didn't want to admit it, even though I'd already worked everything out and told him so.

"I suppose she is... yes."

"What do you mean you *suppose* she is?"

He sighed in a *deep thinking* sort of way.

"Life is a funny sort of business lad. Sometimes it's right there, staring you in the face, with a smile, or a kind word, and other times, well, you have to go out and *find* it, because it's got a bit lost in other things. But then I daresay that doesn't make a whole lot of sense, does it Dylan?"

Of course it made sense. How could it not after everything he'd told me?

"Like the fire opals."

And the little green egg that I still hadn't told him about.

"*Yes*. Exactly like those fire opals."

There was something I had to ask.

"Granddad?"

"Yes?"

"Is she just as beautiful as she was seventy years ago? More than that orchard in May I mean."

He wiped his eyes a bit then. I don't know why, because he was still smiling.

"She is."

I remember half waiting for him to say something else, because it looked like he wanted to, but he never did. Well, I mean he *did*, but it wasn't exactly what I'd expected.

"Cup of tea lad?"

"I don't like tea Granddad."

He definitely knew that already.

"What? Even with honey in it?"

That confused me a bit, because I'd never heard of anyone drinking honey before.

"Wouldn't that turn it into custard or something?"

"It melts, you daft berk."

I hadn't thought of that.

"What does it taste like?"

He gave me a funny sort of look; the usual sort.

"*Tea with honey in it.*"

"And is it nicer than that dandelion and burdock stuff?"

"That's like asking me if red is nicer than blue. It's different is all."

"Go on then."

I was a bit thirsty after chewing on all those cold hot dogs, especially the green one.

"Go on then *what?* I wasn't offering you none – we ran out months ago."

"Then why did you go on about it like that?"

He grinned.

"It was *you* that went on about it, not me. All I did was to offer you a cup of tea."

With honey in it.

I got up to get a glass of water.

Unfortunately the cleanest glass I could find had something brown and crispy in the bottom which looked more or less like the top layer of a cow pat after being baked in the sun. I once stood on one of those thinking it was a stone... it wasn't though. Luckily I didn't have any shoes on or they might have been ruined.

"Why don't you ever clean anything Granddad?"

"Oh, your mother will take care of—"

Except she wouldn't, not any more, because that's what she'd said, and my mother never said anything unless she really meant it, and even if she *didn't* really mean it, which she *did*, the fact that she'd said it, meant that she would... mean it I mean. It was like he suddenly remembered. And that made me remember too. The storm. The argument. *She'd left me.* And only the day before too. If it had seemed like a lifetime ago that same night, then it must have been more like *two* lifetimes ago the next morning... unless you're a tree of course, because they live for thousands of years, so it'd be more like one sixth of a lifetime or something.

"What time will she be here?"

"I don't know... didn't say. And I'd rather not think about it to be honest with you lad."

"Why not?"

"Do *you* want to think about it?"

I had to think about that.

"No."

"Well then, probably for much the same reason."

That can't have been right. I didn't want to think about it because it was *me* that my mother had left, and I still didn't know if she'd really meant to or not. But thinking that she *had* meant to made my stomach feel hollow and my heart hurt a bit, or at least something in that general area. It might have been kidney ache for all I knew. I wonder if kidneys can even ache; it's not as if you ever feel them is it? Not like *big toes* or something. Anyway, the point is, my Granddad *hadn't* been left, because that was where he lived, and besides, he was an eighty-seven-year-old man (at the time) and I was just a nine-year-old boy, so it wasn't the same at all.

"Are you coming or not?"

He was standing in the doorway looking back at me with a mug of tea in his hand.

"Coming where?"

"Let me see... how about the Taj Mahal? I've always fancied seeing that. Or perhaps the North Pole? Old Saint Nick's got a lot to answer for – hasn't given me any presents for eighty years."

I stared at him.

He stared back at me.

"*The garden.* Where do you think?"

"Did it work Granddad?"

"Did *what* work?"

"Did you dream about flying last night, like you said you would?"

If I could fly in my dreams then I think that's where

I'd go first... to the North Pole I mean. And maybe the Taj Mahal too; although I didn't know where that was at the time, or even what (it's a big palace in India in case you're wondering).

He smiled a bit, on the other side of his mouth this time.

"Dreams are like secrets Dylan. Given to you and you alone. Not things to be waffled on about willy-nilly. Why, a man's dreams are just about the only place that he's truly free."

That didn't seem like much of an answer.

"Does that mean *No*?"

"It means I'm not bloody telling you lad."

He could have just said that in the first place instead of waffling on like that.

"I will tell you about something else though; something altogether more real than dreams, if you've an ear to listen, and a mind to sit under that tree for a while – instead of trying to climb it that is. And in case you'd forgotten; it has just about *everything* to do with flying."

The umbrella tree.

I think I had forgotten.

"All right."

He grinned at me.

"So you *are* coming then?"

I followed him to the doorway.

"Yes."

"Good, because my tea's getting cold."

I bet it wasn't nearly as cold as those *fried* sausages had been.

"Granddad?"

"Dylan?"

I was walking by his side then. The grass was still wet.

"What's her name?"

He stopped.

I stopped as well.

"That girl I mean. You know, the one with the pink—"

"Yes, I know lad."

He looked at me in a thoughtful sort of way. And then beyond the gate to the orchard and forest, as if he was remembering I suppose. Not that he can of needed to. He must have seen her only that morning.

And then he smiled.

"Tiger Lily."

Properly I mean... on *both* sides of his mouth.

"Of the Valley."

22

UMBRELLAS

"Do you know much about *time* lad?"

It was mid-morning by then, and the air had mostly warmed up, so it didn't taste quite so new any more. In fact it felt like summer again. I remember thinking how strange it was that only the night before the world had been battered by that storm, sort of like a very big haddock I suppose – you know, like the type you get in fish and chip shops. Except when haddocks get battered the batter stays on them, but the world just seemed to shrug it off, as if it never really happened... apart from being left very soggy I mean.

My socks were still wet.

"What do you mean?"

"Well, for instance, have you ever noticed how sometimes it seems to *speed up*, so that after it's passed, you wonder how it could ever have gone so quickly? Or indeed the opposite; how sometimes it seems to *slow down*, so that a whole year's worth of memories seem to gather up in just a handful of days?

"Oh."

I used to think that was just me, but then it usually turns out that most things I thought were just me really aren't just me at all.

"Yes Granddad, I notice that all the time."

"All the *time* eh lad?"

He looked at me with a strange sort of smirk on his face. I've no idea why.

"All the *time*... get it?"

"Get what?"

"Never mind."

I suppose he was just very old.

"The point is; time doesn't always play by the rules, even in our world. But in magical places, where Energy is *alive* and free to do as it will, time is even less constrained. That is to say, the chime of an hour can pass like the tick of a second, and of course, the tick of a second, like the chime of an hour. So when I reached that umbrella tree on the morning of my fifth day beyond the gate, it really didn't feel like five days at all, even though the sun had set five times, and I'd slept five nights – five horrendously uncomfortable nights I might add. But in truth lad, it felt more like five months than five days, and that's even how I remember it now, odd though that may seem."

It didn't seem that odd, perhaps because it'd taken him just as long to tell me it all.

"Why did you go there Granddad – to that umbrella tree I mean?"

"Because that's what the king told me to do, and I was in no position to argue, not if I wanted to make it back alive."

"Yes, but *why*?"

"Why what?"

"Why is that what the king told you to do?"

"Oh. Didn't I mention that part lad?"

He hadn't.

"Because the king seemed to think that was the quickest way."

"What was?"

How could a tree be the quickest way to anything? Apart from the sky that is, but only if you don't happen to have a ladder to climb... or an extremely bouncy pogo stick.

"Haven't you been listening Dylan? *Flying*, of course."

That just made me even more confused.

"You mean the tree could actually *fly* Granddad?"

"Don't be ridiculous. Trees can't fly. There aren't any umbrellas big enough for one."

"What have umbrellas got to do with it?"

"It's *umbrellas* that do the flying lad."

I tried to imagine an umbrella flying about – it was actually quite easy. I've noticed that whenever it's slightly windy umbrellas get turned inside out, and then whoever's holding the umbrella gets angry and tries to turn it back the right way, but it only stays that way for about three seconds, so they end up throwing it in a hedge or something. That's why over the course of my life I've found about thirteen umbrellas sticking out of hedges, usually turned inside out and a bit bent, on account of people first trying to beat the hedge to death before giving it to them. Anyway, I expect that's why umbrella makers make them that way, because if umbrellas didn't turn inside out at the slightest puff of wind then people would start taking off all the time, and then the fire brigade would keep getting called up to rescue old ladies out of trees... instead of their cats I mean.

"Is that because in magical places trees can talk?"

I remember watching his face then; I think he was trying to work out what I meant. It reminded me of toilets for some reason.

"To the old ladies I mean... the ones who get stuck in them."

I think there might have been a middle part I'd forgotten to explain.

"Because of the wind blowing them up there all the time... with their umbrellas that don't turn inside out."

I expect confusion is another one of those things that people catch off of each other, except unlike laughter, or nervousness, or all those other things that get caught, it must somehow leave the first person when it enters the second, because I didn't really have it any more, at least not for about forty-two seconds, which was when I caught it all back. Maybe the only way to get rid of confusion forever is to make someone else even more confused than you were, and then run away really quickly, so they're stuck with it. I expect that's why people talk to plants and things... to get rid of all their confusion I mean. It's no wonder they don't always grow straight.

"Because the umbrella makers—"

"*Stop.*"

He smiled at me. It was the sort of smile that looked as if someone had poked chopsticks in each side of his mouth and pulled it up as high as they could.

"I've no idea what you're talking about Dylan, but I've certainly heard enough to deduce that it has nothing to do with the truth, which is quite simply that umbrellas fly because Energy *wants them to*."

"Wants them to why?"

"Wants them to *fly*."

That smirk reappeared.

"Are you going deaf again Granddad?"

I said that a bit loudly just in case.

He rolled his eyes then – at least that's what people call it when someone does that, but it's not like they *actually* roll or anything.

And then he sighed.

And then he looked straight at me.

"Listen very carefully lad, for I shall say this only once..."

"Why?"

"Just shut up a minute."

Nothing happened for about three seconds.

"In magical places Energy is alive – we've established that much I daresay. And things that are alive tend to be somewhat unpredictable – that much you know too."

I remembered the bagpipes.

"Yes, Granddad, which is why instruments have to make sound dance, because if they didn't, it wouldn't bother doing what they wanted.

"Precisely. But sound is just *one type* of Energy. There are lots of others."

"I know that too. Light, and heat, and electricity, and..."

"Yes?"

"And *stars*."

"True. But do you also know about the hidden sort?"

"What hidden sort?"

"There's a type of Energy that exists in things without being seen, or heard, or even felt. It has to do with gravity you see. When a thing is lifted up, like say, an umbrella, the Energy used to lift it, by your arm for example, is transferred right into it as *hidden* Energy. And that's why if you were to let the umbrella go it'd fall right to the ground, because of all that hidden Energy to *make* it fall.

"Now that's all well and good in our world, where Energy does just what gravity tells it to do, but in magical places, where it's alive and unpredictable, it means that anything and everything has the potential to, well... *fly*. And the trouble is, hidden Energy is the most peculiar type of Energy of all, and does seem to have a tendency to get muddled at times, either that or it just has a very unusual sense of humour – the acquired sort I daresay. The point being, it seems to have determined quite unanimously – that means it all agrees – that umbrellas belong in the sky, not on the ground, which is why instead of making them *fall down* it makes them *fly up* instead.

"As for that question of yours; *why* Energy wants umbrellas to fly, I really couldn't say for sure, not being able to talk to it myself, but perhaps it's because umbrellas look a bit like clouds, or because people are always holding them up in the air, and it simply put 2 and 2 together and came out with 5, if you catch my meaning lad."

That must be something else you can catch.... meanings I mean.

"Like balloons Granddad?"

"Balloons?"

"People are always holding them up in the sky, so that's where hidden Energy must think they belong, in our world I mean, because they float, don't they?"

"Ah, well that's not quite the same lad. You see, balloons only float in our world because they're filled with a special type of gas that's lighter than air, and that *makes* them float. They still have hidden Energy pulling them down, it's just not as strong as the gas is... until the gas runs out of course, just like a battery would – haven't you ever seen what happens then Dylan? Why, if you were to let one of those balloons go right now, it might well float for miles up into the sky, but sooner or later gravity would catch up with it, and bring it back down to earth, just like everything else."

"Except for birds."

"Birds flap their wings. If they didn't, they wouldn't

stay up there very long."

"And clouds; what about them?"

"What do you think rain is lad? Clouds falling to the earth, that's what."

"What about *heat* then? That rises up, doesn't it?"

He smiled.

"Very clever. You're a bright little thing, aren't you? But heat's just another type of Energy."

"So why doesn't it do what gravity tells it, in our world I mean, like hidden Energy has to? That's what you said."

"Well now, I'm sure it would, if gravity were to ask nicely enough, but the simple fact is, gravity doesn't tell heat to do anything, so it goes more or less where it wants."

I had to think about that.

"Granddad?"

"Yes lad?"

"What if the balloon floated over that valley, and into the magical place; would it still fall back down to earth then?"

I remember watching him slurp down the last bit of his tea. He must have liked it very much, because he even sucked a few drops straight out of the tea bag. And I suppose that explains why he'd left it in the mug to begin with. I had been wondering, because my mother never did that, and she drank just about as much tea as my Granddad... except without the eight spoonfuls of sugar of course.

"That, my boy, is an *excellent* question, but sadly one I cannot answer. Balloons don't exist in magical places, so I daresay it might come as quite a shock were hidden Energy to discover one. It might just do what gravity tells it, like it would here, or it might ignore it, and fly that balloon all the way to the moon. Hard to say really. Why, it might even get the hump – come over all jealous that is – that a strange unknown thing was able to fly without its help, and turn into heat, bursting it on the spot. Or, equally, it might admire it for defying gravity, the very tyrant which tries to tell *it* what to do, and turn into light, making that balloon glow like a little star. But I'm just guessing Dylan; I suppose we'll never know is the truth of it."

Just like the sycamore seeds that fell from the top of that tree we were sitting under... we'd never really know what happened to them either.

"There's still something I don't understand Granddad."

"Oh?"

"If hidden Energy makes umbrellas fly in magical places – all of them that is – then how can there even *be* any umbrellas? Don't they all just fly right up into space the moment they're made, sort of like rockets I mean?"

He snorted a bit then. I suppose umbrellas taking off like rockets was a funny sort of thing to imagine. It made tea come out of his nostrils. I don't think he noticed though, probably because my Granddad's nostrils were nearly always dripping... the drips were just more brown than green this time.

"People put things on them lad... to stop them floating away."

"Like what?"

"Oh, all sorts. Plant pots with flowers in, bird cages, bath tubs, you name it..."

"Bath tubs?"

"Certainly. Remember, people in magical places aren't all the same size, more or less, like people here are. I've seen bath tubs no bigger than thimbles lad. In fact, I've even seen umbrellas with entire cities built on them, if you can believe that."

"And they don't float away?"

"Well yes... sometimes they do, when the people

who live on them want to that is. And sometimes they don't, when they've a mind to stay in one place for a while. It's a wonderous spectacle I tell you lad, when an entire city floats right over your head, even if it is no bigger than an ant hill."

"But how do they make them stop, going up I mean?"

"By making their city heavier of course. Energy has its limits lad – it isn't some kind of god, as I've already told you. However much it might push a thing up, instead of down, if the weight of that thing is sufficiently heavy, then the hidden Energy just can't win, as much as it might want to."

"Yes, but *how*?"

"How what?"

"How do they make their city heavier when they're up in the sky floating about? It's not like they can just stick a plant pot on it, or a bath tub or something."

He grinned.

"Now then lad, give it some thought and the answer to that question will surely present itself. After all, you did say it yourself only minutes ago."

I tried to give it some thought.

It was quite obvious really.

"They must have a giant lasso which they use to capture birds right out of the sky, and then they tie them down to the umbrella like those little people did to Gulliver I mean. And that way it gets heavier, and starts sinking again."

For some reason that made him laugh even more. Luckily there wasn't any tea left to come out of his nostrils.

"I daresay they *might* do that lad... in emergencies. But a giant lasso would be a tricky thing to operate would it not, especially for people no bigger than ants? And birds aren't exactly predictable, much like Energy isn't; what if there weren't any around when they needed one? It'd be bound to happen sooner or later, and then they'd just float up into space where there's no air to breathe."

I suppose he had a point there.

"It's the clouds that they capture lad, or rather, the water within them, up there in the sky. And the more they capture, the heavier their umbrella becomes, until they eventually start to fall. Of course, if they want to go up again, they just tip some out, like the very clouds they capture it from do."

"You mean the umbrellas start *raining*?"

"Precisely."

"But what if there aren't any clouds to capture the water from in the first place? They're unpredictable too Granddad, just like birds and Energy."

I remember looking up into the sky then. It was blue and bright, at least the bits that poked through the leaves of that sycamore tree were. I couldn't see a single white bit anywhere.

"You might not always be able to see it lad, but the sky is full of water, enough to weigh down a flying umbrella at any rate. You only really *see* clouds when there's an awful lot of it that gets together, but that's not to say it's not there when you don't."

"Oh."

We just sat there for a while then, on those old deck chairs, in the shade of that tree, on the border between this world and a place where umbrellas fly about in the sky carrying entire cities on their backs. I suppose that's what I must have been thinking about, but I think my Granddad was just *sitting*, in that old man sort of way that he did.

And then it suddenly occurred to me.

"*An umbrella tree.*"

"What's that lad?"

"You still haven't even told me Granddad."

It's funny how he could explain something without actually explaining it at all.

"Umbrellas fly because hidden Energy thinks they should, and trees don't, because there aren't any umbrellas big enough to make them; I understand that now, at least I think I do, but then *what is* an umbrella tree? Apart from just something the king told you to find I mean."

"Well now, to answer that Dylan, I'd better tell you just what happened when me and that Courage Monster finally got there. But first, there's a little something I want you to get for me, if it's not too much trouble..."

23

THE MATRON D'TREE

I'd never really paid any attention to all those photographs in my Granddad's house. I knew they were there of course, on shelves and cupboards, window sills and mantelpieces; mostly black and white ones with torn edges in fancy golden frames that my Nan had spent thousands of hours dusting. I'm not sure why I'd never really paid them any attention; perhaps because they'd always been there, so I'd never really had any reason to notice them, just like I hadn't ever really noticed those elastic bands on door handles, or extra bits of carpet where they weren't supposed to be – not at the time I mean... only after.

"Did you get it lad?"

"Yes Granddad."

It was one photograph in particular which he'd asked me to fetch that August morning. I didn't know why, at least not to begin with, because he'd refused to tell me.

"Now then Dylan; describe her for me."

The photograph was of a lady, and *ancient* at that –

the photograph I mean, although the lady can't have been much younger. She looked like one of those Dickens characters; dressed up in poncy old-fashioned clothes which didn't quite fit because she was so fat, and with her head stuck up a bit too far, sort of like ladies do in swimming pools to try and keep every last bit of hair perfectly dry. I hate it when they do that. I think ladies should be banned from swimming pools because they're too slow, always expect you to get out of the way without ever moving themselves, and start shouting at you if you accidentally splash even one tiny drop on them. It's ridiculous that is. You'd think if they hated water that much they wouldn't climb into a great big hole full of the stuff.

"How do you mean?"

He rolled his eyes again without actually rolling them.

"It's quite simple lad; *tell me what she looks like*."

"Old."

"And?"

"Fat."

"And?"

"Posh."

He laughed a bit.

"What else?"

"Strict."

"Now we're getting somewhere. But what makes you say that?"

"The way she's looking down at me – like she's better or something."

"Excellent Dylan. Very observant... couldn't have put it better myself in fact. Anything else?"

I squinted a bit at the photograph. I really don't know why, because it's not like I couldn't see it perfectly well *before* squinting at it.

But there *was* something else. I couldn't tell what it

was at first. And then I realised.

"She looks a bit like you Granddad."

His eyes grinned at me then, in that funny sort of way that they often did. It's odd how grins are sometimes made by mouths, and sometimes by eyes, and sometimes by both together. And sometimes even just by words – at least that *one time* anyway. I wonder if ears can grin too, and noses?

"Who is she?"

"Who she is doesn't matter Dylan, it's who she looks like that really matters – *apart from me* that is."

That was a very strange thing to say.

"And who does she look like apart from you Granddad?"

"The Matron d'tree of course."

"The what?"

His mouth joined in with the grinning.

"The very first person we met when finally discovering that umbrella tree. Not that it was possible to miss exactly. I've never in all my living days seen a thing quite like that umbrella tree lad. Twice as tall as any of the giant trees I'd seen up until then, and standing on its own in the middle of a glade right in the heart of that forest, surrounded by colourful signs, and queues of people; hundreds there were, every shape and size and species imaginable, all chattering away, or bickering with each other in all manner of voice and language.

"And when I looked up, into the boughs of that mighty tree, well... it near took the breath right out of my lungs. There were ladders and ropes and bridges and platforms, and even little shops and stalls standing in serried rows along branches as if they were streets. But it was the sheer number of people that really awed me lad; all moving this way and that in neat little lines, like ants in the jungle. And then there were the wardens; each as different as the next, but all dressed in the same navy blue uniform with white stripes and oversized hats strapped to their chins, like little policemen, poking people in the right direction if they should ever step out of line.

"Why, I should say it looked more like a circus than anything. And it might well have been too, without the Matron d'tree that is, to keep charge of the whole affair. By George, was she ever a woman..."

For about half a second I might have wondered if that was a question, because if it *wasn't* then it was a stupid thing to say, but then my brain just refused to think about that, and went back to imagining everything he'd described – a sort of circus in a ginormous tree, with ropes and ladders and bridges and shops *and people* – hundreds of them, like ants, but each different. I suppose giving brains things like *that* to think about is sort of like giving mouths sugared cola bottles to eat, or ice-cream... or sugared cola bottles *in* ice-cream.

"And that's precisely why I wanted you to get that photograph lad. It's not the Matron d'tree herself of course; I shouldn't think there are any photographs of her, even beyond that gate. There are no cameras you see, not in magical places – they just wouldn't work – but it's as close a likeness as you might ever find, right down to that ridiculously over-sized dress, which somehow manages to cover every scrap of flesh up to her cheeks whilst still being three sizes too small."

"You mean you met a woman Granddad, at that umbrella tree, who looked exactly like the woman in this photograph?"

He stopped grinning and gave me one of those chopstick smiles again.

"So much for bright."

He mumbled that for some reason.

"Yes Dylan, that's *precisely* what I mean... *and said.*"

"Even the hair?"

The woman in the photograph had all her hair tied up in a big knot right on top of her head. It looked sort of *solid*, like it wasn't hair at all, but an oddly shaped hat painted to look like hair. I can't really explain why, because it's not like hair ever moves in photographs, even ones of normal people, so it should always be sort of solid, but hers was *even more* solid somehow. The closest I can think of was when my sister used to put so much hairspray on that no one could enter her room for about six minutes or they'd probably die from breathing in toxic fumes. I suppose she must have had a gas mask in there or something, because *she* never seemed to die from breathing in toxic fumes.

"Yes Dylan, *even the hair*. Only the Matron d'tree had more of it... and it was less natural looking."

I think my imagination sort of broke when he said that, because all I kept imagining was a big tree stump on her head.

"But that's not even the amazing part lad... have you ever seen a lady climb a tree?"

I'd seen a girl climb a tree. I wondered if that counted.

"One looking exactly like *that* I mean."

I looked down again at the photograph.

"And not up those ladders or ropes or bridges like her customers. The Matron d'tree shimmied up and down that trunk with her bare thighs, and swung from branch to branch with arms that were almost as thick. For as fat as she might have been on the outside, she was *ten times* stronger underneath."

My imagination must still have been overloaded, because all I could picture that time was a great big orangutan dressed like Queen Victoria. I tried to imagine it shaved and with a tree stump on its head, but that just didn't work for some reason.

"Did she say anything to you Granddad?"

He spat out a bit of air that made another drip fall from the end of his nose.

"She most certainly did Dylan. How else do you think I know all this; about hidden Energy, and why umbrellas fly, and that remarkable tree of which she was mistress and master both. Yes, we shared a cup of tea together if you must know, and a rather large tray of home-baked gingerbread, which I must say, went down a treat, as up until then I'd only eaten berries, and apples, and nuts, and other natural sorts of things that are abundant in orchards and forests, especially in magical places; and nice though they were, I did feel rather relieved to fill my belly with something *warm* for a change, and deliciously sweet at that. I think she took a liking to me is the truth of it, probably out of pity, though not at first I shouldn't think."

"Why not?"

"Probably because I didn't have the first clue where I was, or why I was where I was, wherever that was, or who she was, or more particularly, where it was that I was going, which happened to be what it was that she was most curious to know."

"Oh."

"It was the very first thing she asked me you see, after introducing herself that is, bowing in a rather self-important manner, and then turning her nose up with a disgusted sort of air... possibly because I hadn't washed or changed my clothes in nearly a week, but then that was hardly my fault.

"But I simply *didn't know* where it was that I was going. All I knew was that the king had sent me to that umbrella tree having told me it was the only way to get back home. And I'd believed him, because trying to find my way back to that gate alone had only seemed to take me farther from it, much to his amusement. But he hadn't told me what to do next, or indeed, *where to go*, so I was rather at a loss as to how to answer the Matron d'tree's question. And I don't think she much liked that, being such a busy lady and all."

"So how did you make her give you all that hot gingerbread then?"

I remember wishing I had some gingerbread right then, or at least something to take away the after-taste of cold hot dogs; I'm sure bits kept coming up from my stomach for some reason.

"I didn't *make her* Dylan. She just... warmed to me is all; likely when she realised I was more of a clueless outsider than the regular sort of idiot that she'd apparently taken me for. But I'd rather not dwell on that to be quite honest with you lad.

"What I finally told her, after a rather lengthy and somewhat uncomfortable discussion, was that I'd been lured through a gate at the bottom of a garden on the pretence of finding a girl, who would apparently be the most beautiful thing I could ever in my life see. At that the Matron d'tree smiled, and seemed much more agreeable it must be said, although she did ask me in a rather blunt tone why I hadn't just said that in the first place."

"And why hadn't you Granddad?"

He sighed in an annoyed sort of way.

"Because... well, it's an embarrassing thing to just come out and say is why."

That didn't make any sense. What could be embarrassing about wanting to see the most beautiful thing in the world, even if it was just a girl?

"Having apparently now established where it was that I was going, though I had not the foggiest idea how, she went on to enquire as to how much I weighed, and whether or not 'the giver' would be coming with me, by which she meant the Courage Monster, who, I might

209

add, had simply stood there, trembling like a leaf, and a cowardly one at that, but not saying a word, the entire time. I looked at him. He looked at me. And I knew there was no need to even ask the question. He *was* coming with me, whether I bloody well liked it or not.

"As for my weight, well, I didn't know exactly... so I more or less guessed. About 12 stone and 3 pounds, is what I think I said. But the Matron d'tree wasn't much impressed with that. You see, they don't have stones and pounds in magical places, or any of that new-fangled metric malarkey. So she instructed me to stand on what I can only describe as a giant scale, like that old-fashioned sort you sometimes see in waiting rooms. It turned out that I was 4,313,279 Tardigrades – a unit of measurement taken from the very *smallest* customer the Matron had ever encountered: the *Tardigrade*. It's a type of water bear, and so small that he or she can't even be seen without a magnifying glass, which of course she always carried about her person, just in case one were to arrive. Apparently they have to take megaphones whenever they travel just to be heard, and even then, so the Matron explained, they sound barely louder than a flea... with laryngitis."

"What's—"

"A very sore throat."

"Oh."

"Alternatively, if it's of any interest to you lad, I weighed 0.000004 Armillarians – that being a unit of measurement representing the very *largest* customer the Matron d'tree had ever encountered. She didn't seem keen to tell me much about them; I suspect the memory of being visited by one wasn't particularly pleasant, to be quite honest."

Listening to my Granddad go on about Tardigrades and Armillarians made me want to ask a hundred more questions, but it suddenly occurred to me that for all that extra explaining he'd done, I *still* didn't even know what an umbrella tree *was*.

"Having first weighed me, the Matron then proceeded to weigh the Courage Monster as well. And much to my astonishment lad, it turned out that he weighed *minus* 20,657,204 Tardigrades, or *minus* 0.000019 Armillarians. Now bear in mind this was a creature the height of an elephant, and certainly not on the skinny side either.

"Of course, it turned out – so the Matron also explained – that *givers*, such as the Courage Monster was, often weigh negative amounts, on account of the things they give being entirely what they're made of – which in his case was *courage,* though I saw no sign of it, instead of flesh and bones like you or I lad. And courage, it seems, is a thing which *takes weight away*, so when a thing is made of nothing else, it's quite literally lighter than air."

It really did feel like my head was about to explode. I wanted to say something, but he just kept on talking and talking.

"Of course, the reason the Matron d'tree needed to know our weights was so she could calculate precisely what size umbrella to give us, and from which branch, having exact measurements as to the height of every single one in her tree, we should, well... *take off from*.

"Impressive, eh lad? Even more so if you consider that that umbrella tree was *growing* every single day, so those measurements had to be retaken each morning or else a customer might end up plummeting into a bog somewhere, or worse still, flying right around the world and all the way back again."

I might have started panting then – like a sort of dog I suppose. I think they do that to cool down, but I wonder if it works on brains too.

"Are you all right Dylan?"

He looked at me in a concerned sort of way.

"Granddad?"

"Yes?"

"Is there any chance you could just tell me what an umbrella tree is... before my head bursts I mean."

"What the bloody hell do you think I've been doing lad?"

"Yes, but what *is it* Granddad?"

"Oh, you mean just like that, do you?"

I suppose I must have.

"Well that's simple lad..."

The panting got a bit worse.

"I thought it was obvious is all..."

There was a sort of race going on in my brain: a million little water bears squeaking through megaphones at a giant Armillarian, which was being poked by funny little wardens wearing police helmets, and all of them being shouted at by a shaved orangutan that looked like Queen Victoria except with a tree stump on her head that was actually hair but didn't look like it.

And then it happened.

"Dylan?"

I turned round towards the house.

"Mum?"

She was standing there looking right at me.

24

PRIDE

It was exactly like the day I'd got lost in that supermarket and they'd had to call my mother on the tannoy thing to come fetch me. The very same face. And the very same look. Her eyes were red, but she smiled at me like I was the only thing in the entire world.

I can't explain how, but I knew in an instant that she hadn't meant to leave me, and that she'd never do it again.

"I'm so sorry Dylan."

I knew that she loved me, and would *always* be my mother.

"I should never have..."

She even gave me a hug – the type that you can't get out of because the other person won't let go. For some reason I pretended to be a bit embarrassed, but I don't know why, because it's not like I really wanted her to let go.

"I was just... angry I suppose, but that's no excuse, I mean..."

The words didn't matter – not that time.

It's funny how the worst feeling there is to feel can turn into the best feeling there is to feel, like the two are sort of *connected* somehow. I hadn't wanted to think about her until then, because I must have been afraid that she'd wanted to leave me forever, to get rid of me... but knowing that she didn't, and *wouldn't*, no matter what... that made me feel strong, as strong as I'd ever felt in my life, like I could have marched through that gate and taken on a whole army of Tardigrades, or Armillarians, or even Matron d'trees, however thick their thighs might have been. I'll never forget that feeling.

She looked at my Granddad then.

"Dad, I didn't mean—"

"Yes, you did."

He got up in the same sudden sort of way that he had done that morning in the kitchen, and then started walking back towards the house.

"And you had every right to."

He wasn't angry, or upset, or even that strange *something else* which he had been when I'd told him I knew that magical girl was still alive; Tiger Lily of the valley, that's what he'd said she was called. This was different again, sort of *stubborn* I suppose, but being stubborn isn't a feeling, is it? Being stubborn is something that happens *because* of a feeling.

"No, I was just angry. It's been a really tough month Dad, that's all."

My mother followed him.

And I followed her.

"No need to hang around girl. You'll be wanting to get back home, won't you? Got things to do no doubt."

She stopped dead.

I looked at her face. It was sad, and sort of lost, like she really *was* a girl. I'd never seen my mother look like that before; she'd always seemed so grown-up all the time, and in control. But not then.

"You don't need to do this."

He stopped too, and turned to face her.

"I won't be a burden to you, or anyone else for that matter, so don't trouble yourself about the cleaning. I'll get someone in to take care of it."

"*Get someone in?* And how are you going to pay them? You've barely enough money to keep the electric on; do you even realise that?"

"*That's my business, not yours.*"

I think he might have shouted that, only without really making his voice any louder.

"I said don't trouble yourself with it... so don't."

It was like that terrible storm had suddenly reappeared out of nowhere, even though it was August, and the sun was shining, and the sky was bright blue, and the birds were singing in the trees. It just didn't seem to fit somehow.

"So you don't want me to come any more, is that what you're saying?"

There was nothing I could do to stop it. Nothing at all.

"I won't be a burden, and that's the end of it."

"Who's to say you are?"

"*You.*"

They weren't even looking at each other. That made me feel angry, because if they had been, they might have seen all those hidden things in each other's face that I could see standing there looking up at them both.

The words were lying. They weren't real.

"And the message was clearly received. So you better leave me to rot in this precious garden of mine, hadn't you?"

My mother turned away.

"I don't need this."

She was talking to herself then.

"I don't know why I ever thought things would be

different."

I wanted to tell her that he didn't mean it, that he was just pretending, that the inside part which he wouldn't show went about smiling and calling things '*my sweet*'. I wanted to... but I couldn't. I don't know why, it was as if what was happening was bigger than me somehow. I felt so small and unimportant, like I couldn't possibly understand, or know what to say, let alone how to solve any of it. I felt as if all I could do was stand and watch. And that's what I did.

"We have to leave Dylan. Your Granddad doesn't want me here any more."

This time I went with her. And it didn't feel wrong, not for a second, because she was my mother.

"Wait."

We stopped.

"The lad will keep visiting I take it? You know he likes it here."

My mother looked at me then, as if she wanted me to say something, but I just looked back at her not saying a word. I couldn't even nod.

"How?"

He looked away as if he didn't have an answer. But my mother was right; how *could* I visit without her to take me there? And that was when everything that was happening suddenly crashed into me like one of those huge waves on the beach that seem twice as big as all the other waves put together.

My Granddad had told her not to visit again. And that would mean that I couldn't either.

Everything was ending.

I'd never find out about Tiger Lily of the valley. Or ask him about the little green egg. Or discover what was in that red box hidden in the sycamore tree. But none of that really mattered...

Because I might never see my Granddad again...

and that thought just filled every bit of my brain until all the other stuff was pushed right out. I wonder if that's why I started crying, because the tears got sort of squeezed out too.

"I'll pay for a car."

My mother shook her head.

"Have you any idea how expensive that'd be? It costs more than you spend on food every month just for the petrol to get here."

He sort of grimaced then – at least I think that's what it was. I'd expected him to tell my mother to mind her own business again, and that he'd find the money somehow. *But he didn't.* I suppose he really can't have been able to afford it. I wonder if that was the real reason we'd had nothing but cold hot dogs for breakfast instead of fried sausages. Perhaps it had nothing to do with my Granddad not being able to taste anything; perhaps he just had no choice. I didn't understand. Why didn't he have any money? It's not like people who are eighty-seven can get jobs or anything... not like my mother could. She had two, and even then we never seemed to have enough.

"Unless I were to drop him off—"

"*NO.*"

That time my Granddad really did shout.

My mother turned away again. It was as if that word had hit her right in the face. She looked... *broken* somehow. It scared me to see her like that.

"Can't we pay for the car?"

"I can't afford it either Dylan."

Nobody said anything. They just stood there, both of them, not saying anything.

That was when I heard myself – crying I mean – in the silence. It was horrible. I felt like a baby – a useless little baby that couldn't do anything but bawl its eyes out.

My mother looked straight at me then. Normally whenever I started crying she'd look away, as if she was ashamed of me. But it was different that time. She *wasn't* ashamed; I could tell when I looked back at her. She was something else. *Proud.* I can't understand why, even now remembering it all. Why would she be proud of me standing there crying like a useless little baby?

"But I might be able to scrape together enough for the train once a month. If you can arrange to have him picked up from the station, and dropped off again."

My Granddad nodded. I think his lips might have been trembling a bit.

She nodded back.

We all stood there for a moment not doing anything. It was as if there was so much more to say, but nobody could quite say any of it.

"Goodbye then Dad."

And that was it.

We left.

SEPTEMBER

25

THE METAL DRAGON

Summer holidays are supposed to be the happiest time of the year... but I remember that one differently. The days and weeks didn't fly by, like they had every other year; they *dragged*, as if time had been slowed down, like my Granddad had talked about.

Nothing seemed quite as fun as it should have: spending time with my friends, going swimming in the beck, catching sticklebacks in jars, even pilfering strawberries from the 'Pick your own' field and being chased for about three miles along a ditch by a man waving a 'Keep out' sign over his head.

It was as if I wasn't really there – not all of me at least, because my mind was still sort of back at my Granddad's house, with that storm, remembering how it'd torn everything apart. Had he really told my mother not to visit any more? That just seemed impossible. *Why would he?* I kept replaying bits in my mind, like when you listen to the same song over and over again because the tune gets stuck in your head. Well that storm had got stuck in my head too, except it didn't make me smile, or sing, or feel happy, like a song would have. It just made me angry, because I kept thinking what I should have said and done differently. And I could have too... if I hadn't just stood there crying, like a baby.

My mother couldn't really have been proud. The more I thought about it on those long summer days – sitting alone on hay bales, or under trees, or in ditches stuffing myself with strawberries – the more I sort of realised that I must have been wrong... that I must have just been imagining it. Maybe because that's what I wanted to see, so my eyes just sort of lied to me, like how people do sometimes, to try and make you feel better about something. *White lies*. That's what they call it.

I wanted to poke them out for that. *I hate lies*. I know I'm not perfect, and I probably get things wrong all the time, but I don't think I'd ever lie about something – even that white sort. People always say that the truth hurts, but I think not knowing it hurts even more, because that just makes you imagine things that are even worse than the truth.

My mother wasn't the same after we got back. She didn't seem as in control as she had been. She pretended to be though; sort of strong, and a bit too bossy, but I knew it wasn't real, because her face never quite matched the words. I didn't bring any of it up – about my Granddad, or what he'd said, or what she'd said back – I don't know why, because I remember wanting to, almost every day that whole summer. I must have been scared or something, that things might get even worse I mean.

I think that's why I felt sort of glad sitting on that train on the first weekend in September. Glad that it was also the very last weekend of the summer holidays. And glad to be leaving behind all that time to think. But not glad in the same way I had been the day they'd begun. It was different somehow; a sad sort of glad I suppose.

I thought I might have been scared (it was my first ever train journey alone), but when I was sat there, staring out of that window, watching rain drops race along the glass and the world pass by beyond, I didn't feel scared at all. It was the worrying about it that was scary, not the actual *doing it* part. What I really felt, more than anything I mean, was *free*... like I was escaping somehow. And for the first time in my life too. I wonder if that's the feeling you get when you start growing up.

There'd been lots of phone calls first of course – between my mother and Granddad. I hadn't heard any of them; she'd made sure of that by using the phone in her bedroom, and always keeping the door closed, so that even when I pressed my ear right up against it all I could hear was a sort of mumble and the odd word which didn't make much sense. They'd been short though – the phone calls I mean – and there hadn't been any shouting... I knew that much.

It was a long journey, and my mother thought I'd get bored, like I always seemed to in the car, so she made me bring things to do. All I can remember is packing one of those word-search books. It was the most boring thing ever invented; just reading through line after line of letters trying to find hidden words. So I didn't bother in the end. Because staring out of the window turned out to be far more interesting.

The carriage was big, with forty-six seats (I counted), not like the type you see in films where it's like a little room. But there were only two other people sharing it with me – I remember them perfectly. One was a businessman in a grey suit who spent the entire journey reading a great big newspaper with tiny print. I expect he must have read every single line by the time he finally arrived. The other was a woman – a young one I suppose. She had an earring in her nose, and pink hair.

I'd never seen anyone with either of those things before. I think she spent most of the time staring out of the window, just like I did, but every so often she'd look at me and smile, and so I'd look back at her and smile too. I didn't even know her name, but it felt sort of good, like we were friends somehow, sharing something together. I remember watching her leave; she had a huge backpack, about twelve times the size of mine, which was so full, I thought she must have packed just about everything she'd ever owned. And it was sort of *worn* too, like socks get about a year after you're supposed to throw them out. I wonder where she is now, that girl with pink hair and an earring through her nose. I'll never forget the way she smiled at me.

The only other person who passed through our carriage was the ticket inspector; a tall man in a flat hat, like the type traffic wardens wear, who always seemed to be in a rush, which didn't make any sense, because there can't have been many tickets for him to inspect. I remember looking at mine right after he'd punched a little round hole in it. There were three parts: the outward journey, the return journey, and the receipt. The receipt said how much the ticket had cost. It was *so* expensive. She hadn't told me – my mother I mean – but I wondered then how she'd even been able to afford it. I'm sure it was more than the cost of petrol to drive there would have been, because she always complained about that on the journeys. But she hadn't complained about buying that train ticket... not once. That must have been why she had to work all those extra hours – it seemed like more every week – just so I could go and sit with my Granddad drinking weeds and eating cold hot dogs. Why hadn't she just said *No*? I'd always thought my mother was an expert at saying No, but not that time.

I remember the noise it made too – the train I mean. It wasn't a *chug-chug-chug* like I'd expected, more a sort of *clickety-hum*, but over and over again. I liked it though, which is a strange thing to say about a boring old noise like *clickety-hum*. I suppose it felt like the train was alive somehow, and working especially hard to protect us all; as if it was a great big metal dragon, fighting the wind and the rain and the night so that everyone inside was kept warm and dry. That must sound a bit stupid though, because trains aren't alive, and dragons don't even exist.

It was dark by the time we finally arrived at my Granddad's station, or at least the one that was nearest to his house. There hadn't been a morning train, not a direct one anyway; I'd have had to swap from one to another in some big city that I hadn't heard of, and I didn't like the sound of that... not back when the whole thing had seemed scary I mean.

I think that must have been the last stop, because there didn't seem to be anyone left when I got off. Even that businessman with the huge newspaper had already gone, two or three stops before mine. It was strange looking up and down the platform and not seeing anyone. It hadn't been like that when I'd got on the train. There'd been a lot more people then, and I'd sort of just followed them, doing what they did, because everyone went in the same direction, and did the same thing, which made it all seem a lot easier.

I started to feel afraid again. I think it was leaving the train so suddenly – that big metal dragon which had kept me safe for so many hours – and then being all alone, sort of in charge of myself and not knowing quite what to do or where to go. And the darkness made it seem worse. I don't know why, because I'd never been afraid of the dark, not like those people who have to sleep with the light on or anything, but just then, standing on that platform and hearing the train leave behind me, it definitely seemed to make my heart beat a bit louder in my chest. There were so many shadows; the type you're only supposed to see out of windows late at night when you know nothing can get to you. And then I remembered.

The type that turn into darkling grubs like Beamer Eighty-Six. Her face suddenly appeared in my head; two fire opal eyes and a great big smile, *beaming* right into me. She looked just like that girl on the train – the one with pink hair and an earring through her nose. I don't think darkling grubs have pink hair or earrings through their nose, but it didn't matter, because seeing that smile, whoever it really was, made me smile too. And that made me stronger somehow... less afraid.

I'd see my Granddad soon. I'd sit with him in that old house and listen to more of his strange adventures from beyond that gate whilst watching him drink endless mugs of extra sweet tea. I might even have another one of those sponge puddings... just without all that dandelion and burdock to make me need the toilet all night. For some reason thinking about that made me smile even more. I must have looked odd just standing there smiling like that, if there'd been anyone to see me that is.

But first I had to get there. And that meant finding the right person. My Granddad had arranged it – that's what my mother had told me. *'There'll be someone there to meet you Dylan.'*

Except there wasn't.

I was alone.

"Is that you lad?"

I don't know how I didn't scream when I heard his voice. I suppose my heart must have shot right up into my throat and sat on my voice box or something, because I couldn't even speak, not at first. I remember looking around in a mad sort of way, trying to work out where it had come from, because I'd been so certain that no one else was there.

And then I saw him.

It wasn't a big station; only one platform, with a little building next to it – just a grand sort of shed really – and a lot of benches lined up along the tracks, like the type you see in parks. There was a man sitting on one of them; a man in a long brown coat wearing one of those old-fashioned hats, just like the sort of old-fashioned hat that I'd seen on that dresser in my Granddad's house. And he had a stick too. A big wooden one. But I couldn't see his face, because there was a lamp-post right above his head, and it seemed to paint everything under his hat almost completely black, like a sort of shadow puppet. That might *really* have scared me, if I hadn't recognised him I mean.

"*Granddad*?"

"Who the bloody hell else would it be?"

I felt so much better then. Safe somehow. Even though he was eighty-seven and blind, he still seemed every bit as strong as that metal dragon. And every bit as good at fighting off the wind and the rain and the night.

"What are you doing here?"

"Fetching you of course."

"Yes, but... weren't you supposed to be sending someone?"

"Like who? I'm the only person left that I know, so that's who I bloody well sent."

It took him a while just to reach me on the platform; waving that wooden stick from side to side like *real* blind people do. I think it might have been the first time I'd ever seen him do that. I suppose he knew the house and garden so well that he didn't really need to.

"But my mother said—"

"I lied. She wouldn't have let you come otherwise. And you'd better keep it a secret Dylan, or she won't again."

A secret? That's just lying too, isn't it? But he was right; she wouldn't have let me come if she'd known. I tried not to think about that.

"How did you even get here? You can't drive Granddad."

I could finally see his face. He was looking down at me from under that big brown hat covered in a thick layer of dust. It was a familiar sort of look; the type that usually came with a sigh, or that eye-rolling thing he did.

"Why, it's a good job you told me that lad, or I might have plain forgotten I've been blind for near half my life."

He reached for my arm.

"We're walking."

"*Walking*?"

"It's a long way; took me an hour or more to get here, and that was in the daylight when I could see shapes and what not. Can't see a damn thing any more, so you'll have to guide me back, all right?"

"But I don't know the way Granddad."

"Then what an amazing stroke of luck you'll be arm-in-arm with someone who's been living here for eighty-six years. Someone who knows every inch of this route like the back of his hand. Someone, for instance, *like me*."

"Seven."

He looked at me then, sort of open-mouthed.

"Unless of course you moved here when you were one or something. But I think you probably just forgot how old you are, because you're always forgetting how old people are. That's okay though, because I bet most eighty-seven-year-olds forget even more than you do. But then you are blind, and sort of deaf too, so I expect that balances it out a bit."

His mouth closed, and turned into a smile. It got bigger and bigger until it looked just like that smile I'd seen in my head.

"I've missed you lad."

I smiled back.

"Now come on... before my feet get any colder."

26

ANGER

Anger is a funny sort of thing. Sometimes it can be trapped inside you for ages and ages without you even knowing it's there, just waiting I suppose, for the right moment to come out. And sometimes that can be when you least expect it, even when you think you're happy, like I did seeing my Granddad again that September evening. I wasn't though, except maybe on the surface, but that's not where anger really comes from. It was buried much deeper, in the same part of me that hadn't really been there that summer holiday, because it had been worrying, and hating, and blaming instead. It needed to come out though. I suppose it had to, one way or another. I just didn't know that then – not until it finally happened I mean.

"Left here, over the bridge, and then down that lane. There's no lamp-posts for the last bit, which is why I brought this."

He pulled a little torch out of a huge side pocket on that big brown coat and handed it to me.

"What an adventure eh, lad? I haven't been out at

night like this for... oh, a decade or more I should think. Used to love walking though. I must have trod this very path a thousand or more times before now. But I stopped in the end, didn't want to worry your..."

He turned away.

"Nan?"

And then he nodded without really looking at me. It was as if he couldn't even say her name.

"Not that it matters any more. I can do what I bloody well like. And I will too, because what's the worst that can happen now? A heart attack? Stroke? Collapsing on the road and getting run over by some idiot joy-rider?"

He actually laughed then. And that scared me more than any amount of shadows could have. I don't think I'd ever heard someone laugh about heart attacks or strokes or getting run over by joy-riders – it just wasn't right somehow. People aren't supposed to laugh about things like that.

"As well it happens now as in a month or a year."

I suppose what he'd said back in July during that argument with my mother must really have been true, even though he'd pretended that it wasn't afterwards. He didn't care any more... about going on living I mean.

"And while I'm actually bloody *doing* something for once. I've never much liked the old *peacefully in your sleep* routine – too boring by half. And besides, I'd rather be awake to see it happen, whatever *it* happens to be. After all, it's not like you get a second chance at dying, and you never know, it could be quite a show come the—"

"STOP IT."

All I remember is the echo. It was like the night was screaming right back at me.

He stopped.

Walking. Talking. *Everything*.

We just stood there for a minute, or two, or three... not saying anything, until somehow my brain found the right words.

"You're *selfish* Granddad."

And the courage to say them.

"You think just because Nan is dead there's nobody else who cares about you. But you're wrong, because I care about you, and my sister cares about you, and even Mum cares about you. I don't know why though, not after you told her not to come see you any more. It's just not right... none of it is. Families are supposed to love each other, not go on arguing about *nothing* all the time and making each other miserable."

I wasn't even crying. The words wouldn't let me. They were too important I think.

"She made a mistake, shouting at you like that, but she said sorry too. And she meant it, I *know* she did Granddad. That means you have to forgive her, and get on with living, instead of keep wanting to die all the time. Because people who love each other have to stick together, even when things are really hard. So you don't get to just give in like that. *Not like him.*"

He just stared at me.

I don't think those last words had come from the same place as all the rest. Because those thoughts belonged somewhere even deeper, somewhere that was probably right at the bottom... that I'd been trying to forget about for half my life.

I started walking again, pulling my Granddad by the arm. It was easier that way – giving my brain something to do I mean. I tried to concentrate on every step. And there were lots of them before any more words came. I don't know how long we walked like that for, in silence, apart from the odd bit of wind, or the sound of a car on some faraway road, but it seemed like forever to me. I just didn't know what to say. Perhaps because it wasn't my turn to talk.

That lane was long, and very dark, and very empty. I wasn't scared any more though. Letting anger out seems to get rid of being scared... it frees you somehow, from caring about the little things I mean.

We must have been half way back before my Granddad finally spoke.

"I always thought it was your mother..."

But so quietly that I don't think he'd even meant me to hear.

"My mother?"

He looked at me then, as if sort of realising that I was still there.

"...*who gave in.*"

I didn't want to remember. But I couldn't help it. It was like one of those big waves I talked about; the type which catches all the other little waves and just sort of soaks them up, getting bigger and bigger, until it's the only one that's left. And you can't ignore it, because you know it'll catch you, however fast you try to get away.

"What happened Dylan? Why did he leave like that; *your father*? I always thought it was because she drove him away."

"What do you mean?"

"Your mother used to be very different lad: imaginative, joyful, and with such heart – worn right on her sleeve too, just like your Nan. And that's what he fell in love with. Not the machine she turned into; working every hour God sends, or planning, or *worrying*... she's always bloody worrying about things. She didn't used to worry about anything. The world was hers to conquer, and by God I thought she might too. But instead she just became... *like me*. And what a waste of life that is."

"*She's my mother.*"

It was the only thing I could say.

"And she *always* comes back. *He never did.* He

might have promised to, but that was just a lie, because he still hasn't."

My Granddad stopped again. But I just wanted to keep walking... it made the memories easier to bear somehow.

"She might not be perfect, but *she* didn't give in, and *she* didn't run away, and *she* didn't make promises and then break them like he did. So don't you say that, not any of it."

He pulled me towards him then, and wrapped both arms around me. He smelled of dust, and mould, and unwashed clothes, but it didn't matter, because it felt good all the same.

"I'm sorry lad, I really am. About all that dying business too. It's not that I want to. It just makes it easier somehow, pretending that I don't care any more. The truth is, it's just about the only way I can cope sometimes, still being here, without, well... on my own that is. It's no excuse though; I should have stopped to think how saying those things would make you feel. But I didn't.

"And I didn't mean to tell your mother not to come either. I'm just a prideful old man, that's all; a prideful old man who hates to think he's somehow *dependent* on anyone. But I know she only said that to hurt me, because I'd said things to hurt her. And she bottles everything up, just like her father, and perhaps her son too."

I think he might have been smiling then.

"It must be hard; raising you and your sister on her own, with next to no money, or support. I should have been there for her really, more than I ever was, instead of grieving over the person that she used to be. We all have to grow up eventually, don't we lad? Life sees to that, one way or another. And you've certainly done some yourself today. My God, I never thought I'd be humbled by a ten-year-old."

I think that was the only time he ever got my age wrong the other way – that I was older than I really was I mean. And I think it might have been the only time I didn't put him right too.

"You're so very like her Dylan; I can't tell you just how much. Right down to those endless bloody questions you ask. And always managing to see things in a way that no one else can. She could do that too."

I looked up at him them, but he didn't look back. His eyes were a bit watery and he was still smiling, in a strange, remembering sort of way.

"You've taken me right back there lad, these past few months. Gods, I had everything: a house, a job, a beautiful wife who laughed at my every joke – however bad it might be – and a daughter... with such spirit and fire as I've ever seen. It was a gift – a gift that I lived, and I loved, because what man wouldn't have? And now I'm old. And the only thing left is that house, filled with the memories of everything I've lost. Until you came along that is, and made it all seem real again."

I pulled away from him then. It's not that I really wanted to, but it just didn't feel right to me... everything he'd said. I felt sort of like I wasn't *me* any more; like he'd turned me into a character in a play or something. Not a bad one I suppose. But it still didn't seem right. Because what's the point in looking back all the time if it makes you forget how to keep going forward?

"She's not lost Granddad. You just got rid of her."

He finally looked back at me.

"Mum, I mean."

But he didn't say anything, not at first.

"You just have to fix it is all."

"It's too late lad."

He turned away as he said that, and started walking again. We must have been nearly back at his house, because the lamp-posts finally ran out, like he'd said they would, and I had to turn that torch on. Except it barely worked, so I had to use the light on my calculator watch instead.

"What do you mean?"

"The damage is done. The mistakes already made. You can't undo forty years of hate."

"But you said it was wrong. You said you were sorry – just now. That you should have been there. So why do you still hate her?"

"It's your mother who hates *me* Dylan. And she's got every bloody right to. But can't we talk about something else? I've had enough of memories for one day."

That made the anger come right back. I suppose it had never really gone. People can't just end conversations when they get hard... because that way things that have to be said don't ever get said. And that's when they get stuck in your brain, just like they had in mine that summer, until there's nothing left to feel but anger. The sort that just gets worse and worse. And who wants a brain filled with nothing but anger? I had to get it out.

"She doesn't hate you. You just have to tell her what you told me, that's all. Get her to come back again."

He didn't say anything. He just looked straight ahead, as if he hadn't even heard me.

"Granddad?"

"*It's too late Dylan.*"

"Why?"

"It just is."

"*But why?*"

"Because I'm eighty-bloody-seven. Because I've let everything go to shit. *And because she's dead.*"

He must have meant my Nan.

"But *you're* still alive Granddad... even if you don't

really want to be."

He was breathing a bit hard then. He had been the whole walk, even though we'd been going so slowly, but it seemed to get worse and worse the farther we went. And just then it got so bad that I started to get scared. It was as if he really might die... right there in the dark. There were no houses to run to, or people to hear if I screamed for help. Only trees; the type that couldn't talk. And I didn't want to watch him die. I'd never seen anyone die before, but my stupid brain just started imagining it all of a sudden, and what I saw terrified me. It was the loneliness that I was most afraid of – the part which comes *after* I mean.

And then I saw the house. The familiar trees. The little drive that was overgrown with nettles. The white chimney. The walls that looked like they were about to fall over, but never did. The sign next to the door.

The smell.

If only my Nan had been waiting inside – waiting to greet me with a smile. Then everything would have been okay.

I'd have given anything to hear her laugh right then, even though there was nothing to laugh about. Just hearing it would have made things better somehow... taken everything bad away, like the anger, and the fear, and the being alone.

People shouldn't be allowed to go away.

Not when you need them so much.

27

WORDS

I was four and three-quarters when my father left us. It was the week before I started school... for the very first time I mean. I suppose him leaving like that made it easier somehow. I remember all the other children being terrified those first few days. But I wasn't. It's hard to be afraid of something ordinary like that when the world doesn't seem to make sense any more. I just didn't understand. I still don't really.

He said he'd come back. That he just needed time to work things out. To make everything better with my mother. But that was just a lie, because he never did come back. And you don't make things better by running away. You just hurt the people who love you.

I suppose he was just a coward or something. He probably still is. I often wonder if he's got a new family now, with someone else to call him Dad, like how I used to. I try to forget. I try not to think about it, or imagine stupid things that I don't even know are true. But I can't help it somehow. Whenever there's a hole in my thoughts he just seems to creep in from that deep place in the bottom of my brain.

My mother never used to talk about him, and she'd just walk away whenever me or my sister brought him up, so we stopped trying in the end. I think I understand why now; it made her sad, like she wanted to cry, but she couldn't, not in front of us anyway. I suppose she just wanted to look strong or something, but I think if she'd just been weak everything would have been easier. Because then we could have been weak too. And sometimes being weak is what *really* makes you strong... instead of just pretending to be.

My Granddad didn't have a heart attack, or a stroke, or get run over by one of those joy-riders. He just got angry instead... with himself I think. I suppose he must have caught it off me, except it was different somehow. It didn't come out in screams or shouts or even just ordinary words, like it had for me. But it didn't get buried in his brain either; hidden in a box full of fireworks waiting for a little match to make it explode. *It was just there*; in his eyes, and his thoughts too I suppose, screaming a silent sort of scream to himself. I could almost hear it just by looking at him.

We didn't talk that night after finally making it into the house. Or the next day. It wasn't just my Granddad though. I didn't much want to either, even though there were so many things to say. I think sometimes you have to let words sort of sink in a bit... before you know if they've really worked I mean. It's just like catching sticklebacks I suppose. When you first throw the jar in they all swim away, because it's new and scary. And if you pull it out too soon, it'll be empty, because it takes time for them to get used to it. But if you wait, and watch, then eventually they'll just swim right in and make it there home, as if that jar had always been there. Unless of course your friend comes along with a big net and scoops them all out right in front of your nose. But

then there weren't any big nets in my Granddad's house...
so the words just got caught in his brain instead.

I can't really remember what I did that day in
September, not in any sort of order anyway. The little
bedroom in the attic which had used to belong to my
mother was just the way I'd left it, even down to the
window being a bit open, where I'd sat and watched the
sun rise that first day in August.

The view out wasn't quite the same though. The sun
seemed to stay hidden behind a thick layer of white
cloud; the type that never turns into rain, but won't go
away either, as if the sun had put a million woolly
jumpers over its head and refused to take them off.

And nothing else was quite the same either. The
leaves had stopped being quite so green, and turned
yellow and brown and red instead – and every colour in-
between too. Sort of like the trees were having a contest
with each other to see who could stand out the most. I
suppose it was still beautiful, looking out over that
garden and forest beyond, but a bit sad too, because
everything was dying; letting go of life; *giving in.*
Summer was saying goodbye. Except not forever, and
that's why it was only *a bit* sad, because summer never
really leaves, it just moves on to a different place, and
you know it'll come back again the next year, even
though it doesn't tell you it will.

I think I must have got it wrong about promises.
They're just a lot of empty words really. That must be
why summer never bothers making any. It just gets on
with things, and always finds a way to come back,
because it knows it has to. I suppose there are just some
things you can trust, and other things you can't, and no
amount of words can change that.

There is one thing I remember about that day:
walking out into the garden, painted grey beneath the
clouds, and looking up into that giant tree that me and

my Granddad had sat under for so many hours. The tree with the little red box hidden in a hole in the top of its trunk, like some ancient secret that only me and it shared... and perhaps a squirrel or two, but they don't really count.

It was a sycamore tree. You know that already because I've told you. But I didn't... not before that day in September when I looked up and saw thousands of little helicopters beside each dying leaf. It was like that old tree had taken one final breath – an extra long deep one – and then turned every bit of it into seeds, as a sort of reminder to the summer, that it had to come back again. Because if it didn't, then how else could any of them grow?

I suppose you can trust trees too; it's not like they can ever go away and not come back, is it? Even in magical places, because my Granddad had said there aren't any umbrellas big enough to make them fly. I wonder if it's really just people you can't trust. Or maybe it's only the words they use.

Words mean things. That's what I used to think. Except perhaps they don't... not really. Perhaps they only mean what each of us wants them to mean. Perhaps instead of only listening to the words, you have to listen to the *person*. Just like the trees listen to the summer when it's time to grow, and the summer listens to the trees, by always coming back. Words are just there to point you in the right direction I suppose, like those people in shops who tell you where things are. You still have to use your eyes, and your legs, and your brain, and that other brain inside you brain, to actually find the things. And even then sometimes they don't tell you right, so you have to start reading those signs above the aisles, and trying to work out if Bird's Custard Powder is more like 'Sauces and Spices' or 'Baking Produce' or 'Sweeteners and Condiments' (whatever they are).

He wasn't ever there, my Granddad... not that day. He stayed inside, in his room mostly, or the lounge, just sitting there looking out of the window. I suppose all those words caught in his brain must have been pointing *him* in the right direction too.

It wasn't until I was about to leave that Sunday morning that I finally knew just what that direction was.

"I'm coming with you lad."

He was standing there in his brown coat and brown hat covered in grey dust, just like he had been at the train station two days before, except with a little shoe box under one arm containing three tins and a tin opener – I only know that because I looked inside when he went to go to the toilet for the third time.

"There's nothing else for it. I'm getting on that train if it kills me."

"Why?"

"Because I'm not apologising into a bloody phone, that's why."

He wasn't angry any more. He might have sounded it, and those words he used might have suggested it, but I knew better. I knew that that anger had turned into something else. *Strength.* I couldn't have stopped him if I'd tried. Not that I even wanted to.

"And because someone reminded me that I'm still alive... so I might as well get on and do the right bloody thing for a change."

28

TAKING OFF

Being proud isn't always a bad thing. Not when you feel it for someone else. Because feeling proud of someone else, in a *real* sort of way that isn't even a bit pretend, seems to make people *better* somehow. It gives them courage I suppose – just like words, even the wrong ones, except a *million* times stronger. Come to think of it, I'd say being proud of someone is just about the best gift you can ever give; better than any kind of present, even all the sugared cola bottles and ice-cream and sponge puddings in the whole world.

And that's the sort of proud I felt for my Granddad that day, as we walked back to the train station together. I wasn't angry any more, even a little bit, and nor was he. We'd got rid of it all somehow.

I've heard people say that sometimes you have to *swallow* your pride, which I used to think was one of those stupid expressions which doesn't mean anything. But now I know just what it means, because that must be what my Granddad did that September; sitting alone with all that anger in his eyes. He had to swallow the *bad sort* of pride, so that the *good sort,* from me, could fill him up again.

"You don't have a ticket Granddad."

We were standing on that same little platform waiting for the train to arrive. It wasn't nearly as scary in the day, but one thing was just the same: there was no one else there. It felt like we were the only people in the world who even knew that that station existed.

"I don't need a ticket. I'm blind."

"But a tall man wearing a flat hat like a traffic warden asks for your ticket and then punches a little round hole in it Granddad. How will he punch a little round hole in yours if you don't even have one?"

"With difficulty I expect."

He was smiling. As if not having a ticket was somehow funny.

"What do you think they're going to do Dylan... throw me off the train? A decrepit old bugger like me, who can hardly walk, let alone see? And separate him from his little grandson ta boot? Gods, maybe they'll have me shovelling coal to pay for the fare."

I suppose that might have worked seventy years ago, but I was pretty sure that trains which go *clickety-hum* don't even run on coal.

"It's the electric sort Granddad. And I don't think you can shovel electricity."

He looked at me and grinned.

"Relax lad; it'll be fine. And besides, there's no choice in the matter. Your mother was right about one thing; I don't have the money to pay for train tickets going half way across the country. Not that I thought I'd need to of course, but then you never quite know what's round the next corner... even when you're a stubborn old so and so like me."

I might have been worried, but I wasn't. I just knew somehow; that that ticket inspector couldn't have stopped him any more than I could.

That time the train really was empty. At least to begin with it was, until we started passing through other little towns, with other little stations, just like my Granddad's, and one or two people started getting on, and then one or two more, until eventually all those *ones and twos* started adding up to make *tens and twenties*. I suppose each of those people must have had a story, just like I did, even though most of them only sat there, not saying anything – like that girl with the pink hair and earring through her nose. It's funny how you can miss people when all you've done is *look* at them, without even hearing their voice, or knowing their name. I think it's because as soon as they leave, you know you won't ever be able to look at them again, because they'll just sort of disappear back into the world, like drops of rain that fall on the ocean.

"By God, it's been a long time since I've sat on a train Dylan. I'd forgotten just how invigorating the whole thing is. There's something about train journeys... can't say quite what though."

We were sat facing each other on one of those little table seats, right up against the window. My Granddad was beaming. I don't think I'd ever seen him quite like that. It must have been all that pride I suppose; the good type, sort of leaking out of him a bit.

"What's the view like? Fields I expect – a big patchwork, with fences and hedgerows and houses stitching it all together?"

I looked out of the window.

"I don't know."

"What do you mean you *don't know*? Got eyes haven't you... ones that work, unlike these?"

I remember him looking up then, as if there was a pair of eyes sitting on top of his hat or something. I suppose he was just trying to point at the ones in his face, except you can't really point at the thing you're trying to point with. That'd be like an arrow that somehow points at itself. Unless you use your arms of course, because then you can point with one, and point at the pointing one with the other. But anyway, that's beside the point, because unlike arms, eyes can't point in different directions... unless you happen to be a chameleon or something.

"I can't see any of it I mean."

"Why the devil not?"

"Because the clouds have all fallen down."

It was like the sun had taken off all those woolly jumpers and thrown them down on to the world in a sort of huff... probably because they were the knitted sort that are too big and make you itch, like Nans always give people for Christmas, and cats seem to like piddling on.

"*The clouds have fallen down*? Talk sense lad, what's that supposed to mean?"

"That's what it looks like Granddad. It must be *mist* or something, only so thick that you can't see through it, except for about one metre, but that's only far enough to see another lot of mist that's an extra metre away."

It almost felt like we were driving through an endless white tunnel; or the train really was a metal dragon, and it'd taken off somehow, right up into the clouds.

"Is that so?"

He smiled again.

"Almost like we're flying eh, lad?"

And then sort of half winked at me.

"That reminds me... I forgot to bring an umbrella."

It's funny how brains know what's important and what isn't, at least what *isn't* when something else *is*, if you see what I mean. It wasn't that I'd forgotten about the magical place, or the courage monster, or the umbrella tree, or the matron that looked like Queen

Victoria if she was a shaved orangutan... or any of the hundred other things that my Granddad had told me about. My brain had just decided, without even telling me, that what was happening *then* and not seventy years ago, was the most important thing to think about, for the time being at least. It's a good job brains know how to do that, because just imagine if they didn't. People would spend months, or even years, thinking about things that aren't even slightly important; like how big their bottoms look, or what the meaning of life is.

But just then, when my Granddad mentioned *flying* and *umbrellas*, my brain seemed to fall right back into that world beyond the gate, and the strange adventure that he'd still only half told me. It wasn't that I remembered every little detail or anything. It was more a sort of *feeling* instead; the same feeling you get when smelling freshly cut grass every spring, or peeking through closed curtains late at night to watch snow falling.

"It's a sort of airport isn't it Granddad? That umbrella tree. Only you never did tell me. Not that that's your fault exactly, because you were just about to that day, before my mother arrived I mean."

An old woman with deep lines in her face covered in about twenty layers of make-up smiled at me just then. She was pushing a trolley down the aisle of the train, piled with newspapers, and big kettles full of tea and coffee, and sandwiches, and chocolate bars, and lots of other strange little things wrapped in crinkly bits of plastic.

"Why yes, I daresay that's *just* what umbrella trees are; only with branches instead of runways, and umbrellas instead of aeroplanes."

"And Matrons instead of those girls at desks who check your passport?"

He had to think about that.

"Well, no... not exactly Dylan. For a start there's only *one* Matron d'tree, and she does a whole lot more than check passports. And furthermore, people in magical places don't have passports, so even if it were her job to check them, which it probably wouldn't be, she couldn't anyway, because there aren't any."

"Why not?"

"Why not what?"

"Why don't people in magical places have passports?"

"How should I know? Probably because there's no one to check them."

I suppose that made sense.

"What about pilots?"

"What about them?"

"Well what's instead of *them*? To fly the umbrellas Granddad?"

"There aren't any Dylan. Just like there aren't any seats, or seatbelts, or pretty girls in bright uniforms to tell you where the Emergency Exits are... or indeed Emergency Exits for that matter."

"What about that *hidden Energy?* Doesn't it sort of fly the umbrella – like a pilot I mean?"

"More like an *engine* I'd say. Only one that's alive, and a bit more unpredictable; not that I've ever had much faith in the mechanical type either lad. There's something wholly unnatural about being held thousands of feet above the ground by a few bits of spinning metal."

I was just about to ask him what made flying umbrellas *not* 'wholly unnatural' when something suddenly occurred to me.

"That doesn't make any sense."

"What doesn't?"

"How can there not be any Emergency Exits on an umbrella? Don't you just have to, well... *let go*... to exit I mean?"

His eyebrows sort of met in the middle for a second – even more than normal that is.

"That's a very good point lad. I stand corrected."

"But you're *sitting* Granddad."

He sighed.

"That I am, and on a comfortable seat too, quite unlike my younger self. Have you ever tried to sit on an umbrella Dylan?"

"Yes."

Well I had.

"At the same time as someone else, who just happens to be about the same size as an elephant?"

I suppose my sister hadn't been *that* big.

"Whilst balancing on the end of a branch, about a hundred feet above the ground?"

Why did people ever used to measure things in *feet,* when feet come in about a million different sizes? I suppose that must be why metres were invented.

"Only to suddenly find yourself no longer balancing on the end of that branch about a hundred feet above the ground, but hanging on for dear life, about a thousand feet in the air?"

"What size feet?"

He didn't seem to want to answer that, although it would have been useful to know.

"With one leg hooked over an extremely flimsy looking handle, and a Courage Monster sitting above you, trembling with such terror that the umbrella suddenly feels more like an out of control washing machine... only umbrella shaped?"

It took me a while to finally answer; probably because I'd been trying to imagine an umbrella shaped washing machine. Where would you put the clothes in? If you were a mother I mean, because they seem to be the only people who know how to work washing machines... even the ordinary sort.

"No."

"No what?"

"No I haven't tried to sit on an umbrella Granddad... not like *that* anyway."

"*Well I have*. And I'll tell you this lad, it was the single most terrifying experience of my entire life – at the time that is. I quite honestly felt as if I might slip off and plummet to my untimely demise at any moment. If it hadn't been for the dozen wardens prodding and poking at me, and the repeated assurance of the Matron d'tree that I wasn't to worry because I'd certainly reach the very thing I was searching for, then I can't imagine how I'd even have got that far.

"But the truth is Dylan, it all happened so wretchedly quickly that I hadn't time to be afraid... not until it was too late that is, and I was already floating among the clouds, feeling altogether assured that my life was about to suddenly end. By then of course, I had all the time in the world to be afraid... at least until I let go, at which point blind terror must have taken over."

I remember the sun punching a hole right through the fallen clouds just then. It didn't really last very long, and it wasn't big enough to see out of, but it did make the whole inside of the carriage sort of light up, like when you first switch a Christmas tree on in the dark, or when you burn it down two months later because 'for heaven's sake Dylan, January is nearly over and I'm sick of getting pine needles stuck in my feet'. Anyway, that's what it looked like. I suppose the sun just wanted to remind us all that it was still out there somewhere, sort of watching things I mean, and perhaps even listening too.

"*Let go*?"

It was as if those two little words had somehow been hidden by all the others, like strawberry flavoured fruit gums (the best kind) right at the bottom of the packet.

"That's what I said."

"You mean you let go of that umbrella from thousands of feet up in the air?"

"I hadn't a clue how high I was at that point lad – the clouds were too thick – and besides, I hadn't the courage to look down."

"But... *you're not dead Granddad*?"

He rolled his eyes then – at least I think he did, unless he was just trying to point to something on his hat again.

"*Really*? It's a wonder that, isn't it?"

"You *didn't die* I mean?"

"I didn't."

"Why not?"

He didn't answer that right away. But it seemed like an easy enough question; I mean it's not like a person can die without knowing why (if they weren't dead to not know I mean) so how can a person *not die* without knowing why too... because then they're not even dead to not know.

"I can't rightly say. But it certainly bloody felt like I had."

"What do you mean?"

Surely being dead doesn't feel like anything... because that's the point of being dead, isn't it? That you stop being alive to feel things.

"*My back, my head, my arms, my arse...* The ground isn't any softer beyond that gate Dylan. Even my pride was a little bruised."

"Your *pride*?"

"Yes."

"Which type?"

He looked at me in that funny sort of way which I'd got used to by then.

"The type which doesn't expect to plummet to the earth in abject terror only to lie there like a mangled blob, gazing up into the eyes of the most beautiful thing in the world."

My heart suddenly started pounding. I don't know why, because it wasn't like it was happening to me, though I remember sort of wishing it had been... even the getting bruised part.

"*You mean you found her Granddad*?"

"Yes Dylan, I did."

29

THE GIRL WITH YELLOW PIGTAILS

It's a strange sort of name... Tiger Lily of the valley. But then I suppose people in magical places can't very well have the ordinary sort. Although there are tigers in our world – in India I think, probably guarding the Taj Mahal or something – and lilies too, to keep frogs from drowning in ponds. Not that it's not a normal sort of name as well, because it is, just an old-fashioned one that you don't really hear any more. But I can't understand why someone would want to name someone after a big floating weed which keeps frogs from drowning. Then again, I suppose it is better than naming someone after a big floating weed which *doesn't* keep frogs from drowning. I wonder who gets to decide names, because it seems strange that you never hear of anyone called *Mushroom* or *Turnip* or even *Seaweed*; I mean at least you can eat those things, which must be better than just keeping frogs from drowning. It's not like they can't swim, is it?

"But I'm getting ahead of myself now lad, because I did somehow manage to cling on to that flying umbrella

252

for several hours. At least I think it was several hours; it might actually have been several days is the truth of it."

"What did you do?"

The train was still wrapped in those fallen clouds; it seemed like they might never go away. Not that I really minded, as long as they stayed outside, and the train didn't run out of tracks to tell it what direction to go in.

"What the bloody hell do you think I did? Sit down to a three course meal? Write my memoirs? *Paint the view?*"

I don't know why he thought I'd think that.

"What with?"

"Eh?"

"I'm not stupid Granddad. You can't paint a view without anything to paint with."

"*I didn't paint the bloody view.*"

"Then why did you say—"

"Never mind that Dylan. Look..."

He leaned over the table a bit closer to me.

"There's only one thing you can do when hanging on to an umbrella floating through the stratosphere thousands of feet above the ground with a terrified Courage Monster for company... *and that's panic.*"

"Panic?"

"*Panic.*"

"What... non-stop... for several hours?"

"*Of course non-stop for several hours.*"

I couldn't really imagine panicking about something for that long.

"Didn't that get a bit... well, boring?"

"*Boring?*"

"Yes."

I've noticed most things get boring if you do them for too long, even really good things, like sleeping. It's funny to think you can get bored of something like sleeping, but I'm sure it happens to me every Saturday morning at about eleven o'clock.

"You can't get bored of panicking Dylan."

"Why not?"

"Because if you've somehow got bored, then it stands to reason that you're not panicking any more."

"Exactly, because you've got bored of it."

"That's not what I meant."

He said that a bit too fast, as if the words were sort of racing to get out of his mouth. It made a few people turn to look at him, including a little girl with bright yellow hair sitting on the seat behind my Granddad. She had pigtails and stared at his hat in a very serious sort of way, which didn't quite match the rest of her somehow.

"Oh."

I don't think he even knew she was there, because she didn't say anything. I expect little girls with pigtails just aren't used to seeing old-fashioned hats covered in forty years of dust.

"Besides which lad, there wasn't the opportunity to be bored. And I'll tell you why..."

He leaned even closer. So much so that I'm sure I could smell his breath. It was sort of like a mixture of cat food and soap... which I suppose makes sense when you think about it.

"The umbrella stopped going up once we reached the clouds, and panic-stricken though I was, that somehow eased my nerves a tad. At least it did until that great lump of a Courage Monster started eating them; I didn't realise at first, for it just seemed to me that he'd stopped howling quite so much. Until I looked up that is, and saw a whale-sized mouth over the brim of that umbrella, gulping mouthful after mouthful of cloud, as if it were candy floss.

"Well, I just stared at first Dylan. I mean who'd have thought it possible for a thing to actually *eat* clouds? Of course, looking back on it now, I should have realised that he'd stop at nothing to keep eating, for therein lies the very life and function of a Courage Monster: *eating and growing*."

"What about all that *wailing in terror* Granddad? Don't forget that."

"Believe me Dylan, I hadn't. Eating, growing *and* wailing in terror."

"But, I don't understand, why did he eat the clouds like that? He can't still have been hungry can he? Not when you said he'd been eating things all the way to that umbrella tree."

"Courage, lad. The more things he ate, the more he stored up inside. Just like the more you eat, the more Energy you have stored up inside. Of course, if you eat too much, and do too little, then you get fat."

"Did the Courage Monster get fat too – fat with courage I mean?"

"I wouldn't say that. You see, he wasn't exactly *not fat* to begin with. So rather than get fatter per se, he just got, well... *bigger*."

"Bigger than an elephant?"

"Bigger than an elephant."

"Even a very big elephant?"

"Even the very *biggest* elephant."

I tried to imagine that for a second.

"How did he fit on the umbrella?"

My Granddad scratched his chin in a thoughtful sort of way.

"Have you ever seen those little paper umbrellas folks stick in drinks to make them seem a bit exotic Dylan?"

"Yes."

"Well imagine sitting on one."

That was easy.

"It'd just break."

"I'm not finished yet."

"Oh."

"Now imagine you're on the moon."

"Why?"

"Because everything's lighter there isn't it? So you wouldn't break it, you'd just sort of... *perch* on it."

That wasn't quite as easy to get my brain to agree with.

"Now imagine that little paper umbrella is rising upwards, just like those balloons we once talked about. Well then, because you're on the moon, making you much lighter, you'd just get pushed up with it, wouldn't you Dylan?"

"Er..."

Something didn't seem quite right.

"But why didn't he just... topple off?"

He went back to scratching his chin for a moment. That little girl with pigtails leaned over to watch him do it. I expect she'd never seen an eighty-seven-year-old man scratching his chin before, because she couldn't take her eyes off him.

"What's the biggest muscle in the body Dylan?"

"Whose body?"

"*Anybody's* body."

"Depends which they use most."

"No it doesn't."

"Why not?"

"Because... well, just *because*."

"Oh."

"It's the *bottom* Dylan. The gluteus maximus; biggest muscle in the entire body. And we've each got two of them ta boot. *Ta boot, hah*!"

He looked at me then, as if that was somehow supposed to explain everything. But it just made me even more confused.

"Oh Gods, do I have to spell it out for you?"

I don't know why he said that, because spelling

things out doesn't exactly making them easier to understand. I mean that's what words were invented for... so people don't have to bother spelling things out.

"He *clenched* Dylan. And with bottom muscles as thick as tree trunks."

"What sort of tree trunks?"

"*The thick sort*."

"Oh."

"But how that Courage Monster managed not to fall off is really beside the point lad, because the simple fact is... *he just did*. What, however, is *not* beside the point, is what began to happen when he started eating those clouds. You see, courage weighs less than air, which means Courage Monsters weigh less than air too."

"I know that Granddad. You told me already."

"Well then; the more clouds he ate, the bigger he got, and the more courage he had stored up, which meant—"

"Eating clouds made him lighter."

He smiled.

"Precisely."

But only for about half a second, because then it got sort of flipped over and became a frown.

"Unfortunately Dylan, the lighter he got, the less weight we had pulling down against all that hidden Energy pushing up. The long and short of which, is that with every mouthful of cloud that Courage Monster swallowed, the umbrella started *rising* a little bit faster, taking us steadily higher and higher, until it eventually occurred to me, hanging on for dear life as I still was, that if I didn't do something, and rather sharpish at that, there seemed very little chance that I'd ever see the earth again, let alone stand on it. Of course, there was one obvious solution, and that was to—"

That was when my Granddad suddenly noticed her – the little girl with pigtails I mean. Probably because

257

she suddenly stuck her head all the way through the gap between those seats, and looked right into his eyes.

"What's that?"

He didn't exactly turn to face her, but she just kept staring right at him, about twenty centimetres from his nose. *I wonder if I used to do things like that, or if it's just little girls with yellow hair and pigtails.*

"A girl."

"A girl?"

"With yellow hair."

I looked at her for a second. She didn't look at me though.

"And pigtails."

"Is she smiling?"

"No."

"Then what's she doing?"

"Nothing."

He reached for that little shoe box then. It had been sat on the table between us.

Then he pulled out a tin.

And a tin opener.

And started to, well... I should think you can imagine the rest.

"What was that obvious solution Granddad – to the umbrella floating up into space I mean?"

"Oh perfectly simple lad; I just had to convince that Courage Monster to stop eating clouds, and, well... to shed a little courage somehow, so that he'd get heavier, and we'd start to fall again. As the alternative was almost certain death, I felt certain that he'd cooperate. Of course... *I was wrong*."

"So you let go? Just like you said you did?"

"Of course not. Do you think I'm crazy lad? If I'd have let go up there I really *would* have died."

"But..."

"I tried to reason with him is what I did. And then I

shouted at him. And then I shouted at him even louder. And then I begged. And then I begged some more in a very pathetic desperate sort of way. And then, well, I think I actually kicked him once or twice – which isn't as easy as it sounds when dangling from an airborne umbrella.

"He just kept apologising in a wet sort of way, and saying that he needed every bit of courage he could get, and that I could save them both, somehow, because I was brave. But by God, I didn't feel brave. And for the life of me I couldn't see any alternative. Unless..."

It was another one of those *rotten fish* tins. Except instead of starting to eat them, like he had the last time, he just pushed the open tin across the table a bit, until it was right under the nose of the little girl.

"Unless what Granddad?"

"*Unless* I could somehow get heavier than he was getting lighter. Because if I could get heavier than he was getting lighter, then it stands to reason that not only would we stop rising, but we might even start falling back down again."

I had to think about that... and whilst holding my nose too. The smell of rotten fish was so bad that everyone in that carriage suddenly started coughing, as if they were choking to death or something.

"But how could you get heavier with nothing to eat?

Everyone except the little girl with pigtails that is. I don't think she even noticed.

"*Nothing to eat*! What are you talking about lad?"

"Well there isn't Granddad... up in the sky."

I mean it's not like there's tins of food floating about up there, is it? And even if there was there wouldn't be any tin openers to open them with.

"Unless you started catching a lot of birds or something."

"Would that be with a giant lasso Dylan?"

There was something odd about the way he said that.

"You mean you had a giant lasso?"

He sighed.

"No Dylan, I did not have a giant lasso."

"Then why did you—"

"*There were clouds lad.* Hundreds of them. Thousands even. Up. Down. Left. Right. We were surrounded by the bloody things. And if that Courage Monster could eat them, then why couldn't I eat them too?"

I looked out of the window again at that mist. It didn't look like the sort of thing you could skewer with a fork, or even scoop up with a spoon.

"How?"

"What do you mean *how*?"

"I mean what with Granddad?"

"*My mouth.* What the bloody hell else?"

The little girl with pigtails giggled then, probably because of my Granddad's face. I think sometimes it just *turned funny* without him even telling it to.

It made her seem a lot more real all of a sudden – hearing that giggle. And I suppose it felt a bit strange, to know there was someone else listening in to his story – someone else sort of sharing our adventure – because that's what it had always felt to me, even though I wasn't exactly *in it* or anything.

"Yes, but how did you get them in your mouth Granddad – the clouds I mean?"

"*By opening it.*"

She giggled again. It was a nice sound.

"Didn't you need a straw or something?"

"Of course not. I just... well, kept sucking is all."

I tried to imagine that.

"Sort of like the opposite of blowing up a million balloons... or one of those rubber dinghy things that take about three hours worth of puff?"

He puckered his lips up and made a sucking sound. I suppose he was just checking or something.

The little girl with pigtails did exactly the same.

"Yes Dylan."

"Granddad?"

"Yes Dylan?"

"Did it work?"

"Ye... *sort of.*"

"How do you mean?"

"Well, as you know lad, clouds are just made of water, except the type that floats, so the more I sucked, the more water ended up in my mouth. And the more I swallowed, the heavier I got, which was of course the intended objective. The only trouble, you see, was that my mouth wasn't quite as... *large* as my opponent's – that is to say, the Courage Monster's mouth. And he was certainly, well, a voracious eater; by which I mean, he never bloody stopped. Now the consequence of this lad is that I found myself *sucking* at a rather desperate pace, non-stop, for rather a long time."

"How long?"

He shook his head a bit.

"I'd say about two hours."

"You sucked clouds for about two hours Granddad?"

"There or there abouts, yes Dylan. And it *did* work. The umbrella stopped going up, at least quite so fast, and more or less levelled off slightly. Though I can't honestly say it started going down again... because it didn't, however frantically hard I kept sucking. Of course, another problem that soon emerged was the limited capacity of my... *internal parts.*"

"What do you mean?"

"Well, Courage Monsters are extremely large creatures lad, and have, I daresay, extremely large

261

stomachs to match... and bladders too no doubt – those are the organs which hold all the water inside you."

"And your internal parts *aren't* extremely large Granddad?

"Er... not exactly lad, no. I mean think about it logically Dylan; there's only so much space to fit them in to, isn't there?"

"Is that why you're always going to the toilet?"

The little girl with pigtails giggled again. I don't know why, because it's not like needing to go to the toilet all the time is funny – it's just annoying really.

He turned and stared right into her. But she just smiled at him without even flinching. I don't think he'd been expecting that.

"I daresay it is, yes."

But then I realised something.

"I'm even smaller than you Granddad."

"You don't say."

"No, really Granddad. I'm about a quarter as big as you are."

"Yes, I know that Dylan."

"Then why do you go to the toilet about four times as often as I do? If I'm so much smaller I mean, and you're so much bigger, and the smaller a person is, the smaller their *inside parts* are, so the less water they can hold, and—"

"That has absolutely *nothing whatever* to do with *anything*. All right?"

He might have shouted that... at least in the quiet sort of way that he sometimes did shout things.

"All right."

"The point is, I wasn't *able* to go to the toilet however much I bloody needed to, because if I had, then the weight of all that water would have been lost, wouldn't it? And if the weight of all that water had been lost, then that umbrella would have started going up again... with me attached to it. And that would have meant—"

"Certain death."

"*Certain death.*"

"So what did you do Granddad?"

"Well, I mean... I *held it in*, didn't I?"

I remember suddenly thinking of long car journeys when he said that; the type where my mother would refuse to stop because 'we'll be there in five minutes Dylan' even though she'd said that same thing five minutes earlier, and five minutes before that, and would probably say it again five minutes later too.

"Fortunately I passed out before it became entirely unbearable."

"You passed out?"

"Yes... it was all that sucking you see. Because when you start sucking up clouds lad, you can't help but suck in a whole lot of air with them – and not just the ordinary type either, because the higher you go, the thinner it gets – the air that is."

That didn't make any sense. I mean, how can *air* get thin? It's everywhere is air, which means it's not thin or fat; it just *is*. If a person was everywhere you wouldn't say they were thin or fat, because a thing has to be *somewhere* to be thin or fat, otherwise what have you got to compare it against?

"Which is why I hyperventilated."

"You hyper-what Granddad?"

"It's what happens when you breathe too fast, or... accidentally suck in too much air whilst trying to eat clouds."

"Oh."

He pulled a few rotten fish out of that tin and started waving them about in the air right next to the little girl's head. But that just made her start giggling again, so he sighed a bit and then ate them instead.

"I'd have surely died but for that voice. For it was her that saved me lad. My God, what a way to greet a man, eh?"

My heart started pounding again.

Even the little girl with pigtails suddenly went back to being all serious.

"You mean..."

"*Lily.*"

He smiled in that remembering sort of way like he often did.

"*Tiger Lily?*"

"Yes Dylan. The very same. She called up to me through the clouds – and with *such* a voice too. But not shrill, or even loud. It was soft, and gentle, like the babbling of a low stream in summer, or the call of a loon across a mist-wreathed lake. And yet as soon as she spoke those words it was the only thing in the world I could hear, or think, or feel."

"What did she say Granddad?"

"Two words lad. No more, no less."

He leaned closer again.

So did the little girl with pigtails.

And so did I.

"*Let go.*"

"And you did?"

"And I did."

OCTOBER

30

LETTING GO

Sometimes letting go isn't enough... whether it's the wrong sort of pride, or being angry, or being afraid, or even just being up in the sky hanging on to a flying umbrella.

I used to think that doing the right thing – the really *hard* right thing I mean – would somehow always put things right. Just like it does in stories I suppose. But those are just stories, and real life isn't like stories. It doesn't end with things being right, because it doesn't really end at all. It just keeps going. Bad things happen. And good things happen. And a whole lot of things that are somewhere in-between happen too. But that doesn't mean that people shouldn't try – to do those really hard things that they know are right I mean – because I think sometimes just the trying part is enough to make the world a little bit better. Even if it all goes wrong somehow, and things get worse. Maybe the part that's got better is just hidden, somewhere secret where nobody can see it. Like in a memory. The sort of memory that goes on for a lifetime. The sort of memory

266

that tells you who someone really was, and maybe even who you are too.

My Granddad had tried to do the right thing that September. It all went wrong somehow, and things got worse. But it doesn't matter, because at least he let go. At least he tried. And that's what I'll always remember.

The little girl with yellow hair and pigtails had still been on that train when me and my Granddad got off. I suppose it was us who were the drops of rain that time, disappearing back into the ocean. I wonder if she still remembers us, or that little bit of my Granddad's story which I think only she and I ever heard him tell. She never did say anything – not a word – but I hope a bit of him is still stuck in her head somewhere, like it's stuck in mine, even if it's just that dusty old hat, or the way his face went funny without him really telling it to, or that look he gave her which was meant to be mean, but just made her smile, because she saw what was on the inside instead.

"What happened?"

It was October. My Granddad had been living with us for over a month.

"He fell Dylan. In the road."

It wasn't easy at first. There hadn't been a storm that time between him and my mother; just an empty sort of politeness which never seemed to go away. The right words were said, but without the right sort of feelings to go with them. He tried. And she did too. It was nobody's fault.

"What do you mean? Why was he in the road?"

"I don't know. But it was miles away; out in the country somewhere."

My mother looked right at me. There was something in her eyes, like a lot of stuck words that she couldn't say. She tried to smile, but it just made me want to cry.

267

"He's cracked his pelvis, that's all. A broken bone. And they can fix broken bones. It's all right Dylan, he's not about to die. Really, he's not."

She even laughed, to sort of make it less scary I think. But it was her eyes I was looking at, and eyes don't lie like mouths do.

I suppose he must have been lonely. My mother had to work every day, and me and my sister were at school. She had exams – my sister always had exams – and it was the first month of my last year at primary school. Everything had suddenly become more serious somehow, like on a Sunday evening. Because on Sunday evenings you just have to get on with things, don't you? Even the things that you don't want to do, like homework, and taking a bath, and going to bed early.

I hadn't forgotten about him – none of us had. We'd just got distracted is all. Because sometimes that's what life does... without you even noticing.

"But why was he there; miles away like that? Why wasn't he at home where we left him?"

He can't have been lonely. Because my Granddad must have known a kind of loneliness that most people can't ever know. The kind where dreams are the only place you ever get to see someone smile, even the people you love. I don't even want to imagine what that must be like.

"I don't know Dylan."

There was something about the way she said that. Like she *did* know.

"But don't start asking him when we get there. He needs rest right now, not a lot of questions."

We were on our way to the hospital. It was a Thursday afternoon. My mother had picked me up from school in the middle of class so we could go straight there in the car. She'd never picked me up early before. I remember how strange it had felt to realise that some

268

things really were more important than school, and not just in my head; because if my mother thought so, then it must be true.

I don't know why my Granddad had ended up living with us. 'How could I ever leave this Dylan?' That's what he'd said that June evening beneath the sycamore tree. I suppose that garden was all he really had left – at least all he thought he had left. Because memories don't ever go away, do they? Not important ones.

I think it just sort of *happened* when we got off that train, probably because he'd fallen into an ocean that he didn't know. And I don't think my Granddad was used to things that he didn't know, like train stations, and lots of people, and being blind – *really* blind I mean. I remember him clinging to my arm so hard that day that it left a bruise; a proper one that went all red and purple. I didn't tell him though, because even then I knew that he hadn't meant it. He was just afraid I think.

"Did he say anything to you Dylan? About... I don't know... leaving or something?"

I'd barely even talked to him since that train ride home. It wasn't that I'd forgotten. Things just seemed different somehow – real again. It was like waking up I suppose. Only I wish I hadn't. I wish that train ride had lasted forever. I wish the three of us had got carried away somehow – me, my Granddad, and that little girl with pigtails – carried away up into those clouds, into that world beyond the gate.

I wish I could go back.

"No."

"Are you sure?"

A whole month and I'd barely even talked to him.

"Yes."

But if he was afraid of the things he didn't know, or had just forgotten *how* to know, like living in a house that wasn't his, and sitting in a garden that wasn't his, and loving a family that *was* his, then why didn't he just leave? Why didn't he just get back on that train and go home? It might have been scary, but he could have done it. There wasn't much my Granddad couldn't do; that much I was certain of.

Maybe it wasn't the things he didn't know that really scared him. Maybe it was the things he *did* know instead. Maybe it was going back to being alone again that he was most afraid of.

"We're nearly there now Dylan. Remember what I said, won't you?"

I've never understood how not talking about things – important things – is supposed to make people feel better. It's not as if not talking about things can make bones heal, is it? Just like it's not as if pretending everything's all right can make anyone happy. It just makes them pretend everything's all right too, even though everything isn't all right, and won't ever get all right unless everyone just talks about it. I hope I don't ever forget that.

"Yes Mum."

But if my Granddad was afraid of being alone again, then why did he go off like that, by himself, and fall over in some stupid road miles away from our house where he shouldn't even have been? If my Granddad was afraid of being alone, then why wasn't he happy *not* being alone? Why did letting go somehow make everything worse?

It just didn't seem right. Not even a little bit.

"All right Dylan. This is it."

We got out of the car.

My mother took a deep breath.

"Here. Take my hand."

31

HOW TO LOVE

I used to hate hospitals.

I used to think they were places people were sent to die. Because that's where my Nan had been sent to die – when she got cancer I mean.

And I remember thinking just that as me and my mother walked along those horrible white corridors with stupid coloured lines everywhere that day in October. It seemed to take forever to reach my Granddad, and that made me feel sort of angry. It was like they'd put him away somewhere on a shelf, right at the back, to be forgotten about. And I think that's what makes people die – when everyone forgets about them.

"Why is it so far?"

I don't think she even heard me. She just kept gripping my hand tighter and tighter.

"It's this way. Come on Dylan."

It wasn't like on television. There weren't doctors everywhere fixing people; putting them back together somehow; rushing about with needles and bandages and medicine. It wasn't like that at all. It was waiting. Just endless waiting. People sitting on chairs, waiting to see people sitting in beds, who were waiting to see doctors, who were waiting for them to die. Everyone was waiting for something. But it always seemed to end with dying.

"What's that smell?"

She didn't hear me again.

"Mum?"

"*What is it?*"

"That smell. I don't like it."

"I don't either. But they all smell like that. Hospitals. Just try not to think about it."

"Is it people dying?"

We stopped. She looked down at me for a second.

"No. It's just... I don't know what it is. But it's not people dying, all right?"

Sometimes it doesn't matter what makes a smell. It matters what you think of when you smell it. Like smelling cut grass makes me think of running out on that field at school, and smelling soap makes me think of my Nan laughing, and smelling rotten fish makes me think of my Granddad telling his story. It's funny how smells work like that; I mean you wouldn't think a bit of grass, or soap, or stinking fish could make me feel happy; just like you wouldn't think boring old hospital smell – whatever that really is – could make me feel scared... but it did.

"This is it Dylan. The Alexandra ward. *Look.*"

There was an open door leading to a big room, with a closed door next to it, and a sign above it, that said 'Alexandra Ward' in big black capital letters. The floor was yellow and made of concrete. It felt cold.

"Just like your Nan. God, what are the chances of that."

She shook her head and smiled in a strange sort of way. I couldn't understand why.

"What do you mean?"

"The name of the ward Dylan. *Alexandra*. That's what your Nan was called. You must have known that?"

It hadn't occurred to me that my Nan might have had another name. Because it seemed like 'Nan' *was* her name. The name I'd always called her. The name my sister had always called her, and my mother, at least when I'd been there. The name she'd always signed Christmas cards with, and birthday cards too. The name she'd always said on the telephone whenever she rang us. 'It's your Nan love. Just calling for a chit-chat.'

"But then I don't suppose you ever heard that name, did you? I don't think anyone called her Alexandra. 'Too proper by half' – that's what your Granddad always said. She was Nan to you, and Mum to me, until your sister came along."

We had to move out of the way then. There was an old woman being pushed into that ward on a trolley with a wheel that squeaked. She didn't even look at us, or turn her head, or do anything that living people are supposed to do. She just stared into nothing... and dribbled a bit.

My mother apologised to the man pushing the trolley – like we were in the way, like we didn't belong somehow – but he only smiled and kept pushing, until they disappeared behind that door.

"Christ, I hate hospitals."

"Mum?"

"Sorry Dylan. Forget I ever said that. I didn't mean it."

We just stood there looking at each other for a minute. And then I think I smiled. I didn't know why at first, but it was because I felt glad; glad that it wasn't just me who was scared, and glad that she hated hospitals too. I suppose we really were alike – me and my Mum. And realising that suddenly made me feel a little bit better.

"Right..."

She took my hand again.

"Let's go and find your Granddad shall we?"

I nodded.

"Just you keep smiling Dylan. If it can give me courage then God knows what it can do for him."

We stepped through the open door, hand in hand.

It was a big room. There were eight beds on each side. Except they weren't beds. They were just trolleys, with wheels, and metal bars on each side, and clipboards stuck on the end with a lot of wires. And they had curtains next to them; normal beds don't have curtains next to them. And the walls were bare. There were no pictures, or ornaments, or anything that felt normal, like how rooms are supposed to feel... at least the sort of rooms that are meant for *living* in.

Nobody moved in any of the beds. They all looked just like that old woman that we'd seen pushed in. It was as if they were the same person, copied somehow, over and over again, because none of them seemed to be real people; like what used to make them real people had been stripped away somehow, and it was only bodies that were left. Bodies that breathed, and dribbled.

I didn't recognise my Granddad at first. But when my brain finally realised it was him, lying there in that bed, like all the others, I just froze, right there on the spot. I couldn't even move – like that day in April when he'd shouted at me not to go through the gate. Except then I'd been afraid of what made him who he was, but in that hospital, lying there in a horrible white gown, staring up at the ceiling like he was already dead, it wasn't who he really was that scared me, it was seeing that taken away from him. It was seeing a shell, without anything inside.

"It's all right Dylan. He's still your Granddad, I promise."

I remember looking up at my mother then.

She never made promises. Not to me. She just did what she said she would. Because my mother was good at doing what she said she would.

"Come on. Let's talk to him. You'll see."

He didn't know we were there, even when we were standing right next to that bed. He just kept staring up at the ceiling. I even looked up too... to see if there was anything there I mean. But there wasn't.

"Dad?"

My mother stood in front of me. Her hand was sweating.

"*Dad?* Are you all right?"

"Who's that?"

He wasn't my Granddad any more. I was sure of it.

"Lil... is that you?"

My mother smiled, but I just backed away. If she hadn't been holding my hand I'm sure I would have turned and run. It was his face – it didn't look right somehow, as if the inside part that I'd come to know was suddenly all different.

"No Dad. It's me... Wen."

"Wendy?"

"Yes. And Dylan too."

She looked at me.

"Say hello to your Granddad."

I couldn't speak. I knew I had to. And I wanted to, but my mouth just wouldn't work. All I could do was stare at him... lying there in that bed, waiting.

"*Go on.*"

My mother squeezed my hand. So hard that it started to hurt.

Nothing happened. And I remember every second of it. You wouldn't think that possible, would you? For me to remember every second of *nothing happening*? Because if nothing happens, then you'd think there'd be nothing to remember.

"*Say hello Dylan.*"

I stared at him. He stared at me. And then all that *nothing* finally ended, and in one perfect moment I knew that I'd got it all wrong. He smiled right at me – in that funny *knowing* sort of way that only he ever did. I don't know how he knew where I was, but I'm sure he looked right into my eyes as he did it. And I knew then that it was still him, not some empty shell, but the same eighty-seven-year-old man who'd shouted at me in that garden that April without really meaning it. He was my Granddad. And it wasn't the shell that I was seeing; it was the *inside part* with everything else ripped away.

He had a tear in his eye. I think I might have too, but I don't remember that.

"Hello Granddad."

"Hello lad."

I reached for his hand. My mother did too. We'd never done that before. I don't know why, but it took all that fear away in a second, and made me feel strong... as strong as I'd ever felt in my whole life.

I suppose sometimes you don't even need words; sometimes feelings are so big, that no amount of words, even the very best ones, can make any difference. And I suppose standing there in that hospital, with one hand holding my Mum's, and the other hand holding my Granddad's, made me realise just how small words really are.

It was my mother who finally spoke.

"What the hell happened Dad? What were you doing out there? Do you have any idea how worried I was?"

My Granddad shook his head a bit – to himself I think.

"I'm so sorry love. I don't know what I was thinking. I just felt... like I had to get away – not because of you, or the kids, or anything anyone's done. I just wanted to walk, without that wretched fear. Like how I used to."

"But you must have known what would happen? Christ Dad, you're eighty-seven, and blind as a bat."

He smiled. They both smiled.

"I just..."

"*What?*"

I used to hate hospitals. I used to think they were places people were sent to die. But I was wrong.

"I don't want to be a burden to you. I don't want to be a burden to anyone."

Hospitals are probably the best places in the world; not because they fix people, because sometimes they don't – sometimes they can't – but because hospitals are the only place I know where people forget how to be anything but themselves – the real part I mean, on the inside. Whether they're waiting in a bed, or in a chair, it doesn't matter, because everyone suddenly remembers the same thing... *how to love.* And properly too. And I think that makes hospitals sort of magical; perhaps even more magical than that world beyond the gate.

"For God's sake Dad, you're not a bloody burden to anyone you daft old fool. We need you. *I need you.*"

"But I always seem to be in the way. And you're so busy all the time – the kids too. How can you need someone like me?"

"I've always needed you. Every day of my life I've needed you, even the times when you haven't been there. God, *especially then.* I might make mistakes, and shout at you sometimes, and say things I don't mean, or worse still, not say things that I do, but you're my Dad... and I still look up to you, and care about what you feel, just as much as I ever have."

She was crying. My mother was actually crying, and not in an ashamed way, with her face turned away, or in silence, but *properly,* like how I did.

They both were.

"But I blamed you. I ignored you for so long. And everything I said..."

"*I don't give a damn about any of that*. Haven't you been listening? You're my Dad, and I love you... just like your grandson does, and his sister."

She wiped her eyes, and smiled again, in that same remembering sort of way that my Granddad often did.

"And just like Lil did too."

My Granddad's hand started shaking then.

"I don't want to lose you Dad. You're a silly bugger, but there's no one quite like you, that's for sure. You might not know it, but she did – all the way to the end. And so do we."

He didn't let go. And nor did my mother.

"So don't you dare give in. Not now. Not ever. *Do you hear me?*"

My Granddad didn't reply. I don't think he could have. I'd never seen him cry before that day, and it was strange at first, but then I realised that it didn't make him any less strong, just like it didn't make my mother any less strong. It just fixed them is all... and better than any kind of doctor or medicine ever could.

"Mum?"

She looked at me.

"Yes Dylan?"

"Who's Lil?"

The question had just appeared in my brain, without me even thinking it first. It took her a while to answer.

"*Lily* was your Nan's middle name Dylan."

Lily? But that meant...

"Tiger Lily. Of the valley."

It was my Granddad's voice, but broken and high.

"God I miss that woman."

32

MY NAN

Sometimes letting go isn't enough. Sometimes you have to fall over in a road that you can't even see because you're blind and eighty-seven and then get sent to hospital where everyone thinks you're going to die even if they pretend they don't. Because sometimes bad things happen to make good things happen in return, which sort of makes the bad things not that bad at all when you think about it.

Nothing was the same after that first visit. My Granddad started wanting to live again, and my mother stopped wanting to forget how. It must have been all those feelings that fixed everything, which is a bit odd, because I think they were what first broke everything as well. I suppose they had to be got out is all, just like how cancer does.

Even though we fixed the important stuff in one afternoon, it took another four weeks before they'd let him leave. We visited every weekend though – me, my mother, and sometimes my sister too. The doctors kept telling us how well he was doing; one even said 'he's the most determined *oxo-getarian* I've ever seen'. At the time I thought that meant he just liked gravy a lot, but apparently it's a fancy word for people who are so old that they're older than eighty, and my Granddad was eighty-seven. I've noticed doctors often use fancy words to explain things, but then when they explain what the fancy words mean it usually turns out that the thing they're explaining isn't fancy at all. I suppose they just have to invent the fancy words to seem more clever, because otherwise people wouldn't want them for doctors.

I think my mother visited him by herself sometimes too – after work, without me or my sister there. I don't really know what they talked about on those visits, but she always seemed a little bit happier afterwards; the sort of happiness that never really goes away, as if she kept finding new bits of herself; bits that had been lost, or buried, or forgotten about somehow. And my Granddad seemed happier as well, but not in an obvious sort of way. He still liked to complain about things, especially stupid things that didn't matter, like how loud the clock above his head always ticked, and how one of the nurses wore so much perfume that it made him sneeze every time she walked past, and how the food tasted far too 'fresh' and the cups of tea didn't have nearly enough sugar in. But it was that same sort of complaining that he used to do, before my Nan had died. And best of all, it made my Mum laugh, sometimes so hard that she even cried a bit (from all the laughing I mean). And seeing her laugh seemed to make me laugh too, and even my sister. Sometimes we all just laughed without even knowing why, just like my Nan would have. It was sort of like she hadn't died at all; she'd just stopped having a body, and become part of *us* instead.

It wasn't until the very last week in October that I got to speak to my Granddad alone. My mother had to take my sister somewhere, so they'd dropped me off at the hospital for an hour or two. It wasn't scary at all that time, even being by myself, and even when I started smelling that smell; because I knew then that it wasn't the smell of people dying; it was the smell of people getting fixed.

He only had one more week left – to stay in hospital I mean – because those doctors with fancy words had told him he had to leave after that, even if it was in a wheelchair, but then I suppose that's a step up from a wheel-bed, isn't it? Or a step down, depending on how you look at it. He seemed very happy about it though, because he complained even more than usual. But I don't think that old woman who dribbled was very happy. It's funny to think how much seeing her that first day had scared me, because she wasn't scary at all – not once she got talking at least, and the *inside part* came out. She'd broken something or other too, but it didn't heal as fast as my Granddad; she probably wasn't eating enough gravy or something. I think they were sort of *friends* though, her and my Granddad, because she seemed to enjoy talking to him, and he definitely enjoyed complaining about her talking to him.

"Just one more week Dylan... one more week of listening to that old crone drone on about her perfect children, and her perfect grandchildren, and her even more perfect great-grandchildren, and her so spectacularly perfect great-great-grandchildren that they aren't even bloody born yet. Gods, it's like she's forgotten how to be British."

"Granddad?"

"Yes?"

"You said she was still alive."

He looked down at me from that trolley-bed in a confused sort of way.

"She's not died while I've been talking has she?"

I looked across at the old woman who dribbled. She was asleep... and dribbling.

"No, but I didn't mean her."

His face went all serious then.

"You said you went to give her that pink cardigan; that day in August, remember? Because it was hers, and because she was still alive. *Tiger Lily of the valley*. The magical girl from beyond the gate. But how can she be Granddad? Because she's Nan, isn't she? They're the same person, aren't they? You said it yourself that first day we came to visit."

But it didn't stay serious – his face I mean. Not like I thought it would. Not like it used to whenever I'd talked about Nan before. Instead he just smiled, and a good smile too; the real sort, that isn't trying to hide things.

"I didn't ever tell you what happened next, did I lad?"

"What do you mean?"

"After I let go of that umbrella in the clouds. After I heard her voice calling to me. It wasn't the end you know; it was more like the beginning."

"The beginning of what?"

The old woman who dribbled was snoring. I think it was the first time that I'd ever heard a woman snore. Not that you could tell, and that was the strange thing, because I thought it sounded just like my Granddad did when he snored... except a bit more wet, probably because of all the dribble that was still stuck up her nose.

"The beginning of my life Dylan – at least the part that really mattered."

That didn't make any sense.

"Why didn't it matter before?"

He'd done so much: fly through the clouds on an umbrella; follow Soundposts through a forest of talking trees; watch a Courage Monster be born out of a fire opal; talk to a king of birds who smoked a pipe... How could all those things *not* really matter?

"She didn't say anything Dylan. She just reached out a hand towards mine, looked me right in the eye, and smiled. I didn't know if I was dead or alive, lying there on my back, but I knew I'd never seen anything quite as perfect as that smile, nor would again.

"There are some things which change your life forever lad, whether you intend them to or not. Things which give you a purpose the like of which you never thought you'd find, because you didn't know it even existed. Things which redefine what it means to be. I daresay what happened before did matter, just not nearly as much."

That didn't make sense either – not at first anyway.

"Was it magical Granddad?"

"Was what magical?"

"Her smile. Is that why you forgot who you were and had to re-decide what to be?"

He laughed a bit then. I don't know why, because that's just what he'd said.

"Everything about her was magical lad. She was born in a wild place, just like those badgers, and otters, and—"

"Green squirrels?"

He smiled.

"That's it lad. She knew and felt things I could scarcely even imagine. And I can't deny it, just seeing her made my spine tingle."

I thought of Nan, and remembered what my mother had once told me. It must have been true.

"Was she really the most beautiful thing you'd ever seen Granddad – when she was young I mean?"

It took him a minute to finally answer. But when he did, everything seemed to go silent, even that old woman who dribbled. It was as if the whole world wanted to listen.

"Flaxen hair; long and loose, that soaked up the sun like sheaves of corn. Emerald green eyes that seemed to see in you all the tenderness and wonder that you saw in them. A voice that carried compassion without pity, as it carried strength without force. And a smile that clung to your heart, and never let go.

"At least that's what I'd write in a poem, for what little skill I have with words. But beauty isn't really what you see or hear Dylan, it's what you feel. And she made me feel more alive than any man has the right to. She made me feel as if I could command the sun to shine brighter, or the rain to fall wetter, or the trees to grow taller. She made me feel as if every second yet to pass was the greatest gift I could ever receive. And yet with her for company, they fell away by the thousand, without me even pausing for breath.

"Seconds became days, and days became weeks and months, until the gift of time ran dry. It was only then that I realised, in blind fear, that I hadn't the courage to tell her."

"The courage to tell her what?"

"It was on the top of that mountain Dylan – do you remember? Across the valley, on the far horizon. Bare and rocky, where the trees can't grow. Sometimes in winter it even snows up there; blown cold by a wind that never seems to stop."

I remembered the mountain, and the valley, and the orchard which it kept hidden inside. And I remembered looking out on them, through that window, so many months before.

"Yes. But I don't understand..."

"That's where I landed when I let go of the umbrella: right on the top of that mountain. What are the chances, eh lad? Had it been anywhere else I'd surely have fallen all the way to my grave. But it was more than just a mountain top, if you can believe such a thing. Because when you enter a magical place, you're as far away from the gate you stepped through as you think you are near—"

"And it's only when you think you're as far away as you actually were when you thought you were near, that you might actually be getting somewhere. I remember that too, Granddad."

"Of course you do lad. Except it was more than just *somewhere*. That mountain top was the *way back*. Only the way back wasn't exactly *back* any more; it was forward, to something new and unknown. Something without her. Because she'd become my home, just as that valley had, and looking out on the world beyond from the top of a mountain made me feel as small and as terrified as I had in all my life."

"But I still don't understand Granddad; what happened?"

He looked right into me then, and it made my heart pound like it never had before. I knew what he was about to say was somehow more than just words, or stories, or memories. It was who he was – who he *really* was I mean.

"I finally found the courage Dylan... to say *I love you* to the only person I've ever wanted to grow old with, and to look into her eyes and know that she loved me too."

My mother stepped through the door, smiling, with my sister at her side. She looked happy – they both did.

"But I was young. And the world was big. And I suddenly found I had more courage than I ever thought possible."

"What do you mean Granddad? I don't understand."

He smiled at me then, but not like he'd ever smiled at me before. It was the sort of smile that can't really be described, just like magic can't really be described... or love.

"I had to leave Dylan. It was the hardest thing I've ever done, but I had to leave."

NOVEMBER

33

GRIEF

Winter came early that year. There was already snow covering the top of that faraway mountain when we arrived at my Granddad's house in November. And it was cold – so cold that I could see my breath on the air. But there was no wind; everything was still and silent. The trees had all lost their leaves, and every last helicopter on that sycamore had flown away into the valley. Nothing moved, just like nothing spoke. It was so different to the spring and summer, and it felt as if those long days sat beneath the sun on mouldy old deck chairs listening to my Granddad talk about the king of birds, and Beamer Eighty-six, and the Life Turner, and everything else, had happened a lifetime ago, back when the world was still alive.

I stood alone in the garden, looking out over it all, just as I had that April right after my Nan had died. The orchard was so different – there were no leaves or flowers – but in a strange way it seemed just as beautiful, and I think if my Granddad had been there, standing by my side, with eyes that still worked, he would have said just the same. Only he wasn't there, standing by my side, and he wouldn't ever be again. I couldn't have known that then, but I probably felt it somehow, and that made me sad – so sad that I couldn't quite breathe, as if something was pushing on my chest, harder and harder until it made me want to scream.

"I just don't understand. Why can't he come and live with us? It'll be different this time; we've fixed everything. We're a family again, like how families are supposed to be. It's not fair Mum. Why won't you let him live with us? *It's just not fair.*"

We were there to collect some of my Granddad's belongings; the things he wanted to take with him to the home.

"It's not that simple Dylan. If he wanted to come live with us then of course I'd let him; I'd welcome him with open arms, you must know that. But he doesn't. And that's his choice to make, not mine."

The house didn't smell of soap any more – not even a bit. It smelled of old clothes, and something else too; something which I'd never noticed before... I think it must have been my Granddad. It didn't look the same either, not like how I remembered it looking that September when we'd both left together. It was a *home* then, a place that was alive, but when me and my mother opened the front door that day everything seemed different, sort of old and forgotten about, like those pretend rooms that you see in museums.

"Then why can't he come back here and things just go back to how they were? We could start visiting him again, and do the cleaning; I'd even help, honest I would. It's not right without him. It's not the same somehow. Why does everything have to change? He's still alive, isn't he? We fixed him Mum – that hospital fixed him. So why can't things just go back to how they were?"

She looked at me and smiled.

"It was you who fixed him Dylan."

"What do you mean?"

I hadn't done a thing, had I?

"Sometimes people get stuck, and however much they might want to escape, deep down inside, they can't, because they've forgotten how; they don't know where to go or what to do, so they just stay stuck, remembering something that's gone, and letting that memory tell them what to be, instead of leaving it behind, and just being who they really are."

"Is that what you did... when Dad left I mean?"

She didn't look away when I said that, or change the subject, or leave, or shout at me without really meaning to.

"I'm so very proud of you Dylan. Your Granddad keeps telling me you're the brightest little thing he's ever known, and my God he's right. You've a way of seeing things for what they are. And to think there's a bit of me in you... it just makes me so proud."

I don't know what that feeling's called – whether it's magic, or love, or something else – but hearing my mother say that she was proud of me that day seemed to change the whole world. It was like I'd been stuck too, without even knowing it. Except it wasn't really the words; it was the feelings that made them spill out. I'd always known that my mother loved me, but that was the first time that I ever really *felt* it.

"Do you know what grief is Dylan?"

I thought I did.

"When you think about someone who's died, and it makes you cry a lot? That's what it's called, isn't it? But it's never happened to me, not even when Nan died. I don't know why."

The sun came out then, through a gap in the clouds. It was strange to see it shine so bright and warm on a world that was so cold and dead. Except it wasn't dead –

it was just sleeping, and waiting to be woken up again. Because real-life doesn't end when things get bad, just like it doesn't end when things get good. It just keeps going, and summer *always* comes back.

"Are you cold Dylan?"

My mother looked down the garden towards the gate.

"Not really."

"Then let's sit down and talk for a bit. I know just the place."

She started walking. I didn't realise why at first.

"Come on."

The deck chairs were still in the shade of that sycamore tree, just as we'd left them that summer; my Nan's blue and purple, with a flower design; and my Granddad's faded orange, and covered in mould. I just stood and stared. It didn't seem right somehow... to be there without him.

"Never mind staring at them. Let's move them into the sun; over there."

She took my Granddad's chair, moved it into the sun and then sat down. I looked at her for a second, sitting there, where before I'd only ever seen him. And then I stopped looking, took my chair, and did the same.

"Someone doesn't have to die for a person to grieve Dylan. It's just what happens when we lose something that's precious to us; something that feels part of who we are, that we've come to depend on. Usually that's a person, but not always. It happened to me when your Dad left.

"The feeling is the same; a sort of loneliness; no, more an *emptiness*, because what's in your head, and what's in the world outside doesn't quite match up any more. But the way each of us deals with that feeling is different. Some people cry a lot, others shout and scream to try and block it out. Some want to talk, and some want to be alone, to hold on to the memories. Others just want to forget; so they work too much, or play too hard, or search for new things to fill that emptiness which just reminds them of what they've lost.

"But it doesn't go on forever, because although you never forget, what's inside your head does eventually get used to the world again. And when that happens, the emptiness goes away, and the other feelings start to come back: happiness, love, even the bad ones, like guilt, and shame. Without them though, without emotion – that's what it's called – a person doesn't quite work properly. They might look all right on the outside, but on the inside they're broken. Does that make any sense Dylan?"

It made more sense than just about anything my mother had ever said to me.

"You were broken, weren't you? When Dad left."

"Yes, I was. And I probably still am a bit."

"Because you were stuck?"

She nodded.

"Because I was stuck."

"Is that why you didn't grieve when Nan died, like how I didn't?"

"I did grieve Dylan, but not in the right way. And I think you grieved too, just without really knowing it. We should have had this talk a long time ago – long before your Nan died – but I didn't have the courage, and for that I'm sorry."

I used to think that courage was something only heroes needed; to rescue babies out of burning houses, or wrestle with bears that are trying to eat people. But that's just wrong! Because the hardest thing in life isn't being brave, it's being the *opposite* of brave; it's showing people who you *really* are, and trusting that they won't hate you for it. Because Superman always saves the world, but he never does it without that suit on, does he?

I think everyone needs courage sometimes... just to let go.

"Did Granddad grieve as well – when Nan died I mean?"

"Yes, with your help, I think he did."

"*My help*? But we didn't even talk about Nan. He wouldn't even say her name. And whenever I said it he just walked off for a bit, or changed the subject."

"It was too hard for him to talk about her Dylan, but that doesn't mean he wasn't thinking about her. And having you around helped him do that. It helped him get unstuck, and remember how to be himself again."

That didn't seem right to me, because I couldn't work out how I'd helped him. We'd just talked about that world beyond the gate, and magical things, like Tiger Lily of the Valley. Except that was Nan – he was talking about Nan all that time. Maybe sometimes all you have to do to help someone is *listen* to them... and keep on asking annoying questions. I suppose I was quite good at that.

"And did Granddad help you get unstuck somehow too?"

"Yes, I think he did in a way. Perhaps by reminding me of everything I still have, and just how valuable that is."

"Like what?"

"Like *you* Dylan, and your sister. We're a family, and we have to stick together."

"Except without Granddad? Isn't he part of our family? Why does he have to go to that home? Why can't we *all* just stick together? If he really is fixed now – if I really have helped him – then why doesn't he want to live with us again?"

It didn't make any sense. Because what's the point in having the courage to let go if in the end it just makes everything worse.

"He needs more than we can ever give him Dylan; he's old and he's blind and he'll be in a wheelchair for months now, perhaps even forever. He needs someone to cook meals for him, and make cups of tea, and he needs to be around people who are there *all day*; people he can talk to, and laugh with, and complain about. Being in hospital has helped him realise that. And we'll still visit. He'll be much closer to us than he was living here. You can see him every weekend if you want?"

"What did he say when you told him all that?"

"I didn't tell him it Dylan... it's what *he told me*."

She sighed a bit then, probably because I didn't understand. But she didn't shout, or tell me to stop asking questions like she could have done – like she used to do.

"Sometimes people have to leave. They don't want to, but they have to."

That's just what my Granddad had said, three weeks earlier, in that hospital. '*I had to leave Dylan. It was the hardest thing I've ever done, but I had to leave'.*

"Did Dad have to leave too?"

My mother turned away.

But only for a second.

"Yes. He did."

"He promised me he'd come back."

She nodded.

"Why did he say that?"

"Probably because he thought he would."

"He didn't though. *He hasn't*."

"I know that Dylan. But I'm sure it's not because he's forgotten. Perhaps he just needs to find a bit more courage."

"You didn't need courage to stay."

"No, because staying is easy. It's leaving that's hard."

That made me angry. More angry than I think I've

ever been; even more than I was with my Granddad that day we walked back from the station and he kept talking about having a heart attack, or a stroke, or getting run over by some joy-rider, as if dying was funny. It was like my mother thought it was right – but how can *leaving* ever be right, or lying about coming back?

"If staying is so easy then why couldn't *he* stay as well?"

I stood up then. I stood up and I shouted right at her.

"HE'S A COWARD. AND I'M GLAD HE NEVER CAME BACK. BECAUSE I HATE HIM. I HATE HIM AND I HOPE HE'S DEAD."

My mother didn't move. She just reached out and took my hand without saying a word.

I felt better somehow... as if I'd been holding my breath for a very long time and had just breathed it all out. Sort of *lighter*. Only when I breathed back in I realised something: *It wasn't true*. I didn't hope he was dead, not really. I hoped he was still alive, and I hoped he still *would* come back one day, even if it was just to visit.

"Granddad came back, didn't he? He must have done."

"What do you mean?"

"In the hospital; he told me that he had to leave, even though he loved her, and she loved him, he *still* had to leave. Only he didn't say why; just that it was the hardest thing he'd ever done."

"You mean leave Nan... when they were young?"

"Tiger Lily of the valley. That's what she was called seventy years ago. The magical girl from beyond the gate."

My mother smiled.

"Oh, he came back all right. It took a good many years, but they were just as much in love – your Nan always told me so."

"Then why did he bother leaving in the first place?"

She looked at me in a serious sort of way. As if she was surprised.

"He had no choice; they sent him overseas Dylan."

"*Who did? What for?*"

"To fight. Your Granddad was in the war. He volunteered when he was seventeen. I thought you knew that."

34

BREAKING A PROMISE

Life doesn't always give you what you want. That's not how it works. Sometimes it gives you something else, like a lot of grief that you aren't quite ready for, or a war to fight in even though you're only seventeen. But that doesn't mean you're supposed to pretend it's okay, because that just makes the *wanting* part never go away. You're supposed to get angry, or sad, or *something*, so that your brain can get unstuck, and you can get on with living. And sometimes getting on with living is all you have to do, because life just makes you wait for things – important things I mean – like love, and family. Of course, I don't expect that makes much sense, because it wouldn't have made much sense to me if it was just a lot of words on a page.

Waiting for things can make them better, like how it does in hospitals, or it can just make them different, like how it did for me that November. For so long all I'd thought about was going through the gate at the bottom of my Granddad's garden, and seeing that magical place where birds can talk and umbrellas fly. Except life wouldn't let me; not for some big reason, because I don't think life even has reasons – *it just is*, and people stick the reasons on afterwards to make themselves feel a bit better. I made a promise, and then more important things got in the way, like fixing people without really knowing it. Until that day in November, when life must have decided that I'd been waiting long enough.

We'd collected all the things that my Granddad wanted to take to the home: fourteen pairs of socks (none of which matched), eleven pairs of underpants (the old-fashioned sort), striped pyjamas, slippers (wrapped in sellotape because they were falling apart), an old blanket which smelled of cupboards, an umbrella, a toothbrush (with twenty-three bristles left – I counted), an electric shaver, a talking alarm clock shaped like a pyramid with a button on the top which told the time, a whole lot of black and white photographs (including that one of the woman who looked like the Matron d'tree), and a lot of other things which I can't quite remember.

"Right then, I suppose that really is the lot."

We were standing in the lounge, me and my mother, just sort of looking, and remembering. I don't think either of us wanted to leave.

"It's funny isn't it..."

She smiled in a sad sort of way.

"I grew up in this house, and I must have walked in and out of this room more times than I've had hot dinners, but not once do I remember really looking at those pictures, even though most have been there longer than I've been alive."

"I think that's normal with really old things."

She laughed a bit then.

"You're probably right Dylan. But seeing this room now – *without* them there – I don't think I'll ever forget. You wouldn't think the most noticeable thing about a thing would be it not being there, would you?"

She laughed even more. And I laughed too.

"I wish we could bring them back, and make everything like it was."

"Now don't say that Dylan. They're better off where they'll be seen than sitting here in an empty house."

"I don't mean the pictures, I mean *them* – Nan and Granddad. I wish we could bring them back."

"So do I love, but life goes forwards not backwards, and all we can do is go with it."

We carried the last few things out to the car. The sun was still shining brightly outside, just to remind us I think, or perhaps to remind that old cottage... that summer would come again, and life and laughter would come with it.

"What'll happen to the house Mum?"

It took her a while to answer that.

"I think it'll have to be sold Dylan; to pay for the retirement home. I'm afraid there's no other way. It's classed as an asset you see, and your Granddad doesn't have a penny in the bank, so we'll have to—"

"I'm glad."

"You are? I thought you might be upset."

"It doesn't feel right without anyone here. It needs a family – a new family, who can grow up, and then grow old, like how you did."

She looked up at the house, standing there all crooked, and then back at me, smiling.

"You're right again Dylan, but less of the old, thank you; I've got plenty of years left in me yet."

The smile turned into a grin.

"I almost forgot... there's one more thing your Granddad asked us to bring – well, he asked me to ask *you* to bring, to be exact."

That didn't make any sense. Why hadn't he just asked me?

"What is it?"

"A box."

She was still grinning.

"What sort of a box?"

"A little red one made of metal. He said you'd know where it was."

I couldn't move. My heart suddenly beat so hard that my chest felt like it might explode.

"It's all right Dylan; he's not angry or anything."

He must have known! My Granddad must have known and not said a thing about it all that time. But why? And how? And if he knew, then that meant...

"It's been hidden up that tree for even longer than those old pictures have been sat on their shelves. And you're not the only one to climb up there Dylan; it was my favourite place in the world as a little girl. I'd sit there for hours, looking out over the valley, imagining what wonderful treasures might be buried in that little red chest. I never had the nerve to bring it down though. He knew, and I knew that he knew just by the way he'd watch me from his chair, or the look he'd give me every time I climbed down. Not once did we talk about it; I didn't dare, and he didn't need to... until now."

I couldn't believe it. And my mouth wouldn't talk. I suppose my brain was too busy thinking things to tell it what to say. My mother knew, just like I did. It was my secret for a few months, but hers for almost a lifetime.

"I didn't mean to find it; it was an accident."

"Of course it was – for me too."

"But what's in it?"

She paused, in a thoughtful sort of way.

"I don't know Dylan, and I'm not even sure your Granddad does."

"But you said he knew, because *you* knew that he knew, so doesn't that mean he put it there, a lot of years ago, before you were even born?"

"Maybe. I certainly thought that when I was your

age, but something tells me there's more to it than that. Your Granddad's never been the type to hide things, at least not where anyone could ever find them. No, I think he discovered it Dylan, just as you and I did, and then he made sure that that's where it stayed for all these years... perhaps because it was never his to move."

"Then why does he want it now?"

She smiled at me again. There was something she wasn't telling me.

"I expect we'll find out... soon enough. But for the moment all we have to worry about is getting it down."

"What do you mean?"

We set off round the side of the cottage; I wasn't sure why at first, and it felt a bit odd to be there, as if the house was watching us somehow. It can't have been though, because houses don't have eyes, or even brains to tell them where to look. But I think if it had of had – a brain I mean – then it wouldn't have been angry, just a bit curious I suppose, like how the king of birds had been that day in April, standing on that upturned plant pot, watching me and my Granddad in a silent sort of way.

"You might have climbed to the top of that tree in summer Dylan, but there's no way you're doing it in winter, with soaking wet branches to slip off, and a box to keep hold of on the way back down. I told your Granddad as much in the hospital."

"But how else are we supposed to get it? It's not like we can fly up on an umbrella, is it?"

She looked at me as if I was stupid then. I don't know why, because it's not like I said that we *could* fly up on an umbrella; I said that we *couldn't*, and that was perfectly true.

"No Dylan, it isn't, which is why it's very lucky that your Granddad has a *ladder*."

"A ladder?"

"Yes, except it's not here."

"What sort of a ladder?"

"The usual sort."

"Like how window cleaners use?"

"I should think so, although probably a lot older. They used to use it to pick fruit in the orchard – your Granddad said it might still be there. Come on."

I stopped.

"The orchard? But that's beyond the gate..."

She looked back at me.

"Which gate? The one at the bottom of the garden?"

I nodded.

"And?"

My mouth opened. And then closed again. And then opened again. My mother looked very confused; I think she must have caught it off me.

"I can't."

"You can't what?"

"I made a promise that I wouldn't go through."

My voice sounded different somehow – sort of shaky, like I was stuck in a freezer on top of a washing machine.

"To whom?"

"To Granddad. He made me promise... so I did. And I don't want to break it. Because promises are important, *aren't they*?"

I wasn't really sure any more.

"It's all right Dylan, your Granddad was the one who told me it might be there. Besides, without it we won't be able to get that little red box down, and that's what he asked us to do."

She was right. It was what he wanted – it must have been. But I just stood there for some reason, not moving.

"*Are* promises important? Only... you've never broken one, not to me."

She looked at me and smiled.

"Would you love me any less if I did?"

I didn't need to think about that.

"No."

"Would you hate me for it?"

"I hated Dad."

"And do you still?"

You'd think it'd be easy to tell, wouldn't you? Whether or not you hate a person. But it isn't, not always. Not then.

"I don't know. I suppose... it's complicated."

"We all make mistakes Dylan – you know that. And perhaps the only reason I don't make promises very often is because I'm afraid of not being able to keep them. Does that make me any better... really? Your Dad said what he felt, and he meant it at the time, I'm sure. But the thing about life – the terrifying and equally wonderful thing about life – is that you never know what's going to happen next.

"You're right, *it is* complicated, and as long as you remember that you'll always be able to tell what's right and what's wrong. I'm afraid that's the best answer I can really give."

My mother was getting good at answering difficult questions. It didn't feel wrong any more – breaking my promise I mean. Not because promises aren't important, but because sometimes other things are *more* important. You just have to work it out.

We walked down the garden together, passed the upturned plant pot, and along the fallen over rose bushes. I think time must have slowed down again, because it seemed to take forever.

It wasn't until we were finally standing beneath that sycamore tree, about to go through, that I suddenly remembered my Granddad's words. Except it didn't feel like a memory; it felt like an echo, one that had taken half a year to bounce off that faraway mountain and come all the way back.

DON'T YOU DARE GO THROUGH THAT GATE.

Only echoes *are* memories when you think about it, just the sort that get stuck in valleys instead of brains.

"Are you all right Dylan?"

My hand was resting on the gate. But I'd stopped again without really knowing why.

"What if we don't come back again? What if when we step through that gate we're as far away from the way back as we think we are near?"

She laughed.

"Then I suppose we'll just have to make the best of it, won't we?"

She stepped through, not looking back.

I watched her walk away, still not following.

"What if we get eaten alive?"

She laughed again.

"What if we don't?"

35

REAL-LIFE

Magic is a feeling – my Granddad taught me that. Not the sort of feeling you get when some old man pulls a rabbit out of a hat, or guesses a card right, or makes a coin appear up your nostril; but perhaps the sort of feeling you get when meeting the king of birds, or seeing a shadow come to life, or shaking hands with a tiny man wearing a green suit and a pine-cone for a hat, or listening to music made of Energy that's alive, or watching a fire opal turn into a monster as big as an elephant, or following paths made of sound through a wild forest, or discovering a gigantic tree that's really an airport, or eating home-baked gingerbread with a lady who looks like an orangutan dressed as Queen Victoria, or flying through the clouds on an umbrella, or standing on the top of a mountain... and looking up at the most beautiful thing in the world.

But then perhaps it's also the sort of feeling you get when seeing a wild creature for the very first time, or discovering a strange green egg that doesn't quite belong, or running so fast across an impossibly huge field on a summer's day that it feels as if you're taking off, or eating sponge pudding out of a tin whilst listening to a storm beating down on the world outside, or climbing a tree and finding a hidden place with hidden treasure buried inside, or sitting alone on a train watching raindrops race across the window and the whole world race by beyond, or just listening to a memory, or a story, or a bit of both, told in a special sort of way, by a special sort of person.

Or perhaps it's just walking through a gate at the bottom of a garden. Perhaps sometimes that's all it needs to be.

The first step was the hardest. The rest were easy; all I had to do was keep putting one foot in front of the other, and luckily the brain of my brain is quite good at that. It's good at most things really – much better than I am.

Looking back wasn't easy though; seeing the cottage get smaller and smaller, and the gate farther and farther away. I kept wondering if the next time I turned round it wouldn't be there, because it'd be far away over that mountain, just like it was for my Granddad. But when it finally did disappear, hidden behind trees, I felt better somehow, because there was no point turning round any more; there was no point looking back... only forward.

There was no shadow with eyes to follow me, or talking bird to sit on my shoulder, or umbrellas that carried cities floating through the sky. There was only silence; not even the trees could whisper, without leaves to be blown, or wind to blow them. The bare branches were still and lifeless, but only waiting, not dead. Because it wasn't a dead sort of silence at all; it was the sort that watches, and listens, and makes you feel things that are terrifying and wonderful at the same time. I was in a magical place, *beyond the gate*, and the world told me so.

My mother didn't speak, or if she did, I didn't hear her. I just kept following; watching and listening, as keenly as the world was watching and listening to me.

And then I stopped. My eyes saw something that I knew very well, but never thought I'd see again. I remember walking towards it, between trees with long arms and hands and fingers – endless fingers that might have been trying to stop me, or might just have been pointing the way. I forgot why I was there. I forgot to keep following my mother. And I even forgot to be afraid. Because all that seemed to matter was reaching what I saw, and letting my eyes decide if it was really real, or just painted in by my imagination.

In a small glade stood a single apple tree; not the biggest I'd seen, or the smallest, or even the strangest, but certainly the most beautiful. It seemed to smile with open arms, as strong and safe as they were old. And the world around it felt oddly warm on that cold November day. Beneath the tree, lying forgotten on a bed of leaves, was my Granddad's pink cardigan. Except it wasn't my Granddad's – it had never been my Granddad's, because it belonged to the magical girl from beyond the gate. It belonged to Tiger Lily of the valley. *It was my Nan's.*

All I could do was stand and stare.

It looked wet and faded, as if the sun had worn it as a raincoat. But the odd thing – the very odd thing – was that not a single leaf, or twig, or rotting apple from that tree lay on top of it, even though there were hundreds and thousands underneath and all around. It can't have been there all that time... *it just can't.*

I reached down to pick it up.

"Don't."

The word rang out in the silence, made louder somehow.

"Something tells me it doesn't want to be moved

Dylan."

My mother stood next to me.

I couldn't speak. I didn't know what to say.

And then something amazing happened – at least it seemed amazing to me. My mother began to bury that pink cardigan in leaves. One armful after another, until it was covered in a mound as tall as an anthill. It looked almost like a grave.

"This was your Nan's favourite tree. She planted it as a girl, and sat and talked to it every spring to make sure the apples grew just right."

My mother laughed. It was strange to hear such an ordinary sound in that place.

"She used to tell me that trees get lonely, because they've no legs to walk with, but the knots in their trunk are really ears, so they can hear every word you say; which is why if you keep them company, and ask nicely enough at just the right time of year, they'll make their fruit with something extra... a little drop of magic."

She laughed again.

"And so that's what I did, just as she had."

I looked at my mother, and then at the tree, and then at the mound of leaves beneath it.

"He told me she was still alive. Out here... beyond that gate. He said he gave it back to her; that pink—"

"And he was right."

She turned away, and began walking again.

"Come on Dylan. We've a ladder to fetch, and it's getting late."

"Wait! What's it for?"

She stopped.

"What's what for Dylan?"

"*The little drop of magic?*"

It took her a moment to answer, and when she did it wasn't in a normal sort of way. Her lips were trembling as if she was cold, only I don't think she really was.

"Your Nan used to say..."

My mother turned away, and then took a deep breath, and looked back at me.

"She used to say those apples could make you live forever. Silly, eh? Nothing lives forever."

She wiped her eyes and tried to smile, only it didn't look quite right.

"That's not true."

"What?"

"Energy lives forever. It just goes from being one thing, to being another thing, and when they die, as things will, it becomes something else. Stars become heat and light, and heat and light becomes plants and flowers, and plants and flowers become animals and people. It's all Energy, because Energy is the spark of life. And it lives forever. It never dies Mum."

She just looked at me. And I looked at her. And that old apple tree kept on smiling at the world.

"Things just go on turning is all. Like pages in a book, except one that never ends. Because real-life doesn't ever really end – not like stories. There's always a next chapter; a new beginning. And new beginnings are exciting, aren't they Mum? Because you never quite know what's going to happen next."

I didn't mean to say any of that; it just came out is all. Perhaps because I understood, and understanding things makes them better. It even makes them more magical when you think about it.

"My God Dylan, when did you get so wise?"

My mother wiped her eyes again, but this time with a smile that *did* look right.

"This year I think, by listening to Granddad go on about things. Sometimes for hours and hours."

She laughed even louder then.

"I can well believe that. Now come on, before it starts getting dark."

It didn't take us long to find that ladder, or to walk back with it. The world kept on being silent; watching and listening, and waiting too; for a new beginning I think, because that's what winter is.

The gate turned out to be just where we'd left it, which in a funny sort of way was exactly where it had to be, because like my Granddad had said: '*when you enter a magical place you're as far away from the gate you stepped through as you think you are near*'... and I didn't think I was very near at all.

My mother stepped back through with the ladder, but something made me stop and look back.

A golden flash above my head, fast disappearing into the orchard.

A king, with a crown. And I saw it too; the finest crown I've ever seen, just to remind me I think – just to remind me of what's really out there.

It was snowing by the time we finally left, carrying that little red box with us. Have you ever seen snow falling as the sun sets over a great valley of trees?

It really *was* magical.

36

OPENING UP

My Granddad was wrong about retirement homes, just
like I was wrong about hospitals. They aren't places
people are sent to die; they're places people are sent to
live. Only they tend to be very old people, and the thing
about very old people, is that they've only got so much
living left to do.

The trouble is, when you see them all there, just
sitting about not doing anything, like I did that first visit
in November, you sort of forget that they're all a bit
different... that they've all got their own stories to tell,
just like my Granddad had. It's only when you get to
know them a bit that they stop being a lot of tired old
faces, and start being real people again – just the sort of
real people who mostly enjoy sitting down a lot, and
talking, and drinking cups of tea all day. And when you
think about it, that's exactly what retirement homes are
made for doing.

The walls weren't bare; there were pictures – mostly
boring old ones of harbours or corn fields or posh
looking houses with too many windows; but that's not

the point, because I don't think most of the very old people could even see what they were anyway. It *looked* like a home, and that was a good start, but it's not really pictures on walls and pots of pretend flowers and Christmas decorations that make places into homes; it's the people that live there, and the people that come to visit them. Because homes are about family, and family is about caring, and there was *a lot* of caring in that place; not just the obvious sort, like making beds and cutting toenails, but the sort that isn't obvious too... the sort that you don't see unless you look really hard for a very long time.

My Granddad's room was on the ground floor, but then so was every room, because there weren't any other floors for them to be on. Nobody answered when my mother knocked. He wasn't there, but it was definitely his room; those black and white photographs were sat on every bit of shelf and table, just like they had been in the house. And it smelled of him too... or at least of those old slippers wrapped in sellotape.

"He'll be in the garden Dylan. He was the last time."

It was my mother's third visit. She didn't look scared at all; not like that day in the hospital when she'd just pretended not to be.

"But it's freezing."

It was nearly December by then. The snow had fallen thick for two weeks.

My mother looked at me in a blank sort of way. I'm not sure how, but I knew exactly what that look meant, even before she said it.

"Do you really think a bit of cold could stop your Granddad going outside?"

I didn't.

"No."

"Well then."

I followed her outside, carrying that little red box

under my arm. My mother had told me to hang on to it, even when she'd taken all his other belongings to the home. That made me nervous somehow, like it was something important – something to be afraid of. I remember walking through those carpeted rooms with extra wide doorways and hundreds of chairs, clinging to that little red box, as if it might have contained a new born star, waiting all that time to be set free. I hadn't opened it – I couldn't. There was no key.

She was right; my Granddad *was* outside, sat there in his wheelchair, wrapped up in that old blanket which smelled of cupboards. There were even two old ladies sat next to him on a very damp looking wooden bench.

And he looked happy – I'll never forget that. It was as if all that grief had been cut out of him, like how doctors cut out cancer; only I'd never really realised it had been there before then. My mother said he looked constipated, but then she always said that when my Granddad looked happy. I suppose he'd just never quite got the hang of it, or his face didn't work like most people's. Even those two old ladies looked happy... just a lot more cold than he did (and probably less constipated).

"Hello Dad."

"*Wendy*?"

"Yes Dad."

"About bloody time; I was expecting you hours ago."

"We got delayed."

"Tractors again was it? Or is that just out in the country? What do you get stuck behind here; milk floats?"

My mother opened her mouth to answer, only the words weren't quite fast enough at coming out.

"You brought the lad then?"

"Hello Granddad."

"Good."

He looked at me.

"And the box?"

I held it out to him.

He reached forward and touched it with one hand. I'm not sure how he knew it was there, but he did.

"You hold on to that Dylan. Come on, push me over there under that tree. I've had enough of listening to these old farts go on about nothing all day."

Neither of the two old ladies said a word; they just kept on sitting there looking happy, sort of like how pots of pretend flowers do.

My mother sighed, shook her head a bit, and then took the handles of his chair in each hand and started pushing. It looked like a lot of hard work.

"We can't go under the tree Dad; the snow's too thick there. This'll have to do."

"Nonsense! The snow can't be too thick under a tree by virtue of the very fact it's under a tree, meaning there's less of it. Talk sense girl."

She sighed again.

"Fine. But if this thing gets stuck I'm leaving you there."

Luckily it didn't – not that my Granddad seemed worried.

"Now then. Is there anybody about?"

I looked around. It was a big garden, almost as big as my Granddad's, only more wide and less long, and much better looked after – at least I think it was by the neat sort of shape things were underneath all that snow.

"Only a bird. On the feeder."

I'm not sure why I said that. I suppose noticing birds seemed a lot more important than it had used to.

"A bird? What sort of bird?"

"Oh honestly Dad, does it really matter what sort of bird? Do you think starlings are conspiring against you or something? I'm sure they've got better things to do with their time; like eat worms, and deposit things on my windscreen."

She grinned. My Granddad didn't though.

"What does *conspiring* mean?"

I hate not understanding words.

This time the words raced out of my mother's mouth so fast that I don't know how she had time to open it first.

"It means your Granddad's probably going senile; just like those two *old farts* that he seems to like so much."

She grinned even more then. And so did my Granddad... at least eventually, after about twelve seconds of looking slightly more constipated than usual.

"It's a robin, isn't it Dylan?"

I looked again.

"Yes."

"There's one lives in that tree. Keeps me company he does; and I daresay he's about the most intelligent company there is in this place."

"Oh shut up Dad! You love all the attention, admit it."

He didn't admit anything, but then I suppose not admitting something is sometimes sort of the same as admitting it... only with less words. He was definitely happy there, even if he was going senile (whatever that meant).

"Go on. Open it up."

I looked down at that little red box; I'm not sure why, because it wasn't like it had changed since the last time that I looked at it.

"I can't Granddad. It's locked."

"Well of course it's bloody locked. Use the key."

"I..."

"Yes?"

The words wouldn't come. I didn't have the key, but there was something about my Granddad which made that seem sort of ridiculous. As if I really *did* have the key. Only I really *didn't*.

We all stood there in silence; except for my Granddad, because he sat there in silence instead.

He finally sighed – but not like my mother's sigh. His was the sort of sigh that just went on and on until I started to think he must have an extra lung just for storing up breath for extra long sighs.

"How daft do you think I am Wen?"

I looked at my mother. Her eyes were wide open.

"*You knew*?"

"Did you really think I wouldn't notice? She kept that key hidden in the same place for sixty-three years. And then a week before she dies it suddenly goes missing. She gave it to you."

"What does he mean Mum? Is that true? Have you really got the key?"

She opened her hand.

And there it was; tiny and silver. It shone like a polished coin in her palm, as perfect and new looking as that little red box was battered and old.

"I can't believe you knew all this time. Why didn't you say anything Dad?"

"Like what?"

"Like... like that I should use it. She obviously wanted me to."

He opened his mouth as if to say something, and then closed it again, as if he thought better of it, and then said something else instead.

"You should use it. *Happy now?*"

My mother smiled.

"Just about. Took your time, didn't you?"

"It's been sat there for sixty odd years... do you really think an extra six months is going to make any

316

difference?"

"*Nine.*"

They both looked at me.

"Nine months. Nan died on the twentieth day in March, remember? That's nine months and seven days ago."

Nobody spoke. It was as if I'd said something that I shouldn't have, but it was only the truth, wasn't it?

"My God, that's the best part of a year."

They were my mother's words.

"Open the box Wen. It's time."

I handed it to my mother. She looked at it for a moment, smiling – I don't know why. And then she put the key in, and slowly turned. The lock turned with it. There was no sound.

And then she opened the lid. It didn't even creak. After all those years – all those decades... *it didn't even creak.*

She reached into the box and pulled something out. A package. Something wrapped in brown paper.

"Well?"

My Granddad's right leg was bouncing up and down. It didn't normally do that.

"What's in it?"

She handed him the package, unopened.

And then the strangest thing happened; instead of unwrapping it, like anyone else would have, my Granddad just held that package up to his nose, and took an especially deep breath.

Then he smiled.

And his right leg stopped bouncing up and down.

"Anything else?"

My mother looked in the box again.

"Yes. A drawing."

She took out a single piece of folded paper. It was badly torn, and stained such a dark shade of yellow that it was hard to believe it might once have been any other colour.

"Lil?"

My mother nodded.

"Yes. It's beautiful Dad. I wish I'd seen it before."

She handed the piece of paper to me then. I unfolded it and looked down at the drawing. It was just a sketch, done in pencil, but so perfectly that it might almost have been an old photograph. I didn't recognise her at first – not until I looked more closely at the eyes. They seemed to look right back at me, just as they had the last time I saw her alive. It was my Nan.

"Who drew it Granddad?"

"Who do you think drew it? Me, of course."

"But you haven't even seen it."

"I don't need to see it Dylan. I know exactly what it is, just as I know exactly what these letters are."

He tapped the brown package with a very old, very bony looking finger.

"I drew that picture near seventy years ago... in Egypt... beneath the wing of a plane in forty degree heat. It's a wonder that paper didn't turn to ash in my hand it was so hot."

"In Egypt? You mean during that war?"

"*That* war? Yes, I daresay I do."

"But how did you know what to draw – if she wasn't there I mean?"

He smiled.

"Do you really think I'd forget a face like that lad? Remembering it was just about the only thing that kept me alive. I could probably draw it again now... if I had a pencil that is."

"There's a pencil in the car Granddad."

"Never mind the pencil Dylan."

"But Mum—"

"You knew all along didn't you... what was in that

box? But you never once opened it... not in all those years."

My Granddad's face changed a bit when my mother said that. It went all serious and sort of proud, but not in a bad way.

"Everyone's entitled to a few secrets, even from the people they love. It was never my place to open that box, but that doesn't mean to say I couldn't guess what was in it."

My mother laughed.

"And how did you *guess* exactly?"

"Oh come off it. Do you think I didn't look for those letters in the house? She'd never have thrown them away – not for all the things in the world."

"Is that so? Awfully sure of yourself, aren't you?"

"She bloody well waited for me, didn't she? And besides, you haven't read them."

My mother laughed some more.

"Quite the poet were you?"

"No. Just an ordinary man in love. *Here*."

My Granddad held out the little brown package from his lap. But my mother didn't take it – not at first.

"You're really giving them to me?"

"Looks like it. Take them would you, before my arm drops off."

"This isn't like you Dad."

"She obviously wanted you to have them. God knows why, but if that was her wish in giving you that key then I shan't deny it. Just promise me one thing..."

"What?"

"That you'll wait until I'm in the ground before you read them."

"Oh honestly..."

"*Promise me*."

"Apparently I don't make promises. But I'll take them anyway, because you're right; it obviously *was* what she wanted."

My mother took the brown package, and then looked at me, smiling. I didn't smile back though; I couldn't.

"Granddad?"

"Oh Gods, not that *Granddading* business again."

"What do you mean?"

"Just spit it out lad; whatever it is you want to say."

Sometimes I wish you could spit words out – instead of having to say them I mean. Because there are some words that are so hard to say that you can hardly say them at all. Only it's not the words – not really – it's the thought of them hurting someone that makes it so hard.

"I broke my promise."

He wouldn't get angry. I knew that before I even said it.

"What promise?"

"I went through the gate Granddad. Into the magical world. I'm sorry... I didn't exactly plan to, it just sort of—"

"It doesn't matter lad."

He was smiling. I don't think it was quite the real sort, but it still wasn't what I'd expected.

"You mean you don't hate me?"

"Of course not. Why would I hate you?"

I couldn't understand why he asked that. It seemed obvious to me.

"Because I lied."

"You did no such thing. And even if you had I wouldn't hate you. Everyone lies Dylan; it's part of life. If you go about hating people for it then you'll soon find yourself very alone. And I don't much like being alone. I only hope you don't hate *me*..."

"For what?"

"Oh, I don't know; for being old, and talking too

much, and going on about dying all the time when I don't really mean it, and... well, for shouting at you that day – for getting angry when I should have bloody well known better."

Isn't it funny how sometimes the words that you think will hurt someone don't hurt them at all? They just make everything a little bit better. I don't think I'll ever understand that. But then I suppose some things just aren't meant to be understood; *not many*, but some.

"I don't hate you Granddad, not for any of that, or anything else."

His lips tightened a bit then, and he nodded in a twitchy sort of way which looked very odd.

"Well that's... that's good. I'm, I'm..."

"I love you Granddad."

I don't know why I said that.

Yes I do. I said it because it felt right, and I think that's the only reason you ever need to say something kind and true.

He didn't reply at first. But that was okay, because my Granddad never told me that he loved me – it just wasn't his way.

Only that time he did.

"I love you too lad. More than I can ever say. And your sister. And your mother. I'd be lost without every one of you."

My mother was crying a bit, but probably in that good sort of way people talk about.

"Like how you were lost beyond the gate Granddad?"

He looked up at me from his wheelchair.

"Yes. I daresay I was, wasn't I? Only a lot of people seemed to care about me for some reason. Just like they do now. Bloody lucky, I should say."

"Granddad?"

"Yes Dylan?"

"The Courage Monster died, didn't he? He gave you all his courage so you could go away to fight in that war?"

I must have forgotten not to tell my mother about any of those things, or perhaps it just didn't matter any more. I've always known that I could trust her, but I think that was the first time it didn't even occur to me not to.

"We all have to die lad. The lucky among us don't have to choose how, because we've the courage to keep living until we can't live any more; but one thing we all have to choose is what we do while we're alive. And that's exactly what he did, just as you have Dylan."

"I don't understand. Didn't he choose to die Granddad?"

"No lad. He just chose to do good is all, like a lot of folks did back then."

His face went sort of sad then, but not for very long.

"Keep that drawing. It's not like I can see it, and I've got the real thing up here anyway."

He tapped the side of his head with that same bony finger. It looked very old, but then eighty-seven is very old, isn't it?

"And Wen, keep hold of that box; who knows, you might just need it one day."

He grinned.

"For love letters? The way those two *old farts* keep looking at you I think you might be needing it first."

She grinned too.

"If anyone in this place starts writing me love letters then the only box I'll need is a box of matches."

That didn't make any sense, because it's not like letters would fit in a matchbox is it? Unless there was about a million matches in there first... but then what would he do with them all?

"Don't worry Dad; you're blind, I'm sure they'll

just whisper you *sweet nothings* all day instead."

That didn't make any sense either, because what's the point in whispering *nothings?* It doesn't matter how *sweet* something is if it's *nothing*, does it?

"They can bloody well try, but it won't be sweet nothings I whisper back, I tell you."

They laughed then. My Granddad and my Mum... *together*. They laughed and they laughed until it made me laugh too. I don't know why, but it doesn't really matter, because I know that we were happy.

And we went on being happy for a very long time.

EPILOGUE

THE BEGINNING

My Granddad once told me that he didn't want to die peacefully in his sleep. '*Too boring by half*' – that's what he said. But then he also told me that the lucky among us get to keep on living until we can't live any more. And that's just what he did.

He was ninety-one when he died... in spring, like my Nan. He just went to sleep one day and didn't wake up, even though the sun was shining and the birds were singing and the world was starting again. I suppose for all those new things to keep being born some old ones have to die off now and again, don't they? Or else life wouldn't be quite so perfect. And ninety-one really is *very old*... even older than eighty-seven.

We visited every week, just like my mother said we would – except for that two weeks we spent in France one summer when my sister got so sunburnt that she couldn't sit down because her bottom was the colour of a lobster; at least that's what I kept telling her. But apart from that—oh, and that week I got flu and my mother told me I had to stay at home or I'd 'infect all the wrinklies' and cause an 'epidemic' (whatever that was).

Anyway, the point is, I got to see my Granddad an awful lot in those three and a half years. And in that time he told me a lot more stories, or memories, or bits of both – I wasn't always sure. Some about that magical place, beyond the gate, and others about other things, like what wars smell of, and how to grow flowers in a desert.

He knew a lot my Granddad, as long as you kept on asking the right sort of questions... and I was good at that, everyone said so. But I didn't ask every question; some I forgot, and some I just didn't want to. Like what that little green egg might be. And why that fire opal was waiting for me. And what each of them might turn into beyond that gate, or some other gate, in some other magical place, still waiting to be found. Because everyone needs a few secrets, even from the people they love. And they were *my* secrets now; my memories to be made, and stories to be told.

I can't help but wonder though, when I hold that little green egg and see it shine so oddly in the light, or stare into the galaxy trapped inside that fire opal: will a new king of birds hatch out one day, and will a monster be born to give me courage when I need it the most? But then I suppose not every question can be answered; some things just have to be found out by living. And stepping through gates. Even when you don't know what's waiting for you on the other side.

I never went back to my Nan and Granddad's house; that funny little cottage on the edge of a valley. The inside part just wasn't the same without her there, nor the outside part without him. I'll never forget it though. And I don't suppose whoever lives there now will ever forget it either. I wonder what secrets they've already discovered beyond that gate; who they've met, and what adventures they might have been taken on when the world woke up again in spring. Perhaps someone is living a story there *right now*, just one that has to wait another seventy years to be told.

There are magical places *everywhere* – my Granddad told me so. Other worlds tucked away inside our own, like strawberries mixed up in a great big cake. Nobody talks about them, because nobody wants to spoil the secret, but they're out there, beyond ordinary looking gates, just waiting to be found and tasted. Only you have to know what to feel when you do... because it's *feeling* things that makes them magical.

We grieved properly after my Granddad died; me, my Mum, and my sister too. We talked, and we cried, and we remembered. And we kept on doing it until what was in our heads and what was in the world finally matched up again, like my Mum said it would. He didn't want to get cremated like how most people do; he said it was 'a waste of good meat', which my mother said was 'disgusting' and threw a box of tissues at his head. We took him to a forest instead – a special sort of forest – where they buried him in a hole, and then let us plant a little tree on top. It was a horse chestnut tree; except now it's a gravestone too, just the sort that one day might have a tree-house built in it.

I think he'd have liked that – being buried under a tree I mean – because all that Energy locked up in his body will get turned into worms, and soil. And then that horse chestnut tree will eat the soil, and grow, and one day things might even eat it too; like birds, and squirrels. Only I'm not sure he'd have liked getting eaten by squirrels; my Granddad didn't much like squirrels... except perhaps that green sort that he kept going on about.

I wonder if that's how they get turned – green squirrels I mean. By eating nuts from trees that have grown out of people. I suppose if my Granddad was still here I could ask him. I think it'd be the sort of question that he'd have the right answer for. Only he's not here, because he's under that horse chestnut tree... getting eaten by worms. At least *part* of him is. The other part is stuck in people's heads; like mine, and my mother's, and that little girl with yellow pigtails'. That part can't ever get eaten by worms... unless of course all those other people die and then they get eaten by worms too, but that won't be for a very long time, and besides, I've written it all down now. She said that I should. Because as long as there's someone to keep reading these words he can't ever get forgotten. And even if there isn't someone to keep reading these words, they'll still be here won't they? Written down. And the paper won't forget.

I suppose I'll just have to go back to that forest where my Granddad's buried. I'll have to watch that horse chestnut tree grow, and see if any squirrels get turned green by nibbling at it. I might even talk to him a bit – the tree I mean – providing he grows some proper ears of course, like how my Nan's apple tree did. I should think he will though; my Granddad's ears were the biggest ears that I've ever seen... sort of like enormous pork chops. Only a lot more hairy.

Made in United States
North Haven, CT
19 May 2023